SOUTH
OF SURRENDER

A HEARTS OF THE ANEMOI NOVEL

SOUTH
OF SURRENDER

A HEARTS OF THE ANEMOI NOVEL

LAURA KAYE

Entangled Publishing, LLC
2614 South Timberline Road
Suite 109
Fort Collins, CO 80525
Visit our website at www.entangledpublishing.com.

Edited by Heather Howland
Cover design by Heather Howland

Ebook ISBN   978-1-62061-034-3
Print ISBN   978-1-62061-033-6

Manufactured in the United States of America

First Edition May 2013

The author acknowledges the copyrighted or trademarked status and trademark owners of the following wordmarks mentioned in this work of fiction: Band-Aid, Cocoa Puffs, Exorcist, Frankenstein, iPhone, Jell-O.

*This book is for everyone struggling to surrender
what they are for what they most want to become.
You can do it, and you are not alone.*

All of our reasoning ends in surrender to feeling.
— Blaise Pascal

I never saw a wild thing sorry for itself. A small bird will drop
frozen from a bough without ever having felt sorry for itself.
— D.H. Lawrence

CHAPTER ONE

Chrysander Notos found his brother right where their nightmarish summer began, on top of the west tower of the Chesapeake Bay Bridge. While he circled through the dark sky far overhead, Chrys watched Eurus pace the narrow catwalk atop the structure. What the hell was he doing here, of all places?

Summoning the powerful energy of the South Wind, Chrys prepared for what was sure to be another brutal battle. He didn't want to fight Eurus. Just the opposite, in fact. But fighting seemed to be all his older brother knew anymore. The accumulated scars on Chrys's body from the past three months proved that, and now he wore his weariness like a second skin.

But someone had to save Eurus from himself and the Olympic gods' death sentence. And Chrys was the only viable candidate. Zephyros and Owen were mated, and Boreas deserved to bask in his new status as grandfather.

Not to mention, Eurus's problems were partly his fault.

After everything, Chrys owed him the effort. Least he could do.

Eurus froze and scanned the heavens, revealing the exact moment he perceived Chrys's presence. No sense delaying now.

In his elemental form, Chrys shot down before Eurus took flight. Shifting into corporeality at the edge of the tower's top platform, he braced for Eurus's attack. He could never predict whether his brother preferred to get right to the main event of kicking his ass—not something he *should* be able to do, not in Chrys's own damn season, anyway—or might be up for a little verbal sparring first.

Eurus turned on his heel, black leather duster whipping around him in the heavy, humid wind. Chrys could sense his brother's glare through the black wraparound glasses he always wore, but the blows didn't come. Up for the sparring, then.

"Behold the do-gooder. How nice for me."

"Why are you *here*, E?" Chrys asked. No way Eurus's return to the exact spot where he'd killed their brother's wife—or tried to; Mars had interceded and brought her back as a goddess—was coincidence. It meant something, but with Eurus it was hard to tell exactly what.

"Mmm, just basking in pleasant memories," he said with a sneer. "What's your excuse?"

Acidic rage churned in Chrys's gut. Their brother Zephyros and his wife Ella were happy now, but that didn't erase his recollection of Zeph's brutal agony when they'd thought Ella gone for good. Chrys shoved the useless thoughts away. Eurus liked to pick at a person's most sensitive scabs. It was one of his specialties. So Chrys caged his anger and refused to take the bait. "I'm here for the same reason I've been dogging you all summer. Come back to the Realm of the Gods with me. Atone. We can work this out. It doesn't have to go down this way."

"Grow the fuck up, Chrysander. I don't want your help. And I sure as hell don't need it." He fisted his right hand, flashing the faceted firestone ring he wore in the bright lights that marked the tower's corners.

Chrys's eyes tracked the movement. That damn ring was half the problem. It belonged to their father, Aeolus, the most powerful storm god of them all, and somehow Eurus had gotten his hands on it. Which explained the entire summer's worth of ass kicking. The sacred stone gave its wearer the power to control all the winds and, thus, him. Bad enough when his father made use of those powers. Catastrophic now that Eurus could.

Chrys hadn't told anyone that Eurus had Aeolus's ring for fear that knowledge would hammer yet another nail into his brother's coffin—not to mention their father's for not making that little revelation himself. Now, that shit was just waiting to hit the fan.

"What's your end game here? Huh? You're playing right into the Olympians' hands, and for what? For now, they're letting the family resolve this situation, but once they're involved, it'll be too late." The humid bay breeze whipped around him. He tugged long strands of hair out of his eyes.

"As if I would tell you, boy." Eurus crossed his arms over his broad chest and sighed. "I tire of your questions." The smug smile that settled on his face was all the creepier for the new, slashing red scar carved into the left side of his face from temple to lips. How he'd gotten the wound—which could only have come at the hand of a stronger god—Chrys had no clue. "In truth, I tire of *you*."

Chrys ignored the way his heart tripped. A lifetime of trying—and failing—to win your big brother's approval made you a bit sensitive, though. Fucking hell. "Eurus, man, come on. I just want to help you. You're my brother. And we can fix this."

The firestone flared to life, a soft red that soon blazed so bright it was hard to look at.

Chrys braced, his muscles suddenly alive with tension. The air constricted around his body.

Eurus's ring finger twitched.

It was all Chrys needed to see. In a heartbeat, he flashed into his elemental form and shot skyward.

Eurus's energy followed.

How many more fights did Chrys have in him? Dark clouds already gathered and billowed around them. Inky tendrils of Eurus's malevolent East Wind gusted over him, crawling through his energy as if searching for a weak spot. Even in his elemental form, Chrys shuddered as he released a burst of power to throw them off.

But it was too little, too late.

Preternatural disturbances in the air rammed him from all directions as if he were a featherweight boxer facing an invisible heavyweight opponent. Icy cold North Wind that Eurus had no business commanding lashed against him like a frozen whip, the frigidity stealing Chrys's breath and power with every cutting impact. Exactly what his brother intended, since Chrys's intolerance to cold wasn't exactly a secret. Chrys dug deep into his powers and poured on everything he could muster, but hell if three long months of fighting a stronger god hadn't depleted his reserves. He rocketed across the bay and over the Eastern Shore, hoping to draw the threatening storm over the Atlantic Ocean where it would do less damage to land and people.

A ripple of electricity shuddered past him, as if conducted by the humidity. *Damn it all to Hades.* The defeated thought had barely formed before Eurus's attack hit home. Lightning belted around him in tight, suffocating, scorching loops.

Chrys cried out, an agonized roar that unleashed a series of deafening crashes of thunder.

Knowing he was out of time, he struggled to twist free and flung bolts of his own, zinging electricity across the sky in flashes of red and purple and orange so unnatural he knew they'd capture the attention of humanity, but he had no choice. Soon, he would be completely at his brother's mercy. Not that Eurus had any. And damn if that gem of an admission didn't highlight the possibility that Eurus was a total lost cause. But how was he supposed to just give up on the brother he'd spent the better part of his life trying to save?

He didn't have time to ponder an answer.

Eurus's electricity attached to Chrys's energy signature, slowly but surely stealing his self-control and siphoning off his life force, like a vampire supping at leisure from his victim's throat. An immortal could only be injured by another of stronger power—and that fucking ring was giving Eurus, normally the least powerful of the four Anemoi, everything he needed.

A monster of a storm opened up all around them, tropical force winds howling, rains pounding down in diagonal gashes, thunder and lightning shaking the very world. The storm, the battle, the manner of Eurus's attack—this was the worst yet between them.

But Chrys refused to go down alone. If this was it, if this was how Eurus wanted it, they were going out together. Eurus was whole galaxies away from perfect, but hell if Chrys was going to let anyone else take out the brother he'd helped fuck up.

With his last burst of energy and control, Chrys yanked hard against his electric restraints and released, slingshotting himself across the sky toward his tormenter, toward his demise.

He'd lived too long for his whole life to flash before his eyes, so a few key moments sank their hooks into his wavering consciousness—all from his young godhood, and all instances of Aeolus denying Eurus affection, touch, and attention, while he lavished the same on Chrysander. Or, at least, his version of affection.

Chrys would've sworn that sometimes, *too many times*, Aeolus's touch had been about proving he could control one or all of them. While other times, he just knew the attention was *intended* to hurt Eurus. The image of young Eurus's humiliated, yearning, accusing gazes were burned into Chrys's subconscious, and he saw those now, too. Each instance of his father using Chrys—the only Anemoi birthed by a different mother—as a pawn in punishing Eurus for his mother's childbed death, left Chrys feeling more and more separate from the rest of them. After a time, he came to associate guilt, resentment, and lack of control with his father's affection so strongly that he shied away from it, finding it uncomfortable to be touched and hard to believe he was actually lovable. Not when his existence so harmed another.

What-the-fuck-ever. Ancient history. Blah, blah, blah.

Clearly, none of that mattered now.

The lash of lightning unwound from his rocketing body. But if Eurus had realized what was about to happen, he'd reacted too late. Chrys slammed into his brother so hard thunder and lightning exploded around them, the force of the impact sending a devastating microburst of air and rain pounding to earth. *Shit!*

They plummeted in a tangle of elemental energy through the turbulent night sky, Eurus roaring ancient curses at him before finally regaining control.

Damnit, E, stop!

I was *saving you for last*, Eurus snarled, using the power of the firestone ring to force Chrys out of the elements and into corporeality.

A preternatural wind held him aloft, his head wrenched backward as Eurus pulled at his long hair so hard his scalp burned.

"No," Chrys mumbled, almost unable to vocalize the word.

Eurus manifested into his human form, a sword of fiery lightning in his hand. He plunged it toward Chrys's heart.

Chrys raised his left arm to block the blow, and the white-hot blade sliced into his forearm and scorched deep into his right shoulder. The unexpected angle of the indirect hit threw Eurus off balance, and he released Chrys's hair.

The air dropped out from under him.

His backward motion un-impaled his shoulder from the rod of lightning. And then he was in a free fall. Struggling to hold onto even the smallest vestige of lucidity, Chrys concentrated with all his might to summon the South Wind, to return himself to the cradling safety of his elemental form.

Flash. He went elemental. Relief surged through h—

Flash. Without trying to, he materialized back into his human form.

He willed the wind to heed his call. Any moment, Eurus would be on him again. If he could just— *Flash.* Neither wind nor body this time, but his sacred animal form. The winged horse. Ancient icon of the power of the Anemoi.

Almighty Zeus. He couldn't will it. He couldn't control it. As he plummeted downward through the black deluge, he shifted randomly, repeatedly, tearing his body apart and reassembling it over and over until he lost track of what he was. Who he was.

And then he lost his hold on consciousness itself.

CHAPTER TWO

Laney Summerlyn hated thunderstorms with a passion, and this was no regular storm. The wind blew so hard it sounded like the roof could lift off the house, and a wet dripping in the living room turned out to be rain forced in through the east-facing windows. The concussive deluge was deafening, not a welcome sensation for someone already nearly blind.

As loud as it was, the screaming of the horses still made it to Laney's ears. And that was driving her crazy. She debated going out to the barn, checking on them, calming them. But she couldn't seem to force herself out the door and into the torrent. Her night vision had been the first thing to go, and getting disoriented and lost outside in a storm when she was nineteen had left her terrified of them.

But those horses were her babies. Her family.

A clap of thunder exploded low and close. Laney jumped, chiding herself even as her heart raced. The lights flickered, once, twice, which she could just make out through the pinpoint of central vision that remained in her right eye, like looking through a drinking straw. The threatening dark got her off the couch and in search of a lantern before the power shut off for good. It might not be many years until she lost her sight entirely. Then she'd be forced to live in total darkness. In the meantime, she intended to soak in every bit of light and color and memory of the physical world she could.

"Stay, Finn," she said to her chocolate Labrador. Not that he was likely to get up, old as he was, but he kept an eye on Laney like the guard dog he'd once been. Laney counted her steps from the couch across the spacious open living room to the adjoining kitchen and finally to the hall closet, then reached in and retrieved the third object from the left on the middle shelf—a battery-operated lantern. Through her mobility training, she'd long ago memorized her way around, as well as the location of everything in her house—such organization made her independence possible. Laney could take care of herself just fine.

She'd no more closed the closet door than a tremendous burst of thunder detonated above her house, shaking the building as if a bomb had gone off. Laney struggled to swallow against the lump in her throat. *In. Out. In. Out.* She focused on the mechanics of breathing to ease her anxiety. Clutching the lantern to her chest as if it could keep her safe, she forced away the panic.

Despite the air conditioning, the air suddenly felt thick and heavy, like something was happening, something was coming. The rain continued to pour down, but there was a stillness that felt...wrong.

A series of cracks ricocheted from outside, then a crash. The sound of the horses' distress went from nervous to outright panic. Laney saw every bit of the farm in her head, like a 3-D model she could turn and manipulate. That damn sound came from her stable. Her gut squeezed.

Forcing herself to take the measured steps that allowed her to count her paces, Laney went for the coat closet in the foyer and found her raincoat. She slid it on and snapped it closed with shaking fingers. Taking a deep breath, she stepped out onto the porch and walked right into the howling night and the soaking rain. Her hair instantly matted to her face and the wind blew so hard it stole her breath.

You can do this, Laney. You have *to do this.*

Lantern in one hand, she grasped the lead line tied to the newel post at the bottom of the stairs with the other and followed the well-worn path toward the stable. The thick blackness swallowed the lantern light and negated what was left of her sight, sending her heart into a sprint. Her sneakers slipped in the mud puddles over and over. If she fell and lost the line… *No. Don't go there.* She held onto it so tight it dug into her palm. But the pain was worth it. As long as she held onto the rope, she knew right where she was because of the plastic tags hanging from it at ten-foot intervals.

The closer she got to the stable, the more obvious the horses' fear became. They snorted and blew, kicked and pawed at the walls, screamed and struck their massive bodies against the grated doors and sides of their stalls. She imagined them pacing, desperate for escape. Her stomach squeezed and sank.

Please, whatever that noise was, don't let it have injured one of my babies.

Soaked, muddy, and breathless with dread, Laney passed the seventh tag on the line, and then her hand encountered the cold metal of the door handle to which the line was tied.

She yanked the door to the right and it glided easily on its track.

Laney reached out, found the panel of light switches, and flipped every one of them, flooding the nine-stall center-aisle barn with yellow light. Adrenaline flooded through her so fast she was shaky, making it hard to focus the sliver of central vision she still possessed. But it was clear the barn had been damaged. Wind gusted through, raising a chill on her wet skin, and an intense shower of rain echoed against the floor at the far end.

She settled the lantern on a shelf and let her raincoat drop to the floor. Cocoa Puff's agitation was clear in the flurry of movements and blows coming from the old mare, who was the most high-strung of them all. Laney moved to the barred grill of the first stall and shushed her like she would a small child. Cocoa let out a high-pitched nicker and tossed her head. Laney wanted to stroke her forehead, but hesitated to get too close when the horse was so riled. "You're okay. Mama's here. You're a pretty girl, Cocoa," she cooed. The rescued Morgan nickered again and pushed her nose into Laney's hand. She snuffed as if looking for treats. "Next time, I promise. I gotta go check on the others now. Okay? I'm right here."

Trailing her hand over the grated fronts of the stalls, Laney moved to the next door and found Casper, a white Sabino gelding that was another of her rescue horses. Casper strained his head toward her, and Laney laid her cheek on his forehead. "You okay, buddy?" She petted the soft white hair covering his neck. "Yeah, you're okay."

Laney's heart still raced in her chest, and she wiped the water from her face as she moved to the next stall. *Three more.*

"Hey, Rolly," she said, finding the muzzle of the Appaloosa spotted almost like a Dalmatian, lots of creamy white with occasional black spots. He blew against her hand then pulled away. Rolly was her newest rescue. Recovering from a supposedly accidental gunshot to the abdomen, he remained standoffish. Couldn't blame him, really.

The volume of the rain tapering off now, Laney crossed the center aisle to an empty stall and turned toward the two remaining horses. Hope rose within her and calmed the worst of her fear. All her senses told her the damage was restricted to the opposite—and empty—end of the barn. Her hand found the next door, and the colt—a boarder—nipped at her fingers. Mouthy thing. Laney smiled as tension eased from her shoulders. She couldn't imagine telling Windsong's owner, a fifteen year old named Kara who had just been diagnosed with retinitis pigmentosa—the same degenerative eye disease from which Laney suffered—that anything had happened to the colt. Stroking his cheek, she said, "Good thing you're so handsome." He licked her forearm. "Ew, Windy." She backed away, chuckling, and wiped her arm on her T-shirt.

Finally, Laney came to the last stall she needed to check, and Sappho nickered softly and reached her head out. "Hi, baby," Laney said, leaning her forehead against the silky black mane of her Friesian, the first horse she'd owned, a gift from her grandfather on her sixteenth birthday. When other kids got cars, Laney got her very own filly. She'd grown up around her pop's horses, so getting Sappho that day had been a wish come true. Less than a year later, she'd started noticing problems with her vision. As her sight deteriorated, more than once she'd cried on this horse's shoulder. Ten years had passed, but Sappho still had the power to cheer her up more than anything else.

"You okay?" she asked, reassuring herself more than the mare. Laney let out a long breath, fear making her feel tired and wrung out, even after determining the horses were all fine. "Let's just hang out for a minute and calm down. How 'bout that?"

Sappho chuffed out a breath against her hand, a soft affectionate agreement. Laney wished she could clearly see the Friesian's eyes, which had always held such intelligence and understanding, but the black-on-black coloring obscured the details. This animal probably knew her better than anyone ever had—her grandfather excepted, though he was gone now. Off to greener pastures. The thought always made her smile.

After a few minutes, Laney realized the rain had stopped. A humid breeze gusted and water dripped occasionally, but otherwise only the normal sounds of the horses filled the space.

She gave Sappho a final pat and turned toward the other end of the barn. Seth would have to give her the full picture of the damage when he got here in the morning. Her long-time farm manager and horse trainer—not to mention best friend—was here every day. In fact, he was here so frequently that her grandfather's will provided for the construction of a caretaker's cottage for Seth. If it would ever stop raining maybe they could finish construction. This summer had been the wettest on record, halting their progress, and this storm was the worst of them all. In fact, given his protectiveness of her, she was surprised Seth hadn't called during the storm. She'd made it quite clear on numerous occasions she was more than capable of taking care of herself, but that didn't stop him from worrying over her every chance he got. It would be annoying if it wasn't so endearing.

A kind of morbid curiosity drove her toward the damage to see what she could for herself. Trailing her hand along the rail, Laney held her breath in anticipation of what she'd find. A twisted piece of metal railing was the first thing that told her she'd found what she was looking for. *Damn.* Just before he'd died two years ago, her grandfather had rebuilt the stable, so everything was new and state-of-the-art. Her stomach dropped as she began to get a feel for the damage, which mostly seemed to have impacted the end two stalls. Crossing the center aisle, she found the tack room walls intact. A quick circuit revealed everything was how it was supposed to be. The damage was confined to the other side, then.

Laney grabbed a rake from a hook and flipped it handle side down as she crossed back to assess the damage. She rarely carried her cane around the farm, but if part of the ceiling had come down, there would be debris. As she stepped into the ruined stall, she tapped the pole in front of her, searching out obstructions that might trip her up. The sound was immediately wrong, metallic, and her foot landed on a sheet of metal that wasn't the normal rubber-over-concrete flooring. Part of the roof had collapsed.

Slowly, she lifted the rake handle and swung it in front of her to ensure no pieces of roofing hung loose from the ceiling. Nothing.

Returning her makeshift cane to the floor, she tapped along a large section of metal sheeting.

But what the hell brought it down?

She expected to find part of the ancient oak tree that

stood behind the barn, but nothing she was finding confirmed that theory.

Laney was just about to give up when the handle encountered something on the floor, solid but giving. She focused and scanned her limited vision back and forth, her brain slowly assembling the pieces of the picture into a whole that made her gasp out loud.

It was a horse. She blinked and squinted. A weird yellow halo flickered across her vision when she looked closer. It really *was* a freaking horse.

How? From where? Laney mentally recounted her steps to ensure she'd checked on all *her* horses. *Cocoa, Casper, Rolly, Windsong, Sappho.* She'd talked to and touched every one of them. She was sure of it.

And even if she wasn't, this stall had been empty for a long time. None of her regular horses used it.

Oh, crap. Could there have been a tornado? They were rare in Maryland, but what the heck else would drop a horse out of the sky? Just imagining that's what happened made her stomach toss.

Setting the rake to the side, Laney crouched, her gut queasy and pulse pounding in her ears, and found the wet barrel of the horse's belly with her hand. The lift and fall of its breathing was immediately obvious, shooting relief through her amazed disbelief. *He's alive.*

She moved from between the horse's legs. Downed horses could thrash or kick. Getting injured was the last thing she needed. She crouched near his head and stroked his golden neck, that strange halo effect growing brighter. Laney clenched and reopened her eyes, but it was still there.

"Hey, friend," she whispered, still struggling to believe

what her pinpoint of sight was telling her was there. She leaned in close enough to see the eye was closed, though flickering. Every once in a while, the horse shuddered out a breath, but otherwise its respiration was just a little fast. She pressed her fingers against the fetlock joint toward the bottom of his leg and found a pulse. Heart rate was elevated, but not as unusual as she might've expected. *How could he still be alive?* Given what had likely happened to him and his unconscious state, she expected him to be a lot worse off.

When she leaned away, Laney's hand brushed something sticky and she traced her fingers over the horse's left front leg. A gash flayed open the golden flesh.

She needed to get help. Now.

Laney fished her iPhone out of her pocket and pressed the extra-large telephone icon in the bottom right corner. "Seth is going to have a cow when he sees you," she murmured. She waited for it to connect. And waited. She redialed but had the same luck. No signal. "Seriously?"

Groaning, Laney pocketed her phone as she rose. There were two land lines in the barn. Overkill for a sighted person, but having both made it easier for her to get to one of them when they rang.

Back in the tack room, Laney dialed Seth's number, but all she got was an odd fast busy signal with lots of crackling static. Why would she still have lights but no phones?

She sighed. Stupid storm. The service would get restored soon. In the meantime, she grabbed the first-aid kit and a couple of stable blankets and returned to her mystery guest. Laney was known for taking in strays, but this was going a little far, even for her.

Inside the kit, the bottles were sized differently and color-

coded so she could tell the different solutions apart. She
poured saline from the white bottle over the wound to clean
it, then did her best to center a gauze pad over the injury
before securing it with Vetwrap. Doing this was probably
stupid, given what his other injuries likely were, but it made
her feel useful. And at least it would stay clean until she
could get the vet out here.

"What else is wrong with you?" she murmured.
Carefully, she worked her way around his head, and
smoothed her hands over his shoulder to his—

"What the hell?"

Her fingers encountered something downy soft. Something
that had no business on a horse's back.

She looked. Squinted. Leaned in and looked again.

There was no way she was seeing what her very low
vision was telling her she was seeing.

No way on earth.

Running her hands over the feathery protrusion confirmed
what her sight had identified.

The horse…the horse had wings.

CHAPTER THREE

Awe and wonder—not to mention a healthy dose of fear—rushed through Laney's veins so hard she became lightheaded.

She pressed her fingers against the downy softness of the wings again and sucked in a breath. Never had she felt something so silky, so plush, and her fingertips were especially sensitive to touch.

Sinking her hand into the complex layers of feathers, Laney had to accept what all her senses were telling her.

A winged horse had crashed through the ceiling of her stable in the midst of a terrible storm.

Dizziness threatened to swamp her. She forced a deep breath.

How was this possible? Maybe she was actually in her bed dreaming right now? Or maybe her sight had finally failed her after all? Though, that didn't explain what she'd *felt*...

Her amazement morphed into concern as her imagination painted a picture of this magnificent beast battling the elements and losing. Were there others like him? Would they be searching for him?

Did the fact she was actually entertaining the existence of a…of a Pegasus certify her as raving mad?

But here he was. In the flesh. Far, far from wherever he belonged.

The thought that he was lost, all alone, and injured made her heart squeeze. And, *oh God*, it wasn't like she could bring the vet out now. What the hell was she going to do? If anyone else saw him, they'd take him away, study him, lock him up.

No way.

Or, they'd take her away, run a series of psych tests, and lock *her* up.

Also not appealing.

"Don't worry, I'll figure something out," she whispered as she stroked him.

Her finger caught on a bent feather. She smoothed her palm over the area and found more damage—the sharp edges of broken feather spines and, again, a stickiness she feared was blood. Red smears on her hand confirmed her suspicion.

Unlike his leg, she had no idea how to treat a wing, for goodness sake. She just hoped he didn't thrash in his sleep and damage it further.

"What am I going to do with you?" she asked. She spread out several horse blankets to provide a barrier between her skin and the puddles and debris, then sat all the way down. Her legs were all pins and needles from squatting, and she just needed a minute to stretch them out. "I'll stay with you, okay?" Stroking his golden neck and mane, all she could think was, *I'm touching a Pegasus!*

After a while, she grabbed an extra stable blanket and pulled it up over her bare legs. Her clothes were nearly dry, but her sneakers were still wet and squishy, so she slipped them off. Thunder rumbled in the distance, once, twice. Laney's stomach dropped and, instinctively, she leaned into the horse's big body. Through everything, horses had always been her greatest comfort. Despite this guy's differences, he still gave her that same feeling of safety and solace.

And, in contrast to the cooling night breeze, he was so *warm*.

For a long moment, Laney reveled in the soft rise and fall of his body, proof that this miraculous beast existed. And that he lived.

His heat seeped into her muscles, achy from the tension she'd borne earlier. Now that she knew all her babies were safe, fatigue roared through her body and Laney couldn't stop yawning. She should get up. Arguably, it wasn't safe sitting here by him—*are Pegasuses even friendly?* The question made her head spin. Five more minutes. She just couldn't pull herself away from something so magical. But it definitely wouldn't be safe to fall asleep. Just a while longer. The shoulder she leaned against rose and fell, rose and fell. Just a little while longer…

⚄⚄

Bone-crushing pain and soul-deep exhaustion told Chrysander Notos he was still alive.

He was adrift in a dark sea of agony, disoriented and alone. His limbs weighed a thousand pounds. Putting the full force of his wavering concentration behind the effort, he forced his eyelids open. The low light stung and he blinked and squinted.

Finally, his eyes adjusted. He scanned his surroundings—an odd red metal floor lay beneath him, and the wall before him was made of some kind of unusual fencing. Chrys couldn't assemble the parts into a meaningful whole, and didn't have the energy to think about it, anyway.

At least his form had stabilized. He lay as a man... wherever he was.

The tighter his grasp on consciousness, the more Chrys became aware of another sensation: luxurious warmth against his back. And as hurt as he was, he craved more of whatever was providing the life-giving heat.

Lifting his head made the world swim, forcing him to pause and breathe through the disorientation. His right shoulder protested the movement, still raw from being stabbed by the leashed lightning Eurus shouldn't have been able to wield, but Chrys had to know what he was feeling.

Easing onto his back, Chrys found himself staring into the sleeping face of an incredibly beautiful woman. Long black hair spilled down around her shoulder, and cherry red lips set off the fairness of her skin. She lay stretched out against him, her head now resting against his bicep.

The comfort her body heat provided was so intense, her laying against him didn't even set off his usual anxiety about being touched. As long as he controlled physical contact, he could handle it, but being touched by others was a one-way ticket to a panic attack. It was a sign of his pain and desperation that he now wanted more of this stranger touching him. His condition yearned for her warmth, demanded it.

He struggled to turn toward her, and was struck by the

burning ache seizing his forearm. From where he'd blocked
the— He gawked. Thick bandages now covered the wound.
She'd patched him up?

The thought that she'd touched him while he was so
vulnerable should've alarmed him, but it simply made him
crave her even harder. Shaking from the effort, Chrys slowly
turned until he faced her. Soft, warm exhalations hushed over
the skin of his chest. He scooted closer, until her lips were but
a breath away from his pecs. A length of her hair caressed his
arm, thick and soft and warm.

It still wasn't enough.

Chrys pressed his legs against hers. She let out a sigh and
shifted. Chrys froze and then nearly groaned as she burrowed
against him, her forehead tight against his chest and her legs
entwined with his. Her incredible body heat flowed into him
and more than compensated for the dizziness sending black
spots around the edges of his vision. He breathed through a
rolling wave of nausea.

Thank the gods for this woman, whoever she was. Bad off
as he was, he couldn't even bother to care. He should. Gods
only knew what she'd seen, but all he could think about was
how her body warmed his from calves to throat. To Chrys, heat
was life. And she was giving him both. A shudder of relief ran
through him.

Not wanting to wake her, Chrys refrained from going
as far as wrapping his arm around her like he wanted to, but
he needed heat so intensely he couldn't muster more than a
passing guilt for using her this way.

His head thunked to the floor and his eyes sagged.

Naked. You're naked, Notos. Shit. Chrys concentrated,
willing material, any material—he'd take a damn toga if that's

what he could get—to materialize over his bottom half. He broke out in a cold sweat and shuddered. You know you're in the shit when you can't even cover your bare ass.

Fuck it. After some shut-eye and a few hours of her heat, he'd be in more shape to worry about making himself presentable.

Fatigue pressed down on him, made even the involuntary action of breathing take way too much effort. His gut soured and tossed. Closing his eyes and concentrating on her heat seemed to be the only way to combat the revolt his stomach kept threatening. He pressed his face into the woman's hair—oranges. She smelled of sweet, juicy oranges.

Soaking in her warmth and her summery scent, Chrys succumbed to his injured exhaustion and passed out again.

∞∞

Laney woke up sweating. The sun streamed in through the hole in the ceiling, roasting her body and drawing out a sheen of perspiration on her skin. The underneath of her hair was even damp.

It's so hot, was her first thought.

The winged horse! was her second.

She jumped up. Only, something heavy braced around her waist. Shaking off the fog of sleep, she reached down to push herself out from the warm weight.

What the hell?

It was a…it felt like a…

Laney wrenched into a sitting position, and an arm fell into her lap. An arm that had been wrapped around her. A… human arm?

Her heart pounded blood through her ears. *No, no. Time to wake up, Laney*. She blinked and rubbed her eyes. Scanned her vision over him until, like a puzzle, the pieces started to come together. And…

Still. Freaking. Human.

A moan of panic tore up her throat. She crab-scrabbled backward, and her hand came down on something sharp. She cried out. From somewhere else in the barn, a horse whinnied, a long, low call of concern. Laney slipped, and something sharp and metallic scraped the back of her calf.

But Laney couldn't fight the blind panic. There was no horse. *No horse!* Only a man. *A freaking man!* Questions flooded her brain, disoriented her, ignited her panic. *How? Who was he? What was happening to her? How could her senses have failed her so badly?*

"What's happening?" the man groaned. "Gods, are you okay? Hey, watch out!"

Laney's back slammed into the stable's grillwork. The impact rattled down her spine and set off a sickening ache in her neck and head.

Shadows shifted in front of her, but her sight was no more than a blurred, unfocused array of pinpoint images. She had to calm down.

"Are you all right?" came a deep voice from right next to her. Warmth radiated close to her leg. "Aw, Hades, you're bleeding."

Laney had to swallow twice before she could muster a verbal response. "Wh-who are y-you?"

"Chrys."

"C-Chrys?" As if that explained anything. The light turned gold directly in front of her. Laney blinked and forced herself to take deep, calming breaths. "You're a man."

"Last time I checked," he said, voice weak but amused.

She scoffed. *Yeah, well...* "Last time *I* checked, you were a horse, so one of us isn't quite in their right mind." Laney groaned. Did she really just say that out loud? She sighed, still shaking. None of this made any sense. "Forget I said that." He didn't respond, making the air feel hot and awkward. "Why are you in my barn?"

"I'm not sure. What's your name?" he finally said, amusement gone from his voice.

"Laney."

"Okay, Laney, can you stand?"

"I can, but I need you to get me out of the stall."

"Uh, what do you—"

"I'm having trouble seeing," she said, unwilling to reveal her disability when she didn't know who he was or what he was doing here. She waved her uninjured hand, accidentally brushing against him. "I'm all disoriented." Thankfully, it was less and less true. The more she calmed, the more she regained clarity in her limited vision.

"Sure," he said in a tight voice. He grasped her good hand. "Go ahead and stand up."

Laney nodded and allowed his strength to pull her to her feet, his hand totally encompassing hers. Her legs were like Jell-O from fright, from her injury. Metal warmed the bottom of her feet. "Do you, um, see my sneakers?"

"Uh, yeah. Got 'em."

Laney held her hands out, but his light touch fell on the top of her foot.

"Lift."

"I can put my own shoes on."

"No doubt. Lift."

Laney obeyed, ignoring the heat of his skin against hers and the soft brush of his hair against her thigh. She fought the urge to reach out and see if it felt as silky against her hand. Silky like the horse's wings. *Let it go, Laney.*

"There you are," he said in a deep voice. The golden light moved away from her.

What the heck was that, anyway? If she was developing halos, her sight was deteriorating yet again. "Thanks."

"Okay, uh, take about three steps to your right, and you're out in the main hallway, but there's a rough piece of metal you need to step over."

Wincing at the sting of her cuts, Laney allowed Chrys to guide her.

"Step up and over," he said. "Good. You're clear."

The rubber beneath her feet confirmed the truth of his words. Then the hard concrete told her when she'd returned to the central aisle. Laney swayed.

His hand gripped her shoulder. "Whoa."

"Think I just stood up too fast. It'll pass."

"How hard did you hit your head?"

Distracted by the weird sensation of vertigo, Laney shrugged and braced her hand against the rail. She hissed. Holding her palm up close to her face, all she could see was red, not the specifics of her injury. Her wounds needed to be cleaned and treated, but no sense revealing just how much they hurt. She dropped her hand, ignoring the stinging, and tried to look him over.

She was used to the limitations of her low vision by now, but sometimes it was *so* frustrating not to be able to see more than a pinpoint of the world at a time, her brain putting the whole together like a slow computer loading the pixels of a high-resolution image. Blond hair. Longish. Angled jaw. Muscled shoulder. *Bare* muscled shoulder.

Laney gasped and cut her gaze away, half of her afraid of what else she might see if she continued to scan her gaze over him, and half of her *dying* to know.

"What?"

"You don't have a shirt on."

"Uh, no."

"This is so crazy," she whispered to herself. She cleared her throat. "Please tell me you're not naked."

"I'm not naked."

Laney looked. Scanned. Jeans. She released a long breath. "Good. That's good."

"Look, I'm sorry," he said, his tone strained and raspy, like it took effort to speak.

"For what?" Adrenaline flooded through her, along with a healthy dose of fear. She wasn't sure what scared her most. Whatever he was about to apologize for? That her impossible Pegasus didn't exist after all? That she'd woken up with a strange and equally impossible man? That she'd apparently imagined the events of last night?

"For scaring you."

"Well, I'd say it wasn't your fault, but it kinda was." Still, there was something about the well-worn regret in his voice that made her want to comfort him, touch him, know him. It was just all so crazy.

"Do you always say exactly what you mean?"

Laney frowned, confusion still making her head spin. "As opposed to saying something I don't mean?"

"I guess when you put it that way…"

"Look, not to be rude, but who are you and what are you doing in my barn?"

He sighed. "It's a long story."

One she was determined to hear, given the eleventy-billion questions she had. "I'm sure I can follow along."

"It's not that—"

"Then what? Huh? I could use a little help reassuring myself I'm not going insane."

She could hear his little movements against the flooring. Soft scuffs, like he was barefooted. "You're not. It's just that I don't remember all of it, and what I do remember isn't going to make any sense." The gold light moved in front of her. "We should take care of your cuts first."

Truth be told, her leg and palm burned like hell, but fear that her senses had let her down so magnificently vibrated panic through her veins. Her senses were her independence. Her survival. Without them, she'd lose everything. "Nice try. Talk."

His sigh resembled more of a groan. "I got in a fight."

Huh? "And…"

"I got my ass kicked."

Memories from last night washed over her. The gash on the horse's forearm. The ruined feathers on the wing. *Stop it*. Clearly, this man wasn't that horse. Still, the fact remained that there was a hole in her ceiling, and he was here. "Are you hurt?"

"I'll live."

"Do you always speak using the fewest possible words?"

There was a long pause. "Let's clean you up. You got a sink around here?"

"Yeah, because that wasn't an obvious change of topic at all."

"Sink?"

"I'll get cleaned up inside. It's fine." It wasn't fine, but he didn't need to know that. Like she wasn't vulnerable enough. Fingertips on the rail again, she took a step. Gritting her teeth, she put weight on her injured leg. Man, did that smart.

Much as she hated to admit it, Laney needed help. And that brought one person to mind. *Seth*. He was going to flip his shit when he saw she'd been hurt. She went for her phone in her pocket— Empty. *Damnit*! She must've dropped it in the stall.

Just keep moving, Laney. There was a landline at the end of the barn she could use.

She moved along the railing, and the cuts on the back of her calf pulled with every step. Chrys's soft treads followed just behind her, like he was prepared to catch her should her legs give out. The hair on the back of her neck raised. Who the hell was this guy and what did he want?

And why didn't she feel as fearful as she thought she should? Being blind, hurt, and alone with a strange man didn't exactly put her in a position of power.

A man who was a horse.

Laney groaned and paused next to an occupied stall, her breathing coming a little harder. "Hi, Windy," she murmured to the colt, the horse's presence making her feel more grounded, less alone. Gathering her resolve, she continued on to Sappho's, where she had to rest again. The mare pressed her muzzle into Laney's uninjured hand and nickered. "Nothing to worry about here, baby." Sappho shook her head, as if disagreeing, and pushed her big, elegant nose against Laney's side, making her stumble a step away from Chrys. She grunted at the quick movement. "Hey, what was that for?"

"I don't think your horse likes me," came the strange man's low voice.

"She's protective of me." A noise caught her attention. In the distance, tires tore up her long stone driveway. Seth's truck, if she wasn't mistaken. Years of relying on them for information about her world made her ears especially sensitive. Relieved as she was that Seth had arrived, she mentally prepared for the massive freak-out likely to happen when he saw her injuries. Blowing out a shaky breath, she said, "I think the cavalry has arrived."

Chapter Four

The barn felt suddenly still. That odd gold light shined in front of her and a warmth caressed her face, then both were gone. "Chrys?" She turned around. "Chrys?"

What the hell is happening?

"Chrys," she said again, louder. Behind her, Sappho nickered. She was totally losing it. Tears pricked at the backs of her eyes. "Please answer me." She scanned her nearly useless vision over the space. The light and the man were gone, as far as she could see and hear. She was alone.

Truly alone, this time.

The roar of the engine in Seth's big pickup drew closer and the strange events of the past twelve hours weighed down on her.

Laney's head spun and her injuries left her shaky. Her knees went soft, and she leaned against the front of Sappho's stall. The horse chuffed at her like she was concerned.

Hot tears gathered and Laney looked to the ceiling to force them away. Had she imagined the whole thing? If she had… She batted away an escapee tear. If she didn't hold it together, Seth would go all Papa Bear when he saw her.

The truck's tires crunched over the gravel and finally came to a halt near the open barn door. His footsteps seemed to retreat, as if he was heading up to the house.

"Seth?" she said, but her voice cracked. She cleared it and called again. "Seth?"

Outside, his pace halted, then quickened into a run. "Laney?" The hard soles of his boots tore into the gravel and finally echoed off the barn's concrete floor. "Sonofa— What happened? Are you okay?" He hovered over her.

"Seth," she whispered, a sob suddenly lodging in her throat.

Calloused fingers cradled her injured hand. "I knew something was wrong. Damnit. Where else are you hurt?"

"The back of my leg," she said, his familiar presence calming her. Seth had always been like the older brother she never had. No, more than that. A true friend. Someone who got her, who understood what was important to her. Someone she could rely on for anything.

He moved around her, examining her wounds. "How did this happen?"

"The barn." Laney pointed toward the far end of the stable. "The roof. In the storm," she managed.

"Why didn't you call me? And why the hell did you try to walk in the debris on your own?"

"Any chance you can save the lecture for when I'm not bleeding all over the place?"

"I'm serious, Laney."

"So am I. I had to make sure the horses were okay. I tried to call you, but the phones weren't working and I didn't have a cell signal. Simple as that."

He grunted a sound that expressed his displeasure. "Think you can walk? We need to get you to the E.R."

Laney nodded, grateful that he let it drop. For now. She knew she had a major shit fit coming her way. Holding onto him, she pushed off the railing. Her head swam.

"Okay, lean on me and let's take it slow."

She limped against Seth's side as they made their way out of the barn and toward his truck. "Is the E.R really necessary? Can't I just call my regular doc?" Last thing she wanted was a trip to the E.R. She'd spent enough of her life seeing one doctor after another.

"You're gonna need stitches and a tetanus shot. The E.R. will be able to take care of everything."

It was worth a shot. She sighed. "Okay."

"Giving in that easy makes me even more worried about you."

She elbowed him in the side. "Shut up."

"And there's my Laney," he said in an almost amused voice. "Okay, two more steps then hold up a minute." He opened the truck door. "I'll lift you."

Laney frowned at the idea, but in truth, she wasn't sure she could get herself up on the seat with the cut on the back of her leg. "Just give me a boost."

His arms came behind her back and knees. "Ready?"

"Yeah." She wrapped her arms tight around his neck. This close, she couldn't help but notice his crisp, outdoorsy scent. Sweet hay and warm leather. She'd recognize it anywhere. The arm under her knee pulled at the cuts. She whimpered.

"Sorry," he said in a tight voice as he settled her on the

seat.

"Not your fault," she managed, breathing through the raw burn eating up the back of her leg.

He closed her door and hustled around to his. With her hand injured and her head such a jumbled mess, she was fighting a losing battle with her seat belt when he got in the driver's side. "Here," he said. He reached across and secured the belt.

"Thanks," she whispered, hating being so helpless. Geez, she hoped she wasn't bleeding all over his truck. Not that Seth would care.

Laney laid her head back and closed her eyes as they made their way down the long drive. What she had seen of the winged horse came immediately to her mind's eye.

"Hang on," Seth said.

She lifted her head. "What?"

"We gotta do some off-roading. Trees down over the driveway. Down all over the place, from the storm. Weather men are saying maybe some tornadoes touched down last night."

Tornadoes? That was exactly what she'd wondered when she found the horse. You know, the one that *wasn't* there this morning. The truck bounced as it left the gravel, jarring the thoughts away. Laney gripped the door handle and breathed through the bumpy ride. Then they were back on level ground.

"I'm gonna call Ben. Get him to come take care of the horses and see if he can get some guys to clear the drive."

Laney nodded. Seth's cousin had worked at Summerlyn Farm most summers while he'd been in school. The horses would be in good hands. Seth's voice in the background, she went back to studying the golden Pegasus plastered on the inside of her eyelids.

Now, she didn't know whether to believe her magical visitor had been real or not. Either her faculties were failing or... What? She didn't even know.

One step at a time, Laney. Yes. Okay. That, she could do.

8)(03

From the doorway of the barn, Chrysander watched the truck depart. He didn't know what bothered him more—the exhaustion he felt down to his bones, the ass-kicking he'd received last night that had drained his power, the relief in the woman's voice at the human man's arrival, or the man's hands all over her. And why the hell the latter two should bother him, he couldn't say. For fuck's sake.

And on top of it all, he was so badly drained after the latest round of ass-kicking that he had no choice but to return to the Realm of the Gods. He'd been avoiding returning as much as he could. He didn't want the Olympians to decide the Anemoi couldn't handle the task of bringing Eurus in, nor reveal just how dire the situation with Eurus was, lest he ruin any chance to appeal to their mercy. But given that manifesting a pair of jeans made him break out in a cold sweat, he was in need of some serious R&R of the sort he could only get in the divine realm.

Not to mention, after last night, he needed to reevaluate just how concerned he was about the Olympians' mercy. But first things first.

He willed himself into the elements and— *Shit*. Nothing but a soul-deep ache. He'd been successful moments before when he'd made himself scarce. *Don't tell me that's seriously all I got.* He tried again. Success! The South Wind surrounded him. He drew it in, trying to—

Human. Again. He couldn't hold his form. "Son of a—"

"Need a ride, sailor?"

Chrys turned. *Ella.* His brother Zeph's mate. "Well, look at you materializing in the human realm," he said, hoping his voice didn't sound as strained to her as it did to his own ears.

She smiled, her brown eyes sparkling with excitement. "I know, right? I'm starting to get the hang of this whole 'goddess' gig."

He chuckled. Ella had lost her whole human family, died a horrible human death, and been thrust into her goddesshood without any say in the matter, yet she was always good-natured. "Apparently so, since you're here. How'd you find me?"

"When he finally got a read on you, Livos let me know you were in trouble." Her gaze scanned over his bandaged forearm and the grisly stab wound and burned flesh on his shoulder.

Chrys frowned. He'd specifically ordered his subordinates to shield his whereabouts and not interfere in his business with Eurus, no matter what happened. And yet the god of the Southwest Wind had opened his yap.

"Oh, drop the grumpy face. I didn't really give him a choice in the matter."

"Uh, not to be rude, there, Sis, but you don't yet have the power to be pushing around any of the Anemoi. Even the lesser Anemoi." He winked. "Except maybe my brother, who is about as whipped as they come."

"No offense taken. But, if you think Livos wants to chance earning Zeph's ire, you're wrong. He works for Zephyros, too. Let's just say I persuaded him to see the wisdom in cooperating with me rather than having to get my husband involved. Besides, you and Eurus thrashed my Bay last night, so you sorta made it my business."

Ella had been an avid sailor in her human life, so Mars, the father of her divine bloodline, had given her the job of guardian of the Chesapeake Bay she knew so well. Chrys tugged a hand through his hair. She was going to be a full-out force of nature when she came into her powers completely. Gods help them all, then. "Remind me never to get on your bad side."

"Happily." She tucked her straight brown hair behind her ears. "So, how 'bout that ride?"

"Where are we, anyway?"

"Near a little town called Princess Anne. Eastern Shore of Maryland."

"I was trying to take the storm out over the Atlantic."

Ella nodded, her expression suddenly serious. "Come on. We should go. You need to do anything else here?"

Chrys wasn't sure what accounted for the change in her demeanor, but he didn't want to push. "No. I'll send Livos back later to do some damage control. But, about the ride— I'm worried this is going to drain you."

"Never know if we don't try. Besides, I'm only hauling your butt as far as my place. Livos is waiting there to take you to yours."

"What about Z?"

"He went to see Boreas at Owen's."

"You've got this all figured out, don't you?"

She smiled and wrapped her arm around his. "No. I'm bluffing my way through most of it."

Chrys bristled at the touch, but there was no avoiding it. *You didn't mind the other woman's touch.* The thought did nothing for his frame of mind. "Well, you're doing a damn fine job," he managed.

She gave him a squeeze. "Here goes nothing."

Throwing what little power he still possessed into the effort, Chrys felt himself drawn into the elements. Hell if she wasn't doing it.

They rose up through the air. His lack of corporeality was the greatest relief. In this state, he remained aware of the utter exhaustion, but not the agony of his injuries. Ella's natural aura added a calmness to his elemental state, further providing solace. Laney's farm spread out beneath them then disappeared behind the clouds. They soared on toward the Realm of the Gods, Ella quiet and determined in her focus.

Don't drop me, he teased in the thoughts he knew she should be able to hear.

Don't tempt me, came a reply full of amusement.

Soon, they reached the divine realm. The compound of the Supreme God of the West Wind appeared before them. She guided them toward an outdoor courtyard and Chrys pulled himself free of her power. Simply being home again gave him just enough energy to finish the job. He materialized into his human form and groaned as he touched down.

"I'll get Livos," she said.

He braced his hands on his knees. "It's okay. He'll know I'm here," he said, forcing deep breaths to chase away the nausea being back in his body caused. "Thank you, Ella. Are you all right? Not too drained?"

"I'm fine." She stepped toward him. Chrys straightened, but almost wished he hadn't. She reached out and cupped his jaw. "I was worried about you. I have been, all summer. I'm the reason you're—"

"No, you're not," he gritted out and resisted his natural urge to flinch away from her touch. "Don't think that for a minute. This is all on Eurus." He pulled her hand away from the uncomfortable touch and gave it a squeeze, then he crossed his arms.

She nodded. Something flashed behind her gaze. "He was at the bridge, wasn't he?"

Shit. Not a conversation he really wanted to have, but if she wasn't going to shy away from it, why should he? "Aw, Hades. Yeah. How'd you know?"

"I go there sometimes, trying to remember. Sometimes I think I can feel him there."

"Ella—"

"Zeph won't tell me, and everything's so foggy." She shrugged.

"That's because it's not something anyone should have to remember. But you shouldn't go there alone again. It's not safe."

Her gaze dropped to the ground, but she finally nodded.

"My lord?"

Chrysander turned to find Livos, Ordinal Anemoi of the Southwest Wind, on a knee, dark blond head bowed. "Sure, *now* you're all full of respect and obedience. Get up."

Livos's expression was serious as he returned to his full height. Anger and concern rolled off him in waves Chrys's body couldn't withstand in its current beat-to-hell state. "To the Acheron, my lord?"

"No." Much as the waters of the infernal river would've sped his healing, his presence in the Underworld might also draw attention he'd rather not attract. The Lord of the Underworld was brother to more than one of the Olympians, after all.

Livos frowned and inhaled as if to argue.

Chrys cut off the debate with a single glance. "Home." The heat of Aithiopia, the southernmost geography of the divine realm where he resided, would sufficiently restore him. He turned to Ella. "Thanks for the taxi service."

She gave a small smile. "You're welcome. But thanks aren't necessary. I would do anything for you, for all of you."

He nodded. Livos came alongside him, but was careful not to touch.

"Chrys?" Ella's voice was soft, hesitant.

"Yeah?"

"Please be careful." She hugged herself. "He's not worth it."

The words hit home, filling him with sadness for this god that no one valued, nor ever had. And even if he wasn't really worth it, how did anyone get okay with making that admission, with letting go once and for all?

He met Ella's concerned gaze and searched for a response that wouldn't offend her. Given what Eurus did to her, he could never deny her the right to hate him. He couldn't deny that a part of him did, too. Finally, he managed a small, tired shrug, and said, "He's still my brother."

Chapter Five

Boreas, the Supreme God of the North Wind and Winter, couldn't escape the deep sense of foreboding that had weighed so heavily on his shoulders all summer. From the moment he'd found his brother Zephyros cradling Ella's human corpse last March, he'd known—no matter how he turned the problem of the feud between the Anemoi brothers over in his mind, not all of them came out alive. And that was before the Olympians had handed down Eurus's death sentence.

This whole situation would only get worse before it got better. That was half the reason he'd been spending so much time these past months at his son and daughter-in-law's home in the human realm—over his dead body would he let the fighting breach the happiness they'd recently found together.

As if reading his thoughts, Zephyros appeared in the center of Owen and Megan's living room wearing human street clothes.

"I've been expecting you," Boreas said.

Anger and restlessness poured off his brethren from the West and ricocheted around the comfortable, welcoming space, filled with family photos and baby toys. "What are we going to do about Chrys and Eurus?" he asked, his vivid blue eyes flaring in agitation.

"Good question."

It was exactly what he'd been mulling over. Leaning against the molding of a window, Boreas let his gaze wander outside as he pondered his answer. He squinted against the bright September sun. In the yard next door, Owen's neighbor Tabitha Wilder knelt in the grass. Boreas watched her patiently weed the flower bed in front of her porch. No matter the season, the woman seemed to enjoy spending time out-of-doors. And while he'd rarely noticed her have company, she always appeared content, the hint of a smile on her face, as if she took joy from whatever she put her mind to doing. Not that he was keeping tabs.

He turned back to Zephyros on a sigh. "Because it is his season, Chrysander is the strongest among us right now. He has decided this is his fight, and he will not be dissuaded." Not that Boreas was happy about it. Not at all. It had been one of the worst summers on record—devastating storms and flooding rains alternated with intense heat and suffocating humidity. It was the kind of weather that had once led humans to fear the Supreme God of the South Wind and the turbulent, crop-destroying powers he possessed.

"He may be the strongest right now, but clearly he hasn't been able to bring Eurus to heel."

"No." Boreas was equally troubled by Chrys's seeming inability to defeat their malevolent brother.

"Something's not right, Boreas."

"I agree," Owen said, coming down the steps into the living room.

"Teddy asleep?" Boreas asked. He adored his one-year-old grandson, the other reason he spent so much time here.

Owen nodded, dragging a hand through his black hair. "They both are. I'll be glad when the baby comes. This pregnancy hasn't been nearly as easy," he said. "Hey, Zeph." The gods shook hands.

"Megan is strong. She will be fine." Boreas hated to see his son's worry, but he couldn't have been prouder of the man, the father he'd become. Since he'd earned a reprieve from his duties as a snow god nearly two years before, Owen had proven himself made for fatherhood.

"How much longer will the Olympians wait?" Owen asked. After the near-tragedy with Ella in March, Mars had delivered the message that the Olympic gods wanted Eurus dead. Thankfully, they were willing to let the family handle it. So Aeolus, the storm god father of the Anemoi, had been forced to agree to the death sentence, but it was Chrysander who took up the task.

Zephyros shook his head. "For now, they're allowing it to remain family business. But Mars has been full of meaningful looks that make it clear their patience won't last forever. Honestly, I'm surprised they've let it go on this long." He crossed his arms and looked between the other gods. "Now, summer ends in three weeks. Olympians aside, this needs to be over before fall starts and Eurus comes into his season."

Boreas glanced out the window again. Tabitha was looking toward the house. The sun's glare probably kept her from really seeing him, but he still stepped back, his heart suddenly in flight from the brief eye contact. Apparently being an ancient god didn't save you from developing a crush on someone your heart and guilt would never let you have. "Let's find Chrys and figure out what is going on."

"That's what I'm talking about," Zephyros said.

"Sometimes, this demigod thing sucks." Owen's lips pressed into a line. As a demigod, Owen's powers were neither as strong nor as lasting as that of the Anemoi. Elemental travel as far as the Realm of the Gods would drain him.

Boreas shook his head. "You have a family to take care of now. Let us handle this."

His son gave a tight nod. "Talk some sense into Chrys, will ya?"

Zephyros scoffed. "Like talking to a damn brick wall."

Owen chuckled. "Yeah, I don't know any other Anemoi like that."

"I never really liked you," Zeph said with a mock glare.

"Except when I saved and protected Ella, you mean."

The corner of his brother's mouth quirked up. "Yeah, except then." Smiling, he clapped Owen on the shoulder. "I'll stay for a longer visit next time. Tell your prettier half that Ella and I say hello."

They clasped hands and knocked shoulders. "I will. And I'm serious about Chrys. I've never seen such volatile summer weather, and it's not like him to be so out of control. Something's not right."

The three of them traded glances, the truth of Owen's observation pressing down on them equally. They said their good-byes and Boreas and Zephyros dematerialized. His brother's agitation was apparent even in their elemental form, sending out tiny crackles of electricity and abrupt gusts of wind.

He's here, Zephyros said as soon as they crossed through the invisible shield of divine energy into the Realm of the Gods. *You up for this?*

Chrysander's residence in the south of the divine realm strained Boreas's tolerance for heat, but he could handle it for short periods at a time. *Yes, it must be done.*

The further they traveled, the more intense the sun became. Golden light bathed everything as Aithiopia came into view. They zeroed in on Chrysander's sprawling compound. His unique energy signature revealed he was here, but it felt...off somehow. A mere shadow of itself. Zephyros's agitation flared.

They materialized in the lush entranceway to the compound, thick green vegetation and brilliant tropical flowers surrounding the area. The temperature pressed in on Boreas, the hot air more difficult for his lungs to draw in and out.

"Chrysander?" Zephyros called as they made their way inside. "Chrys?"

"This way." Boreas led them down the main hallway toward the center of the compound.

"Why don't you change? Aren't they making it worse?"

Boreas frowned.

Zephyros gestured with a hand toward the fur robes Boreas had worn for millennia. He never even gave them a second thought anymore. "I am fine." And, anyway, they'd always reminded him of his long-dead wife, Ori, so a part of him had continued wearing the ancient garb in remembrance of her. Now, it was as much habit as anything.

A blast of heat greeted them as they entered a long

mirrored antechamber outside the ceremonial center of Chrysander's compound. Boreas barely restrained a groan and Zephyros gave him another pointed look. But Boreas's attention was on the two gods in traditional tunics standing watch outside the golden doors of the Hall of the South Wind.

Livos and Apheliotes, the Ordinal Anemoi of the Southwest and Southeast winds, dropped to a knee and bowed their heads.

"Rise," Zephyros said. He nailed Livos, who also worked for him, with an expectant glare as the lesser gods resumed their position in front of the doors. "Let us pass."

The gods exchanged glances. Livos shook his head. "It is not my wish to disobey, my lord, but he cannot be disturbed."

"We must speak with him," Boreas said. "It is urgent."

"Perhaps on the morrow—"

"Damnit, Livos, I will not debate this. Step aside." Zephyros got right in his subordinate's face.

Boreas frowned. Livos would not put up such resistance unless... Apheliotes dropped his gaze and Boreas gave him a long look. Realization slammed into him, making it even harder to breathe. He braced his palm against Zephyros's chest to get him to back down. "How bad is it?"

Livos cut his gaze to Boreas. For a moment, the answer was clear in the younger god's eyes. Good gods.

A storm settled over Zephyros's countenance and added a thick humidity to the dry heat of the chamber.

Seeing his superior's temper about to run out, Livos spilled. "It's bad. He only just managed to fall asleep. That is the reason I resist your demand. He must rest."

"He's so bad off he needs to sleep here?" Zephyros asked, pointing to the ceremonial hall. It possessed the highest heat of anywhere in Aithiopia. Livos finally nodded. "Then why the hell didn't you take him to the Acheron?"

"He refused, my lord."

"Damn it all to Hades." Zephyros backed off a step and scrubbed a hand over his face. "What exactly happened?"

"I don't know. He hasn't said."

"What are his injuries?" Boreas asked. "Zephyros could be of service." His was the strongest healing power of them all.

Livos shook his head. "I don't think so. And anyway"— the god looked between the Supreme Anemoi—"Chrysander expressly said not to involve him."

Zephyros charged forward. "Damn bull-headed—"

Livos blocked him, and Apheliotes finally engaged, stepping into the scuffle to bar the doors. "My lord, please. It is worse than you think."

Boreas grasped his brother's shoulder. "What do you mean, Apheliotes?"

The god hesitated, then his shoulders slumped. "It will be easier if I show you."

➊⟡➉

"This is so ridiculous," Laney grumbled.

"Not if it will help you heal," Seth said as he lifted her down from his truck seat. "I'm going to carry you in."

"I can manage." Fifteen stitches later, five in her hand and ten on her calf, Laney was told to stay off her feet.

"I'm here, Laney, and I'm helping whether you like it or not."

"Fine, but I'm going to go so crazy sitting on my butt."

And with her hand out of commission for a while, she was going to have to hunt and peck her way through the rest of the story she'd been working on. Little chance she'd meet her deadline now.

He crossed the yard and stepped onto the porch. "Yep, I know it."

A heavy weight pressed on her shoulders. The pain, all the questions she had about what had happened last night and this morning, the loss of independence this injury created— Laney was overwhelmed and way too tired to work through it all.

Inside, her chocolate lab was right there waiting for her. Small "I missed you" whimpers greeted her and his nails clicked against the floor.

The animal's presence immediately cheered her. "Hi, Finnster. Sorry I was gone so long." The screen door closed behind them. "What time is it, anyway?"

"Almost four. Okay, here's the couch," Seth said, easing her down.

Laney gasped when she forgot about the injury on her hand and accidentally put pressure on it. Carefully, she repositioned herself until she was sitting long-ways, her legs stretched out over the cushions. "Can you grab some pillows from my bed?"

"Yep. Be right back." Seth retreated from the rooms that formed the connecting living space of her L-shaped home. Moments later, her bedroom door squeaked open. Her hearing was so well developed she could track his movements through the house.

Finn sniffed the bandages on her right hand and whined. He set his big lug of a head on her leg. "You're a good old man, aren't you?" She scratched his ears with her uninjured hand. "I bet you're a hungry man, too." His ears perked up at her words. She smiled.

"Will you feed Finn for me?" she asked Seth as he entered the kitchen.

"Yeah. I brought two pillows. Where do you want them?"

"One under my knee, please?" The roof's metal had sliced into the back of her calf, so she couldn't comfortably lay her leg flat. Luckily, the cut hadn't been too deep. Still, for the next week she had to stay off her feet and dress and redress the bandages. And it could be a month before she could ride Sappho again. The thought made her eyes sting. "The other behind my back," she managed.

He tucked it in behind her, then crouched down beside the sofa. "How about some food? You need to eat with the pain meds."

Laney gave her oldest friend a smile. He was her rock, her guardian angel, and her pit bull attack dog all in one. And despite her grumpiness over feeling so helpless, he deserved her gratitude. "Thank you, that would be great. Can you make grilled cheese sandwiches?"

He scoffed, but gave her hand a reassuring squeeze. "An eight-year-old can make grilled cheese sandwiches."

His mock-offended tone brightened her smile. "Well, you should be able to handle it, then."

"I'm only letting you get away with that because you're hurt." He rose and stepped away.

"Right." She sighed. "I really do thank you. For everything." As much as she strived for independence, she couldn't deny she depended on Seth. Every once in a while, it was a relief to lean on him. Not that she would ever say so.

He'd be like a dog with a new bone with an admission like that.

"Don't mention it. Come on, Finn. You wanna go outside?"

The dog followed Seth to the screen door. As it clicked shut, Seth started pulling what he needed out of the fridge in the kitchen that adjoined the open living room.

Minutes later, Seth settled a plate and a bottle of water in her lap. The grilled bread smelled buttery and toasty. Laney's stomach grumbled. Between the weirdness in the barn and the hospital trip, she'd missed breakfast this morning.

"Sounds like one might not be enough," Seth said.

"I didn't realize how hungry I was. Did you make one for you, too?" Leaning over her plate, she took a big bite and moaned at the warm and gooey cheese. She could already tell having only one hand was going to be a pain.

"Yeah," he said from the chair near the foot of the couch.

"You completely rock at grilled cheese."

He laughed. "I completely rock, period."

Shaking her head and grinning, she devoured the rest of her sandwich. After a lifetime of shared meals, the silence was comfortable, familiar. "I'm glad you're here," she said.

"Yeah." The air in the room shifted, felt awkward and tense. "Laney…"

She looked toward him and concentrated her narrow vision on him. The details of his face weren't as clear at this distance. He rubbed his forehead. "What's the matter?"

His head bowed and his shoulders slumped. "I'm just so damn sorry I wasn't here for you."

"You *were* here for me. Still are. If it wasn't for you, I'd still be sitting out in the barn." She forced a playfulness into her words to reassure him and lighten the suddenly serious conversation.

"I know you don't want to hear this, but maybe you shouldn't—"

"Wait." She knew where this conversation was going, and she couldn't handle it right now. Not when she was flat on her back for the next few days. "I know what you're going to say, and you're wrong. I know I wasn't smart in checking out the barn last night, but I'm perfectly competent at taking care of myself on a day-to-day basis. And you know it."

Tension filled the air for a long moment, and then he sighed. "I know. I just…I really hate that you're hurt."

"Me, too, and I appreciate that. But of all people, I need your support in this." With her grandfather gone, Seth was *the* person who knew her best in the world. His opinion mattered to her. A lot. "Besides, you're here."

"I am. And I promised your pop I'd watch out for you." He sighed, and Laney swallowed around the lump that formed in her throat. Seth had been close with her grandfather, too. "Okay, I'll drop it," he said, though his tone wasn't entirely convinced. He collected her plate. "Want that second sandwich?"

"Maybe later."

"All right. I'm going to go check out the barn and see what kind of damage we're talking about. Then I'll look into getting a contractor out to look at it."

"Thanks. I can help make some of those calls tomorrow."

"Here," he said from next to her. "Hold out your hand." He dropped a pill into her palm. "Just concentrate on getting better. Okay?"

Laney took the painkiller without throwing a fuss about it. Her cooperation would ease his concern. She hoped.

"I'll be back in a bit."

She nodded and laid her head back against the pillow. Between sleeping on the floor last night and the stress of her injuries, exhaustion weighed on her like a lead blanket. When she closed her eyes, though, all she could see were two competing images—of a winged horse and a golden-haired man. With really nice shoulders. Limited as her version was, she'd apparently made note of every sculpted detail of that part of his anatomy.

Seth came back through the door. Laney startled out of whatever hazy dream-state she'd been in. She had no idea how much time might've passed, or if she'd really been asleep at all. *Must be some good drugs.*

"I'm sorry. Did I wake you?"

"No," she said, her voice groggy. "What's up?"

"Well, it's not pretty, but the barn's still structurally sound. Shouldn't be too big of a job."

"That's good."

"Shame about the oak tree, though."

"What do you mean?"

"Looks like lightning split it in half. That's what came down on the roof."

Laney frowned and fought the sensation of the room spinning. "The oak tree?"

"Didn't you see the huge branches sticking in through the roof?"

Branches…? Her scalp prickled. "Uh, no, no, but, uh…" She struggled to swallow and fought back the words *What branches? There weren't any branches!* Just like there wasn't a winged horse. Or a golden-haired man.

What the hell was happening to her?

CHAPTER SIX

Aw damn, so warm.

Chrysander burrowed into the soft body in front of him, arm coming tight around her waist, face pressing into miles of silky hair. His lips found her neck and then he was kissing her, tasting her, drawing her warmth inside himself.

More.

She turned over, bringing her lips in line with his. Her soft skin skated over his, and that small touch electrified him. Chrys slanted his mouth over hers, sucking and teasing her full lips. She moaned low in her throat and he pressed in, his tongue demanding entrance, his chest grazing hers. Her lips parted, and he plunged forward, exploring and invading every part of her sweet mouth. Her heat poured into him, making him ravenous for her.

Her hands came up to surround him.

He pulled back. Control. He needed control. "No. Above your head."

Dark blue eyes on fire, she obeyed. He grasped her wrists

with his hand, then brought himself atop her.

Gods. He covered her from lips to ankles, and she was soft everywhere he was hard. And so warm.

His hips settled into the cradle of her thighs and there, there she was on fire.

He willed the clothing off her body, and the wet heat of her center might've scorched him if he didn't find the sensation so life-giving.

Shouting. From a distance.

Chrysander frowned. He mentally shrugged, hanging on to her heat, her body. In her. Gods, he had to get in her.

The shouting returned. Louder now. Urgent.

He looked away from the woman writhing beneath him. Where the hell was he?

He lifted himself off her. Agony tore through his shoulder…

Chrys groaned as his eyes blinked open. *Fucking hell, just a dream.* How he thought otherwise, he didn't know. He never lay with a woman in that position.

He pushed upright. How long had he been asleep? And who in the name of Zeus was making all that racket?

One thing was for sure, his shoulder didn't feel any better than it had when he laid down, which argued that he hadn't been asleep nearly long enough. He looked down at his chest and abdomen, still a minefield of fresh purple and older, sickly yellow bruises. Examining his left arm, he found the same grizzly slash.

I'm gonna knock some fucking heads together.

He pushed off the cushioned altar. His feet hit the ground and his knees went soft. Bracing against the marble, he steadied himself and willed the vertigo away. The room spun, making the enormous floor mosaic of the compass rose seem alive.

Yeah, I'm gonna knock some heads together, all right. As soon as I'm sure I'm not gonna puke all over the place.

As he concentrated on breathing away the nausea, the voices that had awakened him became clearer. Zeph. *Aw, sonofabitch.* Of all the fucking gods. Z couldn't see these wounds or he'd know, immediately, what had made them. After all, it hadn't been that long ago that Zeph had been on the receiving end of their father's whip of leashed lightning. Only difference was, that power was Aeolus's to wield. Eurus had no damn business possessing such a power, and when the others found out, all Hades would break loose.

Chrys needed more time to work this mess out. But his head was too clouded by how drained he was to be able to think everything through right now. Which meant he needed to get rid of his brother.

Clothing. He had to cover these wounds. He closed his eyes and willed on a long-sleeved shirt and pair of loose work-out pants. His vision went wiggly with the effort. And hell if the light pressure of the cotton wasn't tormenting his injuries. Every small shift of the soft fabric felt like a cheese grater against his skin.

Blowing out a long breath, Chrys summoned every bit of energy he possessed and crossed the room to the ornate, golden doors. He flung one open and glared at the melee. "What. The fuck. Does a god have to do. To get some sleep in his own. Damn. House?"

Four sets of eyes turned on him. Their freeze-frame routine might've been comical if the door wasn't all that was keeping him in a standing position.

"Chrysander." Boreas broke the silence.

He dragged his gaze to his oldest brother. Deep concern poured from the winter god's silver eyes. Above his long beard, his face was a ruddy red. Chrys sighed and pulled the door closed behind him, cutting off the flow of superheated air from the ceremonial hall. "You shouldn't be here, B."

"We are concerned about you."

"I appreciate that. I do. But I just need to rest."

"Bullshit," Zeph bit out, blue eyes flaring.

Chrys glared at him. "While I appreciate the erudite assessment—"

"I'm calling bullshit on this whole situation. What the hell happened last night?"

Gods, he did not have the strength to deal with the agitation rolling off Zeph right now.

When Chrys didn't answer, his brother continued. "You know what? Aphel, what were you going to show us?"

Chrys looked to the dark-haired god of the Southeast Wind. His shirt was partially unbuttoned, like he'd been in the middle of undressing when Chrys opened the door. Aphel dropped his gaze, and Chrys frowned.

Suspicion flooded Chrys's gut. Jesus. And the hits just kept on coming, didn't they? "Apheliotes, get inside," he said, in case he was right. The minor god startled but moved right away, quickly disappearing through the doors to the hall. "Livos, make yourself scarce, you dig?"

The god nodded and dematerialized, leaving Chrys and his brother in a glaring showdown.

"Start talking," Z said.

Fine. He'd tell them enough to make them go away. "I'm drained, okay? It took everything I had to manifest the clothes I'm wearing so I didn't have to walk out here with my bare ass flapping in the breeze."

"What is going on, Chrysander?" Boreas asked. "Why have you dragged out this thing with Eurus?"

"It's three fucking weeks until his season," Zeph interjected.

Like he needed the reminder. Chrys was acutely aware of the passage of time. If Eurus came into his powers while he possessed their father's firestone ring, he would be nearly unstoppable. But if his brothers—or worse, the Olympians—found out that Aeolus had lost the ring and not confessed it, their father—and all of them, really—was likely to be in just as much trouble.

"Dude. I'm well aware of the calendar. I've been trying to reason with him, to bring him in voluntarily."

"Why the hell bother? He's dying one way or the other. Just kill him while you're more powerful and put a stop to this," Z said.

If only it were that easy. "Because if he makes a good faith effort at cooperation, maybe we can get Mars to lower the sentence."

Zeph's face went bright red. "*That's* what you've been doing? Trying to *save* him?"

Chrys held out a hand. "Think about it. No matter what, Eurus loses his position and one of his sons comes to power. Do we really want to pass this cluster fuck down to a new generation? If we kill Eurus, or if we don't at least try to save him, all we're doing is guaranteeing a new round of animosity between the East and the rest of us." It was one of Chrys's considerations, if not his main one.

"Chrysander may have a point," Boreas said. "I had not thought of that, but it is true. Not to mention that another of his sons is now *your* heir, Zephyros. We must do what we can to cultivate Devlin's and Alastor's friendship and end this once and for all."

Zeph tugged his hands through his hair. "Devlin's a lost cause. Eurus's influence on him has been too great. But either way, I'm telling you right now that the Olympians aren't going to sit around and wait for us to make inroads with them. They've let the family handle this largely out of deference to Mars, but the decision is going to be taken from our hands. Then the shit's gonna rain down on our heads, too, for not following their orders."

"I know." Exhausted, Chrys fell back against the door. The wounds on his back hit the hard surface and screamed agony through every cell. He grunted and closed his eyes.

"Shit. So this is why you refused the Acheron," Z said.

Chrys nodded, breathing through the dizziness making it increasingly difficult to know which way was up. Finally, he lifted his gaze and looked from one brother to the other. "I just need some shut-eye. Twenty-four hours and I'll get back out there."

Boreas's gaze narrowed. Chrys suddenly felt like maybe B could see through what Chrys wasn't saying.

"Fine. Get your ass back to bed. And ask for some damn help next time."

"No. I got this. You both have families to worry about now." And Chrys was happy for them. He was. Despite his own loneliness. The string of random sex partners was fine for what it was, but didn't leave him feeling connected to anyone.

"You are our family, too," Boreas said. "And we are helping bring this matter to a close whether you like it or not."

"Okay," Chrys said. "Now get out of here before you melt all over my floor, would ya?"

Boreas grinned, winked, and disappeared.

"You, too," he said to the remaining god.

"All right, little brother. But I haven't forgotten how you were there for me when Aeolus dished out his punishment last spring. So know you can call on me for anything."

Guilt at not sharing the whole story mixed with the nausea sloshing around in his gut, but all Chrys could do was nod. When Zeph finally left, he released a breath and lurched back into the hall. The heat shored him up enough to step in front of Aphel, who had dropped to a knee.

Suspecting his secret, Chrys reached down a hand to assist the other god to his feet. "Rise."

Aphel's eyes went wide, but he accepted the help.

"Let's see whatever it is you were going to show them."

"Yes, my lord." He finished removing the shirt, dropped it to the floor, and gave Chrys his back.

"Almighty Zeus." Layers of electrical lash marks flayed open the skin of the god's back. "Eurus did this," Chrys said.

The other god nodded.

"Why?"

"I discovered that he keeps Alastor imprisoned."

"*What?*"

"He wishes to control him, to control the West once Alastor is installed as Supreme God. The boy is not well. I fear he is…tortured."

Chrys's mind struggled to keep up. "Devlin, too?"

"I don't think so. He spends much of his time in his father's employ."

He needed time to process all of this. Pushing through the confusion threatening to take him to his knees, he returned to the altar and heaved himself on top. "We're a fucking pair, aren't we? You'll stand watch in here. The heat will help."

"Thank you, my lord," Aphel rasped, dropping to a knee again.

"Aphel?" The god raised his gaze. "It's good you told me, you dig?"

He nodded, then resumed his position kneeling before Chrys's altar.

Chrys disappeared his clothes, giving the intense heat direct access to healing his body. Not that he'd ever be all the way healed. His body would close the wounds, but since they were inflicted by a stronger god, he had no way to heal the scars they would leave behind—whether the god that inflicted them should've been stronger or not.

Enough.

It was all he could do to lay there.

So he closed his eyes and prayed the gods were merciful, and that his dreams could find their way back into the arms of a certain human raven-haired beauty.

∞

Those twenty-four hours stretched into seventy-two. Finally, Chrysander was restored enough to resume his search for Eurus—and fight him if he had to. He had about two and a half weeks to resolve this situation one way or the other, assuming the Olympians didn't step in beforehand.

It wasn't a safe assumption.

But, no matter where he searched, he couldn't pick up a recent energy signature from Eurus. Not at the bridge. Not at Ella's old house. Not at Owen's place in Northern Virginia, which relieved him greatly.

Where could he—

Shit. Why hadn't he thought of it before? It would be just like Eurus.

Fear flooded Chrysander's gut and sent him soaring through the dead of night to the woman's farm. The woman who had tended his wounds. Who had shared her incredible warmth. Who he'd spent three solid days dreaming about until his body was convinced he knew every inch of hers.

If Eurus had gone looking for Chrys after their fight, the twelve hours he'd spent in her barn would've attracted him like a flare in the night.

Gods, if anything had happened to her because of him...

Under the cover of darkness, Chrys materialized into his corporeal form behind the building into which he'd crashed. Sweet-smelling, fresh-cut logs formed a long stack against the back wall. A huge stump marked the source of the wood, and a kernel of remorse shot through him—before Chrys had sought his rest, he'd sent Livos back to create a plausible reason for the damage to the structure. A felled tree had apparently been the god's solution.

But that wasn't the only—or the most important—thing he found. Without even entering the barn, Chrys could feel the resonance of Eurus's energy. He'd been here. And he'd been here recently, judging by the strength of the signature. The woman was now on his brother's radar.

And that was an exceedingly dangerous place for anyone to be. Ella was living proof of that.

Damnit it all to Hades.

Chrys made a quick sweep of the barn and the yard, his concern and his speed escalating, then circled the house.

Eurus's presence was strongest and most recent around the residence, a fact that shot rage and fear through Chrys's veins in equal measure. Worst-case scenarios formed a macabre parade through his mind's eye. Regret and guilt formed a bitter cocktail on his tongue, curdling his gut. Whatever tragedy he found here was his fault for leading Eurus to her door. He materialized in the living room.

The first thing he noticed was that Eurus had been inside, too.

The second was that a life force still existed within. *Laney's* life force—after their night in the barn, he'd recognize it anywhere. Gods, she was still alive?

The urge to see her, to prove with his own eyes that she'd survived Eurus's attack, surged through him. He bolted through the house, following the twin beacons of Eurus's trail and her energy to the very last door on a long hallway.

Bracing against whatever he was about to see, Chrys pushed inside and crossed toward the bed. His steps slowed, and then relief nearly took him to his knees. The sounds of her soft, even breathing and steady heartbeat were a sweet symphony in the still quiet of the room.

Bewilderment forced him to cross to the side of her bed. She lay on her side, her dark hair sprawled in a fan on the pillow. Safe. Well. Unharmed.

Despite the fact that Eurus had very likely stood in this exact spot not that long before. The energy trail was one of the freshest he'd encountered since the night on the bridge.

Thump, thump, thump.

At his feet, an old brown dog lay curled in a ball. *Good doggy. Nice doggy. Please don't eat my leg, doggy.* He whined, a sound of fear, and Chrys sank into a crouch. Petting the animal's big head revealed he was shaking. Who in Hades knew what Eurus might've done to the poor guy, but no doubt it shaved off a few dog years. The animal heaved a deep breath of what sounded like relief and dropped his head on top his paws.

Even the dog was fine. Ish. Not bad for having had an encounter with his brother.

Chrys rose and studied this woman who had fascinated his dreamself these past days. Part of him was loath to even pose the question, but why in the name of Zeus and all the Olympians had Eurus left her alone? The god had been curious enough to search the property and come inside. Yet, she lived. She slept peacefully. Chrys didn't even sense any of his brother's trademark unluckiness upon her.

Doing no harm was so unusual for Eurus that Chrys just couldn't fathom it. Then again, Chrys couldn't understand most of what went on in the god's mind anymore, and that was half the damned problem.

Thank the gods she's okay. He'd been so sure he'd find tragedy that he couldn't pull himself away from the miracle of her survival.

For a moment, he got stuck there at the side of her bed, torn between the need to pursue his brother and the desire to revel in a moment of her heat. To feel that just one more…

No.

Finding Eurus was the priority. But Chrys wouldn't leave her unprotected—not after Eurus had been so close to her and acted so uncharacteristically. Livos could watch over her and apprise him if Eurus returned.

Just as he turned away, a dim glow caught his eye. He sucked in a breath. A feather lay tucked under her pillow.

Well, hell. It was one of the feathers from the wing of his sacred animal.

Bang-up job concealing yourself, Chrysander.

And, what do you know, Eurus's energy smudged the golden glow of the quill like a stain. Fuck.

He was a big enough god to admit part of him was more than a little satisfied to know she'd taken it to bed with her, but no matter his satisfaction, he couldn't leave a part of himself here. He reached out, his fingers closing on the stiff spine.

Laney's hand fell atop his. "Am I dreaming? Or are you really here?"

CHAPTER SEVEN

Laney couldn't believe it. Seth had shown her enlarged pictures on her laptop of the tree damage to the barn roof. And she'd spent a whole afternoon listening to the grind of the chainsaw cutting it to pieces. With each passing day, she'd convinced herself more and more that she'd imagined the whole thing with the horse and the man. And now, in the dead of night, the same odd golden glow she remembered was all she could see.

His hand disappeared from beneath hers. The golden light receded.

"Please. Don't go again. Talk to me. Chrys?"

Finn's tail thumped against the floor.

He was still here. His footsteps over the carpet gave him away. And if she didn't believe her own ears, she had Finn's tail to bolster her certainty.

"I know you're here. And I know I'm awake." She eased herself into a sitting position and scanned her vision over the room. There. By the door. The light was faint, but it was that unique color. Then it disappeared altogether. *No!* "Chrys?" Tossing the covers back, she swung her legs off the bed. She cried out, forgetting in her impatience to move more carefully. The cut on her leg was healing, but moving too fast still made her feel like her stitches might pop open.

Suddenly, the light returned. The glow came from the foot of the bed.

Laney's heart sprinted in her chest, his reappearance shooting adrenaline through her body. She shivered.

"Are you all right?" came a deep masculine voice.

Goosebumps erupted over Laney's skin. She remembered that voice. God, how she remembered it.

"I will be. Please stay. Please?" She didn't know exactly what she wanted from him. All she knew was she had so many questions. And only he could answer them.

The silence stretched out. Finally, she had him here. He was *really* here. And she couldn't think of what to say. She chuffed out a laugh. "I'm sorry."

Soft movements told her he'd come closer still. The glow brightened. "Why are you apologizing?"

"It's just...I've spent a whole week dreaming about you, convincing myself I'd dreamed you up in the first place. And now I'm all tongue-tied."

"You dreamed of me?"

The air between them heated. And now her heart pounded for a different reason. "Uh, yeah," she whispered.

The glow got closer. "I dreamed about you, too."

Laney's stomach flip-flopped and nervous energy skittered down her spine. He'd dreamed about her? And, what was that scent? Careful of her leg, she leaned toward him, just a little. The scent got stronger. It was immediately familiar, but hard

to describe. It was just…the smell of summer. It was the heat
of the sun and the rich aliveness of nature and the warmth of
the breeze that she'd always associated with summertime.

She wanted to press her nose to his skin to see if she was
really smelling him.

Realizing what she was doing, she sat back, heat roaring
over her face.

Fingers caressed her cheek. "Mmm, that blush is sweet,
and so warm. What caused it?"

How could he see her blush in the dark? She almost
asked, but then his touch disappeared, and it was all she
could do to restrain a whimper at the loss. "Uh, I was just…
nothing." She shook her head. Something very strange was
going on here, and she had to figure out what it was. "Will
you stay for a while?"

Pause. "I can't. I shouldn't."

"Why?"

"It's complicated." His tone was full of regret.

"Does it have to be? I'd like you to stay. And I think…"
She swallowed the rest of the sentence, not wanting to push
too far.

"What do you think?"

Emboldened by the soft challenge of his words, she said,
"I think you'd like to stay, too."

"Do you, now?" Toward the foot of the bed, the mattress
shifted. He blew out a long, weary-sounding breath.

Had he sat down? Victory surged through her. "Thank
you," she said in a small voice.

"Don't thank me yet," he said, his tone serious.

Still, Laney smiled and a sort of giddiness rushed through
her, like she was on the verge of an amazing discovery. "Okay.

Since you're here, any chance you'll answer some questions?"

"Depends."

"Fair enough. So, hold on. I want to get comfortable for this."

He chuckled. The sound of it was deep and rich and sent a delicious shiver over her skin.

Slowly, Laney resituated herself until she could recline against her headboard. Trying to get a pillow under her knee made her moan in discomfort. These stitches couldn't come out soon enough.

"Here," he said in a low voice. His hands brushed the side of her knee as he positioned the cushion for her. She sucked in a breath, the heat of his touch lingering on her skin. "How badly are you injured?"

"Oh, uh…" The last thing she wanted was to make him feel bad. "It's nothing that won't heal."

"I'm glad to hear that, but are you in pain?" His tone was suddenly intense.

It occurred to her that she should be afraid that she'd awoken to find a strange man in her bedroom, but she hadn't once felt that particular emotion. It had been the same way that morning… "A little. It's not as bad as it was."

"I'm sorry for having frightened you."

Man, she wished she could see his face, feel the contours of his skin with her hands. "Thanks. Um, which leads me back to those questions."

"Persistent thing, aren't you?"

She tucked her hair behind her ears. "Is that bad?"

"No. Go ahead."

His light shifted, spread lengthwise across the bottom of her bed. "Did you just lay down?"

"Do you mind?" Now the weariness was in his voice.

Actually, she really liked the thought of it. She wished she could see the full picture of what he looked like sprawled across her bed. Maybe she should turn on the light—seeing a little of him was better than none at all. But she was half afraid of scaring him off. Instead, the image of that muscular shoulder popped into her mind's eye. She imagined him sprawled across her bed shirtless... "No, make yourself comfortable. Here." She tossed a pillow toward him.

"You don't need it?"

"Nah. I have about eighty-two pillows. I'm kind of pillow crazy." She cringed. The thought of seeing him half naked apparently gave her a case of verbal diarrhea. Awesome.

He chuckled. "I'll remember that. So, are pillows what you wanted to talk about?"

She grimaced. "No. No, they aren't. I want to talk about you."

"Hmm," he said softly, just loud enough that she heard the low sound.

"Are *you* okay?"

Pause. "Yes."

She traced the edge of the small bandage wrapped around her palm and decided to just go for it. "Did you...fall through my barn roof?"

Longer pause. "Do you want the truth or the rational answer?"

There was a difference? Suddenly, the air in the room felt alive with some unnamed energy. The hair on her arms stood on end. "Truth."

"Then, yes."

I knew it! There was never a tree! Her scalp prickled.

Laney swallowed, hard. "Okay. Okay. Um...did you fall through my roof as a man?"

His light, his body, shifted closer. "I'm not sure. I don't remember everything that happened that night."

A wondrous excitement skittered down her spine. "Because of the fight?"

"Yes."

"A fight that took place...in the..." Man, she was going to sound so stupid. "In the sky?" She grimaced and awaited his laughter. It never came.

"Do you really want these answers, Laney?"

She shuddered out a long breath. She'd gone all the way down Weird Street and made a hard left onto Crazytrain Avenue. Except, something told her, as crazy as it seemed, it was also real. And if, *just if*, what he was telling her was real, it was also the most amazing thing she'd ever encountered. "Kant said, 'Dare to know.' So, yes, I want the answers."

"You're throwing Prussian philosophers at me now?"

She bit down on a grin, but he probably couldn't see her reaction anyway. "Yeah, why not? I've always liked that motto. And..."

"What?"

She lived alone, worked from home, and didn't have that many occasions to leave the farm, especially since she couldn't drive anymore. Once, she'd had dreams of the world, went to college, expected to marry. Now, her life was the definition of sheltered. Chrys was the most interesting thing that had happened to her in recent memory. Maybe ever. Not that he needed to know all that.

Plus, she recalled the sadness she'd felt as she'd knelt next to the winged horse, worried that he was lost and alone and injured... Something about him reminded her of those feelings, even now.

"Well, to be honest, I want to know you."

His golden light seemed to flare. "Rock on, then," he said in a voice that sounded almost raspy. "And, the answer is yes."

"Yes, as in, you fell through my barn roof after having a fight in the sky?"

"That about sums it up."

Adrenaline flooded through her. "This is...this is...I don't even know."

"Maybe that's enough questions for now."

"Just a few more. Please? You're the only one I can talk to about this without risking a one-way all-expenses-paid trip to the psych ward."

"Well, we wouldn't want that." Did he wear a smile to go along with the amusement in his voice?

She forced herself to focus before he ran out of patience altogether. "Okay. Who were you fighting?"

"Hmm. My brother. But that's all I'm saying about that."

Laney yawned, hoping she hadn't offended him. "All right. So, uh, this next question's a doozy."

"Hit me." He shifted again, and she almost went for the light, just so she could see exactly how he was laying. But for this next question, she wanted the cover of darkness.

Here goes nothing. "Are you a Pegasus?"

When she was just about sure he wouldn't answer, he said, "As in Pegasus, the horse-god son of Poseidon and Medusa?"

Holy crap, he's taking me seriously? At least, I think he is... "Um, honestly, I don't know that much about mythology.

I just know that the winged horse was named Pegasus."

"Well, in mythology, not all of the winged horses were Pegasus."

Her scalp prickled and the hair on her arms rose. "Holy crap, Chrys, what are you saying?" she whispered. When he didn't answer right away, she pushed on. "Okay, I'll rephrase the question. Are you a... No. Can you *also* be a winged horse?"

છ૪૭૪

Chrysander lay on his back and stared up at the ceiling. He should really go. Chase Eurus while the trail was hot. Actually, he should never have returned in the first place. But the sound of her distress had reeled him back into her room. And then he was talking to her, touching her, making himself comfortable on her bed, soaking up her warmth and her smile and her laughter.

It all felt...*so* damn good.

Good like Chrys hadn't felt in who knew how long.

Still, Eurus had to be his main focus right now. And he was getting away. Chrys groaned and tugged his hands through the wavy length of his hair.

"You don't have to answer," Laney said.

Her voice pulled him out of his thoughts. Was she actually willing to accept the idea of him as a man who could also be a horse? Over the millennia, Chrysander had found humans eager to rationalize away anything that didn't fit their version of reality. Why would she be any different? He blew out a long breath. "It's not your questions that bother me." Hell, he *wanted* to answer them. Which meant he should really summon Livos and go.

Her movement on the bed drew his gaze. She pulled the pillow from beneath her knees, slung it to the side, and eased herself into a laying position on her stomach. "Then what does?"

Chrys heard her question but his brain scrambled. The pajama shorts she wore were tiny and made her bottom look so freaking…delectable. He could almost see himself getting up, tugging her hips to the edge of the bed, and sinking deep, deep inside.

Suddenly, the memories of his dreams blurred with reality, and he remembered the incredible scorching heat of her center. He knew it'd only been a dream. He knew it. But the hardness and the tightness of his body made it clear a part of him thought the memory real.

Or at least willing to find out how reality compared to the dream.

Almighty Zeus.

But then his gaze dragged downward, to the length of bandages covering the back of her calf.

She was hurt, and it was his fault.

"Can I have my feather back?" she whispered.

"*Your* feather?"

She smiled, and it was so genuine. "My feather."

Her feather? The idea that she claimed a part of him as hers skittered over his skin, arousing and frightening. The combination of reactions fascinated him. "You have a very nice smile, Laney."

And, bingo. That lovely blush colored the apple of her cheek again. He could feel the heat of it from where he lay, which suddenly felt too far away.

"How do you know I'm smiling?"

"My eyesight is strong."

"Hmm." The skepticism in that soft murmuring made him grin. He couldn't believe how well she was handling what he'd so far revealed. Was it her open-mindedness that most intrigued him? Her acceptance of his truths? Maybe it was that she'd helped him at his weakest moment?

Or, was it that hers was the first skin-on-skin touch he'd enjoyed in…he couldn't even say how long?

Chrys dug into his pocket and retrieved the object in question. Slowly, he rolled toward her, coming to settle in the middle of the bed. Her eyes went wide and he wondered how she saw him so well. She'd never once suggested the lights, yet she seemed to track his movements like she could see him plainly. That he could see her wasn't surprising; his eyesight was as strong in the dark as in the day.

"Maybe I'll make you a trade," he said, spinning the feather by the spine.

"For what?"

"Feather for your hand," he said, the idea unleashing an urgent need in his gut. "Your injured hand."

"Why?"

"Dare to know, right?"

Slowly, she extended her arm across the space between them.

Strictly speaking, what he was about to do violated the rules about the use of divine magic in the human realm. He'd seen firsthand the punishment his father meted out for such an infraction. Then again, Chrys hadn't been able to find his father in a few months. And, given Chrys knew about the firestone, his father needed to be equally worried about what Chrys might do. Any way you sliced it, the god had far bigger things to worry about right now than one of his sons healing a human. He touched the bandage and willed it away.

Laney gasped and withdrew. "What did you…how did you…?"

"It's okay. I won't hurt you. In fact, I just want to make it better."

When her hand crossed the mattress toward him a second time, she was trembling.

Chrys cradled the back of her hand in his palm. She was soft and small and *warm*. His skin tingled with the sensation. Instead of wishing to rush through so he could stop touching her, he found he wanted to touch *more* of her. "Just hold still, Laney." He dragged his forefinger along the crisscrossed string that held her wound closed. With a thought, it disappeared. Laney sucked in a breath as he lowered his head and pressed his lips to the cut. There was that scent again, of warm oranges. Did all of her smell—taste—this way?

What he wouldn't do to find out.

Calling on the heat at the center of his being, Chrys inhaled and blew gently on the cuts. After so many days in the Hall of the South Wind, Chrys's body was strong with healing energy, something his basic nature gave him since marshaling the lush life of the summer season was part of his job. He blew his warm, healing breath until her wound closed and his cock was rock hard between his belly and the soft bedcovers. It took everything he had not to follow the healing by worshipping her skin with his lips. And tongue.

"What did you do?" she said in a low voice, like she was trying not to disturb.

"It was my fault. I just wanted to fix it." His voice

sounded raspy with need, even to himself. But it was a fucking phenomenal feeling to *fix* something rather than to destroy. For once.

She flexed her fingers, carefully at first, then more vigorously when she apparently realized her hand was, in fact, healed. The wonder that lit her expression and eyes was the most amazing reward. "You just *healed* me. I don't...I can't even..."

"Shh," Chrys whispered. He reached across the narrow gap of bed separating them and brushed her hair off her face. Black silk. He could imagine wrapping it around his fist as he...

She grasped his hand. Chrys sucked in a breath at the unexpected contact. No one ever touched him like this. His regular lovers knew not to. And he prevented his random fucks from doing so, in one creative way or another. She pushed herself up a little and pulled his hand toward her mouth. Her lips pressed and lingered against the heel of his palm, nearly mimicking what he'd just done to her. "Thank you," she whispered.

The soft thrum of her pulse played against his fingers where she held him still. Chrys's own pulse thundered in return. Without a thought, he was in motion, needing to possess, claim, take control.

He closed the gap between them, cupped her face in his hand, and kissed her. Aw, gods, her lips were soft and warm and eager. Sugared oranges on a warm summer day. Taking her wrist in his grip, he pressed her arm to her chest, gently trapping her as he leaned in further. She moaned into the kiss and opened her mouth, just a little. Unable to resist, Chrys's tongue surged forward and found her tongue pressing and twirling and exploring right back. *Almighty Zeus,* she was so enthusiastic, accepting, *warm.*

He had to protect her. He had to keep her safe.

She twisted her shoulder to lay flatter on her upper back. Her bottom arm, now freed, slipped around his back. Grabbed tight.

Chrys gasped and reared back, his heart in his throat. Her hand fell away. "I'm sorry," he managed.

She shook her head. "I'm not." She looked away and her cheeks went hot.

He sat back on his knees. He hated knowing his fucking frustrating reaction had probably made her feel embarrassed and rejected. It wasn't his intention. Not at all. Part of his body was screaming for him to dive back into her heat. But a bigger part told him to run far, far away. And he had the perfect reason to go—after Eurus. "You should go back to sleep, Laney," he managed, cursing the raspy strain audible to his own ears. He ushered a soft, lulling breeze through the room, the kind that conjured up lazy summer afternoons in a hammock, and mentally summoned Livos.

"But I don't want to fall asleep." She yawned.

"You're healing. You need your sleep."

"But you'll disappear again," she said, her voice suddenly groggy.

"I'll be here." In one way or another. "Don't worry about a thing."

Livos's energy radiated from beyond the bedroom window.

The moment Laney's breathing settled into the slow rhythm of sleep, Chrys materialized outside. "Stay here and watch over the woman. I'm going after Eurus. Anything threatens her, anything at all, and you summon me immediately."

Chapter Eight

Laney gasped awake. Morning light brightened her room. "Chrys?" Finn whined and his tail thumped a *good morning* against the carpet. "Chrys, are you still here?"

Nothing.

"You said you'd stay," she said. "And I'm talking to an empty room. Awesome."

Disappointment warred with disbelief in her gut. She'd dreamed him. Again. Not surprising since she'd been dreaming of him and the winged horse so much. And damn could dream-Chrys kiss... Of course, last night hadn't been real—

She gasped and looked down at her hand. No bandage. *No cut!*

Tilting her palm toward the light from the window, she still couldn't really make out the scar, but when she ran her finger across her skin, she could *feel* it. He'd healed her. He'd freaking *healed* her. A deep sense of awe swamped her until she felt nearly dizzy with all the questions flooding her mind. She simply couldn't wrap her brain around what had happened, how it had happened, and what Chrys...was.

Because he clearly wasn't...what? Like her. She'd put it that way, for now.

Which also meant...the kiss *was* real. God, it had been so intense, the surprise of it, the way he'd held her, his incredible taste. A tingle of pleasure ran through her body and she trailed her fingers over her lips. She could've kissed him all night long and never tired of it. And, man, no matter how crazy it was, a part of her wouldn't have been against even more.

But then the memory of his rejection chased the feeling away. Her stomach sank. Why had he ended the kiss so abruptly?

Maybe he felt like he'd taken advantage? After all, he'd been the one to initiate the kiss, so he must've felt attracted to her, right?

Laney stared at the shifting patterns of light and shadow on the ceiling and sighed. It had been so damn long since she'd last been with a man. Four years. That wasn't a dry spell—that was the freaking Sahara Desert.

It was a problem she didn't know how to fix. She couldn't go anywhere to meet anyone without Seth's assistance, and Seth didn't do much to help her attract members of the opposite sex. In fact, just the opposite. Half the time, people assumed they were a couple. But, as much as she loved him, she didn't feel that way about Seth. Never had.

Not to mention, she was sorta hardwired to expect guys to decide she was too much to deal with. That had certainly been the case with Ryan, her last lover and boyfriend of two years, who had dumped her because he couldn't handle her deteriorating condition. They'd met in college while she'd still possessed a large percentage of her central vision and before she'd gone totally blind in her left eye. By the end of their relationship, she'd been down to ten percent of her central vision in her left and about forty in her right. He'd always been so supportive, she never realized that he was actually freaking out. He'd seen the writing on the wall, and he hadn't liked it.

One thought about the night he'd said he wanted to talk about their future and that old humiliation swamped her. In her secret heart, she'd been expecting a proposal. Instead, he broke up with her. *It's not you, it's me.*

At least his rejection had made moving back in with her grandfather an easy decision. And thank God she had or she never would've been here to share the last year of his life. She wouldn't have traded that for anything.

But Ryan's reaction was a damn good reason to put the brakes on her runaway libido where Chrys was concerned. If her RP turned off a far-from-perfect man, she couldn't see why it would be any different with…whatever Chrys was.

Ugh.

Annoyed with herself, Laney eased her legs off the bed. "Some guard dog you are," she muttered to Finn, who pushed himself up with a grunt and laid his head on her knee. She gave him what he wanted and scratched his ears for a while. "Okay, out of the way, you." She rose and reached for her cell phone on the nightstand, but what caught her attention was a spot of yellow light.

The feather. He'd returned it to her after all. Warm pressure filled her chest. This was further proof that Chrys existed. That he'd been here. That she wasn't losing her mind.

Smiling, she clutched it to her chest. As she held it, she inhaled the faintest hint of that incredible scent she remembered from the previous night. The feather tickled as she brought it against her nose. *God, that smell is amazing.* A thought came to mind and she couldn't resist. She moved to the bottom of the bed, about where she thought Chrys had been laying, and lifted the covers to her face.

The blanket was absolutely permeated with the scent of the sun and the summertime air and the richness of growing, fragrant things. It was the scent that had surrounded her as they kissed. She would've bottled it if she could, she found it so appealing. And, was it just her imagination, or was this part of the blanket warmer? She rubbed it against her face and a shiver ran through her, like when he'd stroked her cheek.

I am never again washing that blanket. The thought made her chuckle. *Who needs the blanket if you have the man?* her mind helpfully added.

Yeah, well, she'd asked him to stay, hadn't she?

Where the hell was he, anyway?

In the bathroom, Laney cleaned up and changed her bandages. She'd almost walked away from that job and left her hand uncovered, but at the last minute it occurred to her that she had absolutely no way to explain to Seth, should he notice, how her hand had healed so completely so fast. And he'd notice, all right. So, with a twinge of guilt over the lie, she wrapped clean gauze around her palm.

The one Chrys had apparently healed by blowing his warm, ticklish breath against her skin until she'd been hot and breathless. She couldn't even let herself think about the idea of him using the same treatment on her leg without her pulse spiking. God, if kissing him got her this worked up, she couldn't imagine what she'd feel if anything more ever happened.

As if.

The part of her brain shouting that she was freaking crazy, that *all of this* was totally nuts… Well, she boxed that up nice and tight. If being almost blind taught her anything, it was that sometimes things were more than what they seemed at first glance. A whole lot more.

"Where are you?" she asked her kitchen after she finished breakfast. Great, now she was talking to herself. But she couldn't help it. All morning she kept expecting Chrys around every corner.

She settled in at her desk and opened her latest project—her bimonthly column for an international magazine for the blind. Each column featured a person successful in their job, who also happened to be vision impaired. Her document opened across a pair of computer monitors with huge screen magnifiers that made it possible to make out what she typed. When her vision ultimately deteriorated, she'd have to invest in some good voice recognition and screen reader software. This column was about a really interesting massage therapist…except she just couldn't concentrate on him.

Where was Chrys?

Why had he said he'd stay if he had no intention of doing so?

Was he coming back?

One thing was certain, she'd better pull herself together before she saw Seth or he'd know right away something was up. And no way could she tell him any of this. Not if she wanted him to continue to support her independence. He'd never believe her. And why should he? Everything about the past week had been way, way outside the bounds of normal.

Focus, Laney. Right. Another couple hundred words and she'd have this thing wrapped up. She replayed part of his interview to get the quote she wanted. She'd no more started to type when a knock sounded at her front door.

Finn raised his head, sniffed, and growled.

Laney pushed out of her chair. "*Now* you're going to guard the place? When someone knocks at the door instead of just appearing in my room in the middle of the night?" She hobbled down the hallway and through the kitchen, gritting her teeth the entire way. Strictly speaking, she'd been walking more than she was supposed to, and she was feeling the sting of it.

The knock sounded again.

Who the heck could it be, anyway? She rarely had visitors. And anyone who came for horse or farm-related business either met up with Seth directly or made an appointment with her.

She pulled open the front door and scanned to see who was there.

On the other side of the screen door stood an unusually tall woman. Surrounded by a deep red light.

Laney's heart tripped into a sprint and her scalp prickled.

She didn't know what that red glow meant, but instinct told her it was nothing good.

"Can I help you?" Laney managed, her narrow vision focused as much as she could on the woman's drawn face. Finn pushed his body against her leg, whining and growling low in his throat.

"I hope you can," the woman replied in an accent Laney couldn't identify. "I am looking for Notos."

"Who?"

Finn put himself in front of her, his agitation escalating by the moment. The woman tilted her head to the side, as if she was assessing Laney with that severe expression and stony gaze. She wore some kind of a scarf over what seemed to be unusually full hair.

"Notos. He was here. The other one, too," she scowled.

Laney shook her head. "I'm sorry. I don't know anyone by that name." Finn backed into her, like he was trying to push her away from the door. She patted his rump. "Stop it, Finn."

"Ah. Yes, right." The woman narrowed her gaze. "How about the name Chrysander? Is that one more familiar?"

"No, I'm sorry," she said, and then her heart hammered against her breastbone so hard she could feel it everywhere. *Chrysander. Chrys?* Her gut told her that was right. Whoever this person was, she was looking for Chrys. And she didn't bring good news, that much her instincts—and Finn's—were making crystal clear. Laney had to get rid of her. "I don't know anyone by those names. I'm sorry I couldn't help you."

The dark red flared. "As am I." She disappeared.

Laney gasped. She scanned her gaze over the spot where the woman had been standing. What in the freaking world was going on? Finn whined and pushed against the screen door. Trembling, she eased it open and scanned her vision over the porch on either side of the door. Empty.

Finn forced his way out and sniffed the wood where the woman had stood. He kept sneezing and shaking his head.

"Come in, Finn," Laney whispered, her voice stolen by the fear gripping her throat. "Finn, *now*."

When the dog trotted past her, she yanked the screen door closed and secured the door. She fell back against the frame and tried to calm her breathing. What had she gotten herself involved with? Better yet, what had Chrys—no, *Chrysander*—gotten her mixed up in?

She. Freaking. Disappeared.

As in…poof, gone, now you see me, now you don't. Ta-da!

Trembling, Laney limped her way to the coffee pot and poured herself a cup. For several long minutes, she allowed herself to think only of the rich brew. The warm smoothness going down her throat. The mix of cream and French roast. Whether it needed a bit more sugar.

Coffee, she could handle. Coffee was real.

Glowing people and sky-fighting and miraculously healing injuries? At this moment, not so much.

Mug in hand, Laney made her way to her bedroom. A monster of a headache was taking up residence behind her right eye, and a nap was sounding more and more appealing despite the fact that it wasn't even noon. Just an hour, and then she'd get back to work.

A nap would help. She just needed a reset on this whole day.

Already imagining how good her pillow would feel, Laney took a sip of her coffee as she entered her room. A scuff of a footstep. A movement of light. She gasped and stumbled. "Who's there?"

․†․

"Laney," Chrys said, rushing to her as she slammed backward into the door. A drink sloshed all down her front. "It's me. Are you all right?"

Gods, he left her alone for a few hours and a *Fury*

showed up. Tisiphone, no less. If she'd meant harm, Livos might not have been strong enough to protect Laney. And where had Chrys been when the lesser god summoned him? Off losing his brother's trail. Again.

"Shit," she said as she steadied the mug. "Chrys? You scared me."

He stepped in front of her and frowned. Her eyes glanced around wildly, her gaze not seeming to focus. Tisiphone's presence had apparently done a real number on her. Sonofabitch. Next time—no, there wouldn't be a next time. He'd just have to figure out a way to juggle finding Eurus and protecting Laney himself. Which meant he owed Zeph and Boreas some conversations pretty damn quick.

He bent down so his face was in front of hers and cupped her cheeks in his hands. "Shh, you're okay." His thumbs swept over her soft cheekbones. Gods, she was beautiful. He stared into the dark blue of her eyes, but she didn't really seem to meet and track his. *I need you to get me out of the stall. I'm having trouble seeing.* He sucked in a breath. Could she...? "Laney, can you see me?"

She clenched her lids closed and heaved a shaky breath. "Sorta." She tugged her shirt away from her chest. "It burns."

Chrys glanced down. Angry red marred the skin showing above the V-neck of her shirt. "Damn it all to Hades. Take the shirt off. I can help you. Like last night." Emitting and absorbing heat were powers granted by his godhood.

She stood plastered against the door, indecision and fear written all over her face. Blowing out a shaky breath, she tore the wet cotton over her head and dropped it to the floor.

Almighty Zeus, she was spectacular. Dark blue lace formed an intriguing pattern over the swells of her breasts. He dragged his gaze away from feasting on her many appealing attributes. "Trust me, okay?"

She gave a very small nod that looked like it had taken every ounce of courage.

The burn marks ran from her chest to her stomach to her feet. Chrys decided to ease her into it and knelt. He pressed his palms to the tops of her feet and beckoned the heat within to come to him. "Better?"

Shaking a bit harder now, she nodded.

"Do you want to sit down?"

"No, just do…whatever you're doing," she said, her teeth almost chattering from the adrenaline pumping through her system. It was so potent, he could smell it.

He rose and covered her stomach from her waist to just under the blue satin of her bra with his hand. She sucked in a breath, and he plunged onward, placing his other hand between her breasts, fingers reaching upward. The heat poured into him, life-giving and strengthening, but he took no pleasure in it. Not when it flowed from that which pained her.

"Does it hurt anywhere else?" He held his palms against her, making sure he'd absorbed all her pain away.

"No." She bit down hard on her trembling lower lip. "Thank you."

"Don't thank me, not when I caused it."

"If you're going to be popping in like this, maybe we should get you a bell." She attempted a smile.

Chrys dropped his hands, and hers immediately flew to cover her chest. "Can you grab me a shirt from the chest of drawers over by the bathroom?"

He tugged his shirt over his head and held it out to her.

"Here."

She frowned and, after a moment, seemed to see his offering. "I have plenty of my own."

He pressed it into her hand anyway, suddenly wanting to see her in it. Finally, she slipped it on. It was miles too big on her and so freaking sexy.

The moment she was covered, he summoned his brother. *Zephyros, I need you.* "I know, but I want to help. I've been a giant pain in your ass, haven't I?"

She managed a nearly genuine grin. "Yeah, kinda. But you're growing on me."

"Like mold."

"There's a fungus among us." She grimaced.

Chrys chuckled. "That was an…absolutely terrible joke."

She covered her laugh with her hand and nodded. "I know. I babble when I'm nervous. It's horrible."

"Don't be nervous. I don't want to make you nervous." What *did* he want to make her feel?

"You just healed me. Again. And you're half naked now."

Heat stirred within him. "Does that bother you?"

"It doesn't bother me, exactly. But maybe we should keep our clothes on until we get to know each other a little better."

"Annoyingly reasonable," he said with a smile. He materialized a new shirt. "Better?"

He studied her eyes as they worked over him. He knew the exact moment she absorbed the fact he'd produced a new shirt by the way her eyebrows flew up into her hairline. "Oh, boy. I think I better sit down now." She pushed off the door and made for the bed.

Her limp wasn't as pronounced as that first day in the barn, but oh, how he wanted to heal her leg, too. Soon. If she'd let him.

In the meantime, he resisted the urge to scoop her up and carry her the rest of the way. Barely.

It was an odd desire for him to have, wanting to touch someone so freely, so frequently. Moments ago, he'd had his hands all over her. And he wanted more.

Where are you, Zeph?

She leaned against the edge of the bed. "You can sit, if you want."

"That's okay." He scrubbed his hands through his hair. "Look, I know you have a lot of questions about me, and the visitor you just had necessitates I tell you what's going on."

"The woman?"

"She wasn't just a woman, Laney."

"What do you mean?"

Zeph's energy closed in fast. He materialized into corporeality, a scowl on his face.

Laney gasped, slid off the bed, and pressed her back against Chrys's front. Was she just seeking his shelter? Did she think she was…protecting him?

He gripped her shoulders, both possibilities lighting him up inside. "It's okay. He's friendly…ish. This is my brother, Zephyros."

"He just appeared out of thin air. Just like she did," she said.

"What's going on, Chrys?" Zephyros barged forward, the tone of his voice making it clear he sensed the Fury's energy here, too.

"Laney just had a visit from Tisiphone."

"Who?" she asked, looking between them.

"Jesus, Chrys. What the hell is going? And why did you

involve the woman?" he asked in an accusing tone.

"Hey. Give him a break, all right? It wasn't his fault. He was hurt." Heat radiated off Laney, soaking into his chest.

Chrys squeezed her shoulders and kissed the top of her head before he even thought to do it. She sucked in a small breath and leaned into him, the rhythm of her pulse harder, faster beneath his hands. "I'd prefer to explain it when we're all together. I thought I could handle it on my own, but if Tisiphone's visit means the Olympians are ready to intervene, I'm willing to admit I need help. Laney appears to be on *everyone's* radar now, which is my fault. So I need to protect her until this is over."

She pulled out of his arms. "Okay, enough. Stop talking like I'm not here. Someone explain what the hell is going on."

"Fine. I'll call a meeting, but we gotta do this today. Meet at Owen's? Boreas is already there."

"Might be better if they came here," Chrys said, gesturing to Laney.

"Um, hello?" Laney crossed her arms, the heat of anger crawling up her face.

"If you want Owen in on this, it'll have to be at his place. No way he'll be willing to leave Megan and Teddy alone. And given the revolving door of visitors here, maybe you should just move her."

"Stop it. Just stop!" Laney yelled, drawing both gods' gazes. "First of all, talking over me is really pissing me off, especially when you're talking *about* me. Second of all, I'm not going anywhere. Third of all, what visitors? And who is Tisiphone? Start talking *to* me. Now."

CHAPTER NINE

Laney shook she was so mad. And scared. And completely bewildered by the strange woman disappearing into thin air, and Zephyros appearing out of thin air, and the healing. Again.

"I'm sorry, Laney," Zeph said, a blue glow surrounding him. Just like the woman's red and Chrys's yellow. What in the world was that about? Earlier, she'd worried she was developing halos in her vision that meant it was deteriorating, but now she wasn't so sure. "I'll let Chrys explain it all. See you later," he said, and then he was gone.

"Holy crap, everyone needs to stop doing that," she said, turning to Chrys. "You said you'd tell me what was happening here. Now would be a really good time to start."

He heaved a breath. "It pretty much boils down to this—I'm a divine being, a wind god, to be precise, and I accidentally put you in danger. And now I have to protect you."

Whoa. Just...freaking...whoa. "Uh, wait." She returned

to the bed and pushed herself into a sitting position. No way she was standing for this conversation. "Let's, maybe, take that apart a little bit."

The mattress shifted, and Chrys's glow appeared next to her on the bed. She ran her narrow gaze over him. What she could make out was...so freaking gorgeous. Vibrant green eyes. Wavy, tousled blond hair. Warm, tanned skin. She scanned downward... And muscles that out-of-thin-air shirt did little to hide. Geez. "I know how this sounds to you."

Even if she hadn't been able to see the concerned expression he wore, the sincerity was clear in his deep voice. "Chrys, I already know you had a fight in the sky that caused you to crash through my barn roof. And that you're able to heal with your touch. Even though it feels surreal, I think I'm fairly well on board with the idea that you're...different."

"I really am a god. The Supreme God of the South Wind and Summer, one of the four Cardinal Anemoi. We control the wind and the weather and much about the seasons."

She knotted her fingers in her lap, mind torn between fear and absolute wonder. "A god?" Fighting in the sky, healing abilities, appearing out of thin air... "Oh, my God. I mean..." She shifted toward him. "A god? You were the winged horse."

"Yes. It's my sacred animal form. The Anemoi, well, our godhoods allow us to shift between human, animal, and elemental."

Holy crap! She was sitting on her bed chatting with a god. A fantastically hot, eminently powerful god. Maybe that's why he smelled so good? She dragged her gaze over his face, wishing more than ever that she had the full capability of her sight, because she knew she'd never seen anything more amazing than him. And probably never would again.

Her gut sank. No way all those kiss-inspired thoughts were coming true, now. Why would he want her that way? She was just a woman, and not even a particularly impressive woman at that. Hell, she didn't even have all the usual human powers, and he had super powers.

"What are you thinking?" he asked.

She shook her head. "I...just that...what does this mean?"

He looked down for a moment, and his jaw-length hair fell around his face.

Laney had to restrain the desire to run her fingers through it. The memory of the soft blond hair brushing her leg when he'd put on her sneakers for her flashed through her mind. She would give anything to feel the softness against her sensitive fingers. Preferably while they were kissing. *Ugh!*

He lifted his gaze to hers. "I told you I'd been fighting with my brother."

"Yeah."

"It's a serious fight, Laney, and it's been going on for months. Longer, really. But it's turned into a full-blown crisis that I have been unsuccessfully trying to resolve. When I crashed through your barn roof that night, I inadvertently brought the fight to your doorstep. And him. Eurus was here, in your house—"

"And I take it that's a bad thing?" she asked, knowing the answer, feeling it squeeze in her stomach.

"Very. And then, just now, Tisiphone was here. What did the woman want?" Worry radiated from his voice.

"She was looking for you and somebody else—I didn't recognize the name at first because she called you Notos. I told her I didn't know anyone by that name." So, if she was keeping track of all this, *four gods* had been to her home in the past few days? "Wait. How did you know this Tisiphone person was here?"

"One of my subordinate gods was here guarding you. He summoned me immediately."

Another god...so, make that five. And guarding her? Anger bubbled up again. She had enough of men watching over her every move, thank you very much. Seth was enough protectiveness for any woman. "Seriously? I don't—"

"In Greek mythology, have you ever heard of the Furies? Goddesses of the Underworld?" Laney nodded. "We call them Erinyes. Either way, the one who came here is the infernal goddess of retribution. Her job is to avenge murder. She is lethal beyond imagination. That scarf she wears? Covers a head full of snakes."

Goosebumps erupted everywhere and she shuddered. "Are you freaking kidding me? Snakes? Why would she come here?"

"Likely, she sensed my presence and her boss probably sent her to make sure my family was keeping its word to bring a murderer to justice." Chrys reached out like he might touch her, then dropped his hand, rose, and began to pace.

Head swimming with questions, Laney stood and limped to the foot of the bed.

He paused, and for a long moment, he seemed to study her. "I'm sorry I've gotten you mixed up in all this. I promise I'll make it right."

"So, I'm in danger?"

"Yes, but I can protect you. And if we leave—"

"Chrys, I just can't *leave*. My farm manager, Seth, is one

of my oldest friends in the world and he's here every day. There's no way I could explain this to him, and it would kill him if I just up and disappeared without any explanation. Plus…" She sighed. "I haven't been completely honest about something, either. I'm nearly blind. I have a degenerative eye disease called retinitis pigmentosa. I was diagnosed when I was seventeen. It started with the loss of my night vision, then my peripheral vision, and then the increasing narrowing of my central vision. I'm completely blind in my left eye, and I have less than twenty percent of the central vision in my right eye remaining. I can see a very limited amount of what's directly in front of me, like looking at the world through a straw. So traveling…it'd be hard for me."

He walked right up to her, close enough that his warmth was noticeable against her front. "Gods, Laney. I'm—"

"Sorry? Don't be. I'm used to it by now."

Chrys grasped her hand, infusing his strong warmth into her and helping her calm. "I am sorry, but that's not what I was going to say. I'm…impressed. You move around with such competence. Most of the time, I'd have had no idea… Damn, that means you helped me the night it was storming without really being able to see? And, then I shifted forms on you…"

She lifted a shoulder in a small shrug. "Yeah, I guess that's right. And, thanks. It took a lot of time to learn independent mobility. I used to crash into things all the time. I've taken classes that taught me how to organize so I can move around safely, but I can't drive anymore. And if I go out in public, I have to use my cane, as much to let others know I'm blind as to aid myself in avoiding obstacles. So, you see, it's not easy for me to just pick up and go somewhere new. My life is based around order, routine, and familiarity. It doesn't work well any other way. You can't make me leave."

His thumb stroked the back of her hand, and he heaved a breath. "Okay. We'll figure it out, but I won't make you go if you don't want to." Chrys came a step closer. "Last night when I was here, when we were here in your bed, it seemed like you could see me. If you're almost blind—"

She twisted her lips. "I could. Because—I know this is going to sound crazy—but…"

"After everything I've told you? I doubt it."

She gave a small laugh. "I guess that's true. Okay. When I look at you, you seem to…glow."

Laney chewed on her lip, waiting for Chrys to tell her how ridiculous that was. When he pulled his hand away from hers, her stomach plummeted.

"I do? What does it look like?"

She focused on his face, and the gold seemed stronger. His expression was…serious. "You seem to be surrounded in golden light. It moves with you like it's part of you. And not just you, either. Zeph had a blue glow around him. And Snake Lady glowed red." She clasped her hands together as relief flowed through her. "Oh, man. I just realized that if I'm seeing these glows because you're all gods, that means my vision isn't getting worse. I thought the glowing was halos, and…" She shook her head. "Wow. A bit of silver lining in the midst of all this craziness."

The gold surrounding him appeared more intense, more bright. Even his eyes seemed to glow with it. He cupped her cheek in his big, warm hand, and she leaned into it. "I'm glad. Seems like something about the changes to your vision has given you an interesting ability to perceive us."

"Well, score one for the human. I need some way to see you guys as you pop in and out of a room." In truth, though, relief flowed so strongly through her that it helped even out some of the chaos in her mind.

Chrys chuckled, and the sound of it was sweet and sexy. She hadn't heard him laugh often, and she enjoyed the sound of it very much. "I know you don't want to leave for a longer period, but do you think you'd be up for a short trip?" Chrys asked. "My family is meeting to discuss what to do about this situation and I need to go. Given everything, I'd like to bring you."

"Uh…what kind of trip?" And how in the hell would she explain taking a trip to Seth? "I'm not sure if I could get away without it raising questions. It's not like I leave the house very often." She gestured to her face.

"Questions from the human man," Chrys said, an odd tone to his voice. Like he was…no. No way.

"Yes, Seth. There's no way he wouldn't find my getting in someone's car and driving away suspicious."

An odd moment of silence passed. "Er, what time does he normally leave?"

"Around five or six, depending. He's interviewing contractors today to fix my barn roof, so I'm not sure when the last scheduled appointment is."

"Hmm," he said, pulling his touch away and pacing. He turned. "What if we left after he does this evening and came back tonight?"

Excitement and just a little fear set off a troop of butterflies in her stomach. *Dare to know*. "I think that could work."

He returned to her. "Okay, good. Thank you. I know this

is a lot coming at you all at once. You're handling it beautifully."
His voice was soft in Laney's ear. She found herself leaning
toward him. And, *God*, there was that scent again.

Slowly, she raised her gaze. Chrys towered over her,
and heat absolutely rolled off him. In that moment, his eyes
possessed a strange intensity she didn't understand. She only
knew how her body was interpreting all of it, what she wished
he would do.

"I really am sorry," he said. "About all of this."

Laney blinked away the haze of lust that had wrapped
around her. "I know."

"Eurus won't get near you. On my honor."

Right. *That's* why he was here. *Don't forget it, Laney.
You're neither experienced nor tough enough to protect your
heart around someone as powerful and magical as him.* Her
heart? What did her heart have to do with anything? *Yeah,
keep kidding yourself. You were attached from the moment
you thought you'd found a stray Pegasus in your barn.* "How
exactly is that going to work?" she managed.

"I'll stay here as much as I can, and when I can't, I'll have
someone else stand guard."

Stay here? It was exactly what she'd wanted, what she'd
yearned for all morning after she'd awakened to an empty
bed, an empty house. She thought to ask where he'd gone this
morning, but his words raised a more pressing question. "But
how am I going to explain you to Seth?"

He frowned. "Why do you have to say anything to him at
all?"

"Because no one's ever here just to visit me and he'll
demand to know who you are. He's a protective pain in the
ass." You know, in a totally loveable way. But still. His head

would go all *Exorcist* at the appearance of a strange man just hanging around her house.

"Then, we can remain elemental. Never see us."

She frowned. "I'm sorry but that's…creepy. I can't see enough as it is without wondering where my invisible god-protectors are. And how will I be able to talk to you? That's too weird. I'll be a nervous wreck and Seth will be all over me about it."

He made a gruff noise low in his throat. "Then we need a good reason for me to be here."

"What the heck would that be?" An idea came to mind. "Wait. I've got it. Only…any chance your godly bag of tricks includes knowing how to build a roof?"

∞∞∞

Chrys drove the truck up the long gravel driveway. The one demarcated on the road by a sign that read, "Summerlyn Stables, Est. 1945."

Summerlyn. Laney's family name was Summerlyn. He tucked that little nugget away for further exploration.

Focusing on the driveway again, Chrys had one thought: For the love of the gods, this better work.

"What's the plan, my lord?" Livos asked from the passenger seat. After Laney had shared her idea, Chrys had summoned his subordinate to gather all the things needed to give them a shot at pulling this off.

"First step is getting Laney's farm manager to hire me. Second step…well, that one's gonna be a bit more interesting. Just let me do the talking. And drop the 'my lord' crap."

Livos nodded. "As you wish."

"I know you haven't spent as much time with humans as I have, but tone down the formality or no one's going to buy this, okay? How's Aphel?"

"I'll try. And Apheliotes is healed. Thanks to your generosity."

Chrys waved away the compliment. No one deserved to be abused at his brother's hands. Each new evidence of Eurus's malevolence called Chrys's hopes into question more and more. Maybe he wasn't savable. Maybe he wasn't redeemable. But contemplating such a thing about his own brother was a whole lot easier than accepting it in his heart, especially since he was to blame for some part of it.

And now, with the Olympians growing impatient, it was clear that all of his effort was likely for nothing. Little time remained to convince Eurus to do the right thing, assuming he was capable of being convinced. Chrys's doubts were multiplying.

Which meant he needed Seth's cooperation. Because Chrys had every intention of being here to ensure Laney's safety. No matter what. If anything happened to her, because of him… His gut squeezed and Chrys gripped the steering wheel harder. Not gonna happen. Enough pain already lay at his feet.

As he rounded a curve in the driveway, Laney's long white house came into view. Sprawled out in front of it were white-fenced paddocks where a few horses grazed. To the left sat the red barn with its peaked roof, damaged at one low end by Chrys's fall.

Chrys parked the truck and grabbed the clipboard just as Seth emerged from the barn. He climbed down from the driver's seat and met the human in front of vehicle.

"Hi, I'm Chrys Notos. Olympic Construction." He extended his hand, bracing for the touch.

The man had brown hair and eyes, and the kind of brawn that came from doing manual labor. He returned the shake. "Seth Griffin. Thanks for coming out."

Chrys frowned. For a moment, he could've sworn he'd felt the kind of energy only divine beings possessed. But the sensation passed so quickly, he couldn't be sure it wasn't his anxiety over touching playing tricks on him. "Absolutely." He dropped his hand and gestured toward Livos. "And this is Li…Len."

"Len," Seth said with a nod. "Well, come on in and I'll show you what needs done."

"Lead the way."

Len? Livos mouthed, his eyebrows downward slashes on his forehead.

Chrys ignored the god's ire. "Barn looks new. How old is it?"

"Little over three years old. Mr. Summerlyn had it rebuilt not too long before he died. Unfortunately, that contractor has since moved out of town."

"Whoever it was did nice work."

Seth nodded. "Yeah. So, in that storm the other night, a tree came through the roof over here." He led them to the two stalls in the back left corner. "I don't think we lost any structural integrity, but the roof obviously needs to be replaced, as well as some of the grillwork on the end stall.

Chrys stepped into the last stall and looked up at the blue sky through the enormous jagged hole above him. In his mind's eye, Eurus plunged the lightning toward Chrys's heart. Sizzling phantom pain slashed through his shoulder. He looked away, surveying the warped piece of metal framing out the stall. "Floor escaped any real damage," Chrys said, completing his evaluation. In a flash, he recalled the incredible warmth Laney had shared with him while he lay there. A hot breeze blew through the space.

"Yeah, it's the damnedest thing. We're lucky the tree didn't take out this whole half of the barn, big as it was."

Chrys turned to him, ignoring Livos's smirk. "Any special considerations you need taken into account in getting the work done?"

"Matching materials, for one. And with all the crazy storms we've had this summer, I'm giving priority to anyone who can get started right away."

"Well, let me take some measurements. And I'd like to get up on the roof, too."

Seth nodded. "Do what you need to do. Just give me a shout when you're done."

But that was the thing, wasn't it? Who knew how long this battle with Eurus was going to take.

CHAPTER TEN

Laney couldn't stand it anymore. She'd finally finished her column, but that left her with nothing to distract her from wondering whether their plan would work. She knew Chrys was here for his "appointment" because she'd heard a truck arrive about a half hour ago. Much as she should stay off her feet, she couldn't resist going outside for some fresh air and a little snooping.

Slowly, she made her way to the front door. As her hand gripped the doorknob, fear erupted in goose bumps all down her arms. Last time she'd opened this door, a vengeance-seeking, snake-headed creature from the Underworld had stood there. How much weirder could this whole situation get?

Don't even ask that. Right.

She pulled the door open and stepped out onto the thankfully empty porch. Late summer heat surrounded her, and the shift from the dimness inside to the brightness outside momentarily stole her remaining vision as her eye adjusted. Counting her paces, she eased herself down onto the top step—no way she wanted to chance the walk to the barn—and then called for Seth. Finn stood watch next to her, his breath a steady pant.

"What's the matter?" Seth's voice came from the direction of the lean-to storage area that formed one side of the barn.

The sun's glare made it hard to track him in the distance. "Why does something have to be the matter? I was just taking a break from the computer and thought I'd see how things were going."

"Last contractor's here right now. They should be wrapping up soon. I'm not sure how quickly we'll be able to get this done, though. Contractors are always busiest this time of year, and with all these storms—"

"Seth?" a voice—Chrys's voice—called from a distance.

"Be right back," Seth said.

Laney sat up straighter, her ears straining to hear what they said. Who had Chrys brought with him? When their voices trailed off into the barn, she chanted an internal prayer that Chrys would win over Seth. Maybe ten minutes later, their voices emerged again.

"Come on up," Seth said. "Let me introduce you to the owner." Footsteps approached. "Chrys Notos, this is Laney Summerlyn. She owns the farm."

Laney pulled herself up by the railing next to her.

"You don't have to get— Here, let me help you," Chrys said, grasping her other hand.

She didn't really need the assistance, but she reveled in the opportunity to touch him again. "Thank you. I'm Laney."

"Chrys," he said in that deep voice she…really liked.

When the handshake went on for a moment, Seth

cleared his throat. Laney dropped Chrys's hand and met her manager's gaze. "Chrys is with Olympic Construction, and he has a crew available to start right away," he said.

"That would be great." She scanned her gaze between the men. They contrasted like a yin yang symbol, Chrys with his blond waves and golden skin, and Seth with his dark hair and farmer's tan. Seth wasn't a small man, by any measure— he could carry her butt, for goodness sake—but Chrys was at least four inches taller, his shoulders broader.

"Based on his estimate and availability, I'd recommend going with Olympic, assuming the references are good," Seth continued.

"I'd be happy to provide you with some," Chrys said. A sheet of paper crinkled. "But I hope you'll be able to decide soon, because we've got other customers wanting estimates. With so much work around, my crew won't sit idle for long."

Ooh, he's good.

"Understood." Seth held out his hand. The men shook. "I'll give you a call later tonight."

"That'll work. Look forward to hearing from you," Chrys said. "And, Miss Summerlyn, nice to meet you."

"You, too," she said, hoping her voice didn't sound as breathy to Seth as it did to her own ears. What the heck was wrong with her, anyway? She was acting like some lovesick teenager. As Chrys's footsteps retreated down the path, Laney forced normality into her voice. "Well, that's good news, huh?"

"You're all flushed. You feeling okay?"

"Sure." She waved his concern away. In the distance, a truck engine started. Gravel crunched under its tires. "It feels nice being outside after being cooped up all week. Wish I could ride."

"Don't even go there. You know the doctor said—"

"Yeah, yeah, I know." She hated it, but she did know and she wasn't going to do anything stupid. "So, what are you thinking?"

"I'll make some calls and we'll get this set up if everything checks out."

"Okay, great." Bracing against the railing, she hiked herself up a step.

"Damnit, Laney. You're not supposed to do steps." He appeared next to her.

"Done, see? I got it."

He huffed.

"What?"

"I try to help, and I get Miss Independence. Pretty-boy contractor offers you help, and you're all 'thaaank youuu,'" he said in a high-pitched sing-song voice.

"I did *not* do that." *Did I?*

He scoffed.

"What are you? Twelve? I was just being polite." She pushed through the front door and concentrated on the sound of the retreating truck. With Chrys leaving, did he have one of his gods here watching her even now? Man, Seth would go ballistic if he knew…

"You're doing too much walking."

"I know. I just needed a break. I'm going a little crazy in here." Laney took a deep breath and prepared to make nice. "Maybe I'll try the cane again." She settled onto the corner of the couch.

"Yeah? I think that'd be good. I can pick it up for you tomorrow." Her fridge opened and closed. The crack and fizz of a can of soda followed. Proof of how long she'd known Seth. He always just made himself at home.

"Okay," she said with a yawn. This day had taken more of a toll on her than she'd realized.

"I'm going to drive out to the cottage site before I head home. The builder was out again today and I want to see how things are going. Need anything before I leave?"

"Can you grab my iPhone and ear buds off my desk?" Lying here and listening to a book sounded like another plan she could get behind. Seth returned a moment later. "Thanks," she said as she accepted the phone from him. Oh, and a soda, too. Always taking care of her.

He kissed the top of her head. "Stay off your feet tonight, okay? I'll see you tomorrow."

"Okay," she whispered, her voice stolen by the memory of Chrys kissing her hair before. Her body went hot at the remembered feel of his lips… "See ya," she managed as Seth reached the door.

The silence rang loud after he closed it behind him.

"Is anybody here?" Laney whispered to the empty room, feeling like an idiot. No response. Crap, until the roof work started, maybe whoever was here to guard her would have to remain invisible. Not relishing *that* thought, she untangled the cord to the ear buds and heaved a breath.

Her constant lust for Chrys was going to be a problem. But, holy crap, she couldn't help it. Not only was he hot as hell with his sexy, tousled hair and his piercing green eyes and muscled shoulders you could just imagine holding and gripping, but if men could be beautiful, he truly was. Wholly masculine and utterly sensual at the same time. Like a big cat with its stealthy feline movement that could turn lethal predator in an instant.

Unhelpfully, her mind conjured the feel of his hand holding her wrist, his tongue invading her mouth.

To be with him, just once…

Not freaking likely. Him being a god, and all. A supreme god, thank you very much.

Ugh.

Laney slipped in her ear buds and opened the audiobook application on her iPhone. She stretched her legs out, hit play, and settled back into the comfy cushions. God knew she could use a good escape right about now. And how ironic was it that her novel was more believable than her life?

∞CCß

We are running out of time, Boreas thought as he walked back and forth across the living room, Teddy in his arms. The baby was doing everything within his power to resist sleep. His mismatched eyes—one brown and one bright blue, just like Owen's—would droop until his long, dark lashes spread out on his cheek, then pop back open again. Megan was dead on her feet, so Boreas had sent her to nap. He didn't mind his grandfather duties one bit.

And, anyway, it gave him a chance to mull over the problem of Eurus, the Olympians, and the fraternal feud among the Anemoi.

Knock, knock, knock.

Frowning, he approached the door and looked through the spyhole. Tabitha stood on the other side, a covered bowl in her hands. She'd clipped her dark blonde curls up off her neck, but a few tendrils hung down and framed her cheeks, occasionally lifted by the late summer breeze.

She knocked again.

"Boreas?" Megan called. "Who's there?"

Boreas stepped to the bottom of the staircase and looked up. "I'm sorry, Megan. It's Tabitha. It looks like she's here for a visit. I can't really…" With his fur robes and long white hair and beard, he wouldn't fit anybody's definition of normal. He frowned.

"Don't worry about it. Couldn't fall asleep, anyway." Holding the bannister, Megan descended the steps, her large belly leading the way. His granddaughter would be here in two months' time and, like her older brother, she would also be half human, half divine. Megan reached the bottom and held out her arms. "I've got him."

Teddy roused at the hand-off, gave his mother a big toothy smile, and clamped his little fist around a strand of Megan's shoulder-length blond hair. Boreas regretted the loss of the little guy immediately. He shifted into the elements, but remained in the room.

Megan tugged the door open and smiled. "Hey, Tabitha. How are you? Come on in."

The other woman returned the greeting and stepped inside. She smelled of the flowers she loved to tend and of sweetness, like sugar. Boreas guessed Tabitha was in her late thirties or early forties, judging by the laugh lines around her mouth and eyes. He didn't see them as a flaw. Not at all.

After a few moments cooing over the baby, Tabitha held up the bowl and said, "I made too much peach ice cream, and I know how much Owen loves it."

Megan shut the door. "You are going to be his favorite person if you keep bringing ice cream over."

"I'm glad to have someone to try out all these new flavors on. I'm like a kid in a candy store with this ice cream maker."

Megan led her guest into the kitchen at the rear of the house. "Well, I don't think you're going to find a flavor Owen doesn't like."

"Good." Tabitha deposited the container in the freezer. "How are you feeling?"

"I'm okay." She settled at the kitchen table. Tabitha joined her, crossing one long, tanned leg over the other. "I'm tired, but it's not too much longer now."

"Why don't you let me babysit this weekend so you and Owen can go out? Or, seriously, I'll watch Ted overnight and you guys could do a little getaway."

"That sounds like heaven," Megan said as she settled Teddy into the high chair.

"It's only going to get tougher with two, right? And I'd love to do it."

"I'd hate to put you out, though."

Tabitha scoffed. "You wouldn't, at all. I'm home by six o'clock on Friday. And I can paint while the baby sleeps."

Boreas had known she taught art at the community college, but not that she painted. He found himself wanting to ask about her work, watch her as she stood before a canvas and created something from nothing. His ancient guilt over his wife Ori's death surfaced, closed in, lingered. But it didn't stop him from wondering about this human woman who fascinated him a little more each time he saw her.

Maybe it is time to move on. It had been more than a millennia since Ori died.

As his thoughts played with this idea, Boreas only half listened to the rest of their conversation. But he watched the woman, her little movements, her expressive face, how she gave Megan all her attention. And he found himself wanting to give in to his interest.

Zephyros's energy approached.

Go to the basement, Boreas instructed as he materialized in Owen's office. Ever since the fight with Eurus had escalated last spring, Owen had done his work with WinterWatch Environmental Foundation from his home office as much as he could instead of commuting to the headquarters in downtown DC.

Zephyros appeared next to him.

Owen spun in his desk chair, the large computer monitor casting him in silhouette. "What's up?" he asked, rising.

"Tisiphone appeared at a human woman's house this morning looking for Chrys."

"Why—" Boreas and Owen began at the same time.

"I don't know the whole story, but Chrys is going to fill us in tonight. I told him to come here. And he's bringing the woman."

Owen tugged a hand through his black hair. "Okay. Man, I guess the Olympians are done waiting."

Boreas nodded. "Either that or this is just Hades sending out a feeler to see if he should force their intervention."

Zephyros nodded. "Either way, it's time to finish this."

Tabitha's presence moved above him. She was leaving. Boreas's gaze tracked to the ceiling, where he could imagine her lithe frame in those denim shorts…

"Why don't you just talk to her?" Owen asked.

Boreas glanced to his son. "What?"

"Don't act like you don't know what I'm talking about." He grinned. "No disrespect intended, my lord."

Just what he needed, Owen and his brothers wanting to play matchmaker. Boreas scowled and turned to Zephyros. "Should we bring Father in on the meeting?"

Zephyros frowned. "Not yet. Let's get the whole story and go from there."

"Very well," Boreas said. "Now, if you'll excuse me, I know a baby who needs his Grampa." He waited until Tabitha left and the front door closed before materializing in the living room. "My apologies, Megan. I'll take him. You go back up."

She pressed a big kiss against Teddy's neck, making him laugh despite his sleepiness. "Okay, munchkin. Be good for Grampa." She tilted the boy toward Boreas, and he pulled the little lug into his arms. "And you never need to apologize." She patted his arm, then turned for the stairs.

Perhaps he didn't need to apologize but, given all the time he spent here, he did need to make a change. And it was time. Eons past time. "Megan?"

She paused in the middle of the staircase and smiled down at him. "Yeah?"

"After your nap, I was wondering…how are you with a pair of scissors?"

CHAPTER ELEVEN

Chrysander could only hope that the god he was about to visit would offer the help he needed.

Passing over his father's ancestral citadel in Aeolia—yet again devoid of his energy signature—Chrys soared in over the Aegean Sea. The island of Lemnos, now a part of modern-day Greece, took shape in the distance. It was the part-time residence of Hephaestus, god of metallurgy, technology, and craftsmanship. He was the blacksmith to the gods, the maker of all of Olympus's finest equipment and weaponry, and the father of manufacturing and industry. If anyone could help Chrys with Laney's roof, it was Hephaestus. In fact, there was no one more *over*qualified to help.

Only potential snag? He was the estranged son of Zeus and Hera, Olympus's royal and most holy couple—and signers of Eurus's death warrant. Chrys was hoping the "estranged" part would cover his butt.

Coming in over the flat expanse of island, Chrys spotted

tell-tale plumes of smoke in the distance, where the land turned rougher and more mountainous. Triumph roared through him. Hephaestus's forge, and the smoke, confirmed he was here rather than at his more impressive palace and workshop on Olympus. He'd taken a chance coming here. Now he just hoped that luck held out.

The god's compound wound around the base of a mountain. Chrys materialized in a traditional tunic a moderate distance from an ornate iron gate and made his approach on foot. Armored guards blocked his passage.

"I am Notos, Supreme God of the South Wind and Summer and Cardinal Anemoi. I humbly seek council with your master."

"You are received," the guards said in unison. They clicked heels and pivoted, creating a space through which he could pass. The gates seemingly opened automatically.

Hephaestus's power radiated from the forge, making it clear where Chrys would find him. The workshop was a huge complex of buildings and workspaces mostly hidden behind a sprawling villa. A smith's hammer clanked out a steady beat near the tall, pyramidal furnace stack that sat at one end. And that's where he found Hephaestus, bent over his anvil.

Chrys took a knee and bowed his head.

Several minutes later, the hammering stopped. "Notos. To what do I owe the pleasure?"

"I request a favor, my lord."

"Of course you do. Well, rise and let's hear it, then." His tone was gruff, but his grey eyes shone with curiosity when Chrys met his gaze.

"I need to right a wrong, and I was hoping you could spare a few of your artisans to assist me. It would be the work of no more than a few days." Chrys explained the nature of the project.

"And why should I do this for you?" Hephaestus limped around his anvil and eased his hunched frame down onto a bench.

Chrys made sure not to stare at the god's gnarled hands and twisted feet, for which he'd often been ridiculed and shunned. Being Zeus's son offered him no protection in that regard. After all, Zeus had exiled him from Olympus for the very same reason. Or so it was rumored. Far as Chrys was concerned though, the dude was totally badass with a hammer, anvil, and a pair of tongs, so more power to him. "It will help me protect someone in danger. And I know there is no one more qualified to help."

"Bah! Don't blow smoke up my ass, Notos. Who is in danger?"

"A human. A woman. I crashed through her roof, and she braved a fierce storm to tend to me, despite the fact she cannot see."

Hephaestus's head tilted. "She's blind?" He stroked his dark beard.

"Nearly so, yes," he said, hope flaring. Hook, line, and—

"Hmph." Hephaestus rose, a movement that took obvious effort, and retrieved his hammer. Spinning it in his hand, he said, "And what does all this have to do with the death sentence on your eastern brother's head I've been hearing about?"

Tread carefully. "Nothing and everything," he hedged.

The god chuckled. "Oh, this is juicy, isn't it?" He picked up a poker, one end a scorching red, and hobbled toward Chrys. "The Anemoi golden boy. Isn't that what they say? His father's perfect son. Perfect face. Perfect body. Has his pick of the women. And the men." He tilted the business end of the poker close.

Chrys didn't flinch. At this point, what was one more scar? He grabbed the neck of his tunic and wrenched it apart. "I was far from perfect even before all this," he said of the multitude of marks carved into his skin. "But to make the point."

Hephaestus's gaze scanned over the remnants of Chrys's injuries. The one above his right pec, where he'd been skewered by the lightning, remained an angry red, the skin a twisted, ruined landscape.

The god plunged the poker into a barrel of water, setting off a sharp hiss as the red-hot end submerged.

He turned away, his steps slow and halting as he returned to his anvil. He dropped the hammer on top and continued toward the back wall, where tools of every manner hung in a long row. "I can give you two men for three days. And whatever materials you need, they will supply." Chrys resisted a fist pump. From his pocket, Hephaestus produced a ring of keys. After a moment of searching, he opened a drawer on a hidden cabinet.

"Thank you. That's incredibly generous."

He selected an item and slammed the drawer. "Yes, it is. But this is even more so."

Chrys traversed the distance between them, wanting to save him the trouble of crossing the workshop again. "My lord?"

From his large fist, he released a small object bound on a leather cord. A charm? "For your blind human," he said. He spun the larger object in his hand, then offered it, handle out. Chrys wrapped his hand around the fine grip. A dagger. The blade was fierce and gleamed in the firelight of the forge. "For you, to protect against whoever has done this to you." He gestured to Chrys's still bare chest. "These should even the odds a bit. The pieces are made of infernal iron, excavated from the pits of Tartarus by the damned."

Stunned, and hope flaring more than it had in weeks, Chrys cut his gaze to the god.

"If it breaks the skin, this iron is poisonous to a god. A strike of the blade will incapacitate. A hit to the heart will kill. When worn against the skin, the amulet will protect the wearer and serve as a temporary ward against divine power. Use them wisely."

⁊⑃

Chrysander circled in on Laney's farm, making sure Seth was gone before he materialized. The only life forms besides Laney's belonged to her animals. He entered her living room and shifted into his corporeal form. His gaze immediately found Laney, asleep on the couch. Finn lay curled in a ball at her feet. He lifted his head, gave a few half-hearted tail wags, then rolled onto his side.

Her heat drew him closer.

The silky sprawl of Laney's ebony hair, the porcelain smoothness of her skin kissed with a hit of pink on her cheeks and nose, the red rose of her lips. Absolutely beautiful. His gaze scanned down. He drank in the swell of her chest, his mind unhelpfully supplying the image of her lace-cupped breasts when he'd healed her burn. Lower, her legs stretched out, bandages surrounding her left shin. Sooner or later, he was going to heal her there, too. The desire to do so burned in his gut.

So much he couldn't make right. This, he could.

Standing next to the couch, the urge to touch her made Chrys curl his fingers into a fist. How odd, for him. Yet… He gave in and reached out, stroked his knuckles over her cheek. She turned into his touch, a small smile playing around the corners of her mouth.

Chrys eased onto his knees. He dragged a fingertip over her bottom lip. So soft. The scent of warm oranges drew him in. He leaned down, coming closer, closer. He pressed his lips to her forehead. Lingered.

Laney sucked in a breath, her head tilting back until her body was in a full-out stretch. "Mmm, Chrys," she mumbled.

He pulled away and smiled. Still asleep. Could she be dreaming of him?

Her lips dropped open and her body moved sinuously against the soft cushions. She moaned quietly.

The sound wrapped itself around Chrys's cock, had him wanting to trap her body against the couch with his.

"Laney," he said. "Wake up."

Her brow furrowed.

"Laney?" A strand of white hair caught his attention. Looking more closely, he realized it wasn't hair, but a wire that led to an ear piece. He tugged it from her ear and pressed his lips in close. "Miss Summerlyn, it's time to wake up."

She gasped and flew half into a sitting position.

"Hey, hey." He chuckled. "It's me."

"Shit," she said, pressing her hand against her chest. "You suck. Stop doing that." She flopped back against the pillow and tossed a hand over her head. "What time is it?"

"About six."

"I was having the strangest dream."

"Strange, huh? You said *my* name."

She shook her head, as if the strands of the dream still clung tight. "I only remember this man who glowed like you and said he was giving me the gift of sight. But even after he gave it to me, I still couldn't see."

Chrys nodded, the dream making him wonder... "Do you wish for your sight back?" When she hesitated, he wanted to kick himself. "Maybe I shouldn't have—"

"No, it's okay." She sat up higher against the pillow and played with the hem of her shorts for a minute. "You know. I used to. When my vision first started going and I was bumping into things and getting lost in places I'd known my whole life, I definitely wished it wasn't happening to me. When you get news like that, it's just like going through the whole grieving process." She shrugged. "But after a while, you adjust, because, what's your choice? To fight something you can't change forever?"

The words hit closer to home than Chrys ever would've expected. Fighting something he couldn't change was *exactly* what he'd been doing. Not just this summer, but for as long as he could remember. The more he realized she'd accomplished something he'd long failed to do, the more pride in her roared through him.

"Are you always this brave?" he asked.

Her eyes went wide. "God, I don't know. I didn't feel brave while I was in the middle of it."

He imagined her coming out in the storm that night to take care of a creature that had fallen through her roof. "Well, I think you are." She fidgeted under his gaze, and he took mercy on her and changed the topic. "Still up for a trip?"

She tucked her hair behind her ears and turned toward him. "Where?"

"My nephew's house in Fairfax."

Both brows reached for her hairline. "Fairfax, Virginia? That's almost three hours from here. Maybe more, depending on traffic."

This trip wouldn't involve cars. Or traffic. Or their physical bodies. This wasn't a part of himself he usually shared with his human consorts, though, so he wasn't sure how much to explain. "It won't take that long, I promise."

"You never know what the bridge traffic will be." She swung her legs to the floor, her thigh brushing against the outside of his hip. "I so rarely go anywhere. And I'd like to meet your nephew. So...okay." She twisted her fingers together. "Is he an Anemoi, too?"

"No. Owen's a snow god. Demigod, now. He's my oldest brother's son."

"Snow god. Right." Laney shook her head. "And will your brothers be there?"

"Two of them."

She frowned. "Not the one you fought with, though?"

"No." The thought of her and Eurus in the same room again, especially now, was like ice crawling down his spine.

"Okay. Do I have time to shower?"

"Uh." Bare skin. Streaming water. Hot steam. The images shot arousal hard and fast through his body. "No problem."

She tilted her head. "You sure?"

His erection strained against his jeans and demanded he volunteer to wash her back. "Yeah."

"'Kay." She stood and crossed the room. Finn jumped down and followed her.

Chrys tugged himself up onto the couch and fell back against the cushion, which smelled of her summery scent and still held her warmth. Groaning, he adjusted himself, but his mind remained hyper-aware of the fact that, just down the hall, she was getting naked. The whine of the plumbing sounded out from the back of the house.

Now she's naked and *wet*.

For fuck's sake.

He was just on edge. Focused as he'd been all summer on the situation with Eurus, he hadn't allowed himself the usual opportunities to release some of the heat and energy his godhood generated at the height of his season. It was part of the reason the weather had been so volatile. But next to the problem of his brother's imminent death, dipping his wick hadn't seemed a priority.

That's not what these feelings for Laney are about.

Sure it is.

Really, dipshit? Then why are you so compelled to touch her all the damn time?

Chrys shoved off the couch. Great. Now the voices in his head were arguing with each other.

At loose ends and far too wound up to do anything but pace, Chrys wandered around her space. He was careful not to disturb anything—he didn't want to move something from its careful placement. Horse figurines filled a corner cabinet in the living room. Pictures lined the big mantle. A much younger Laney with Sappho. Laney with a group of kids. Several with an older, white-haired man. None of or with people that looked to be her parents' ages. None with men she appeared to be close to. He frowned. Except for one on the end of her and Seth sitting on top of a fence rail, arms around one another, heads tilted close.

"Hey, Chrys?" she called from her room.

He stepped to the head of the hallway. And was immediately awash in her scent, made more potent from the warmth and dampness of her skin and hair. Oh, fuck. "Yeah?"

Dressed in a T-shirt and shorts, she dropped her gaze and shifted her feet. "Do you think you could, um, help me with the bandages? I can do it, but you could do it faster." She shrugged a shoulder. "I just figured—"

Chrys was in motion, the offer to touch, to help, to ease too much to resist. "Of course." He stopped in front of her, and the heat rolling off her brought his cock back to life. "I have a better idea, though."

She tilted her head back. "What's that?"

"Let me heal you."

"Oh, I—"

He pressed in closer, until his chest brushed up against her breasts. "Please, Laney. I want to make this better." He slid his fingers into the sleek length of her damp hair and forced her head back even more.

The sweet scent of her arousal joined her natural perfume. "I...I—"

Suddenly, Chrys needed her taste on his tongue again. Unable to resist the draw to her any longer, he claimed her mouth, devouring, searching, taking.

Laney froze, then was right there with him.

Their tongues met, dueled, twirled. He fisted his hand in her hair and guided her, deepening when he wanted, restraining her when he needed.

Her hands slid up his chest toward his neck.

Chrys gasped into the kiss, but fought the reflexive desire

to pull away. Instead, he pushed her back one step, then another, until her back encountered the door. He grabbed her arms and pressed them to the surface over her head. The control flooded relief through him and fueled his arousal another notch.

"I want to touch you," she whispered around a kiss.

His brain scrambled for a moment, and then he wedged his body in tighter, the ridge of his cock coming in snug against her belly. She unleashed a strangled moan as Chrys plundered her mouth, relished her sweet taste, bathed in her life-giving heat.

Good gods, her body was absolutely alive with her arousal. She clenched and unclenched her hands, her arm muscles flexing where he restrained her. Her abdomen writhed against his, creating a maddening friction against his erection. Her thighs shifted and squeezed.

It was only with the barest of restraint that he resisted willing her clothing away, turning her to face the wall, and tugging her hips out so he could bury himself deep.

Lost in the imagery, Chrys didn't notice the change in her movements until she slowly dragged her injured leg up the outside of his. Her wrists pressed against his hold and a yearning moan worked up her throat. "Chrys," she whimpered, her thigh moving higher and wrapping around.

His pulse lunged into a sprint. *Damnit*. He pulled back and stepped away, the phantom feeling of her flesh trapping his spiking fear through him. "I'm sorry," he said, rubbing his lips, regret a rock in his stomach. He could still feel her, taste her. Making sure she was steady on her feet, he dropped his hands from holding hers.

Hurt flashed through her expression, but she met his

gaze. "Why do you keep apologizing after you kiss me?"

"I'm supposed to be protecting you, helping you, not, uh, taking advantage of you."

She sighed. "Right." She pushed off the door and grabbed its edge. "I'll be out in a few."

Still breathing hard, he caught the door with his hand. "Let me heal your leg."

"And how will I explain that to Seth? Or to the doctor when I show up to get my stitches removed in a few days?"

He frowned. Damn human conventions. "Then let me help. With the bandages." *Anything to make it up to you.*

She stepped clear of the door but left it open. He followed her into the bedroom, then into the bathroom in the corner.

Warm steam still hung in the air. Chrys breathed it in. Her perfume surrounded and invaded him, keeping his body ready and wanting, but at least the heat eased the turmoil roiling through his gut. He concentrated on calming his damn self down. He wanted to kick himself for hurting her feelings.

Facing the mirror, Laney gestured to the medical supplies spread out on the counter. "Everything you need is right here. Just position the long rectangular gauzes lengthwise over the cuts, tape them in place, and then we can put on the tubular bandage to cover the dressings. It's just in a bit of an odd place for me to reach." She braced her hands against the edge of the sink and leaned forward. Her backside pressed out toward him.

Damn it all to Hades. Chrys was immediately rock hard. She couldn't have known what she'd done, of course, or how he'd take it, but this was the position he preferred when he fucked. He could control the act and limit his lovers' ability to touch him. Without question, he was tempted, but he also couldn't ignore the odd prickling of his scalp when he thought of taking her just as he had so many others.

"Chrys? Are you going to help me?"

CHAPTER TWELVE

Laney's heart still hadn't settled down from the kisses up against her door. She studied Chrys's glowing form in the bathroom mirror. Something about the reflection made his features harder to see.

"Yes, I'll help you. Though what I want to do is *heal* you, but I won't." He walked up behind her, grabbed a couple of supplies, and sank down beside her leg.

Generous as the offer was, how would she ever explain it being totally healed? Besides, at this point, it was only a few more days til the stitches came out. She released a shaky breath. "I thought standing would be easiest. Or would you rather I—"

"This is fine," he said, his voice gruff.

Oookay. His fingers moved against her calf, scrambling her already confused thoughts. When he'd kissed her again, he'd caught her totally off guard. But, damn, it had been an incredible kiss. Possessive, commanding, consuming. The way he towered over her. How he grabbed her hair. His restraining grip on her wrists. *Never* had a lover handled her that way. In hindsight, she wondered if Ryan thought her too fragile, and her only lover before him, well, they'd both been too inexperienced to do much more than insert Tab A into Slot B. She pressed her lips into a line to hold back the chuckle that threatened.

"You okay?" Chrys asked, securing another bandage in place.

"Uh, yeah." But one thing was for sure, she'd liked the urgency and intensity of Chrys's touch. The rough pads of his fingers smoothed tape against her skin. She bit back a moan. Actually, she liked his touch any way he gave it. Every way. And she thought maybe he felt the same way about her, too.

So why had he pulled away? Again?

She sighed, doubtful that staring at the ugly marks down the back of her leg heightened her sex appeal in his eyes. Between her puckered wounds and the twists of black stitches, she was totally channeling Frankenstein. Awesome.

The thought about Frankenstein gave her the oddest sense of déjà vu. For less than an instant, her mind conjured the image of a deformed man, but then it was gone, and she couldn't bring the picture back into focus.

"Almost done," he said in a low voice. "How much does this still hurt?"

The question yanked her from her dazed thoughts. "Oh, um, not nearly as bad anymore. Unless I pull at the stitches somehow, it's just—" She twisted to look down at him, and the rest of her words lodged in her throat. He'd glanced up at her in return, and she would've sworn his eyes flared with golden light, more focused and intense than the aura that usually surrounded him. "...uncomfortable. Your eyes," she whispered.

He rose and crowded in close to her, bringing that preternatural glow nearer. "Can't be helped. It's literally everything I can do to not hold you down so I can heal your pain. But once I start, I don't think I could stop exploring your body with my mouth."

Laney's jaw dropped open and her heart tripped into a full-out sprint. His words resurrected her earlier arousal. Her nipples pressed against the cups of her bra and her panties grew damp. "That, uh, sounds…really…good," she managed, her brain struggling to string the sentence together. She reached out.

"Don't." He grabbed her wrist.

Her stomach flip-flopped at the tightness of his grip. A trickle of sweat ran down Laney's back. Was it getting warmer in here? Or maybe it was just her body preparing to spontaneously combust. All around her, the air felt suddenly charged. The hair on her arms stood on end.

"Chrys?"

The sound of her voice seemed to startle him. He dropped her hand and stepped back. "What else do we need to do?" His gaze fell to her leg.

She forced herself to focus. "Just the tubular bandage to cover the dressings. Um." She slipped by him to sit on the toilet lid. "Probably easiest if I sit for this."

Tension rolled off Chrys's body and seemed to fill the small room with male heat. Having already cut a bunch of bandages to the correct length, Laney grabbed one and slipped it over her foot.

"Here," he said, brushing her fingers away. He slid the material up her leg, stretching it so it settled over the dressings on her calf. His knuckles grazed over her skin and she sucked in a breath. He bit out what sounded like a curse, from the tone of it, though Laney didn't recognize the language. "That it?"

She nodded. "Yeah. Thank you."

"Good. Let's go." In a series of quick movements she couldn't quite make out, he was up and out of the room.

"Maybe I should just stay here," she called. Not that she wanted to miss out on the time with him, or meeting his family, but Chrys was clearly agitated by her.

"Come on, Laney. Please."

She pushed herself up and limped into her bedroom, her gaze first finding his unique light and then settling on his face. "I guess I'm ready."

For a moment he didn't respond, and then he stepped in front of her. "I want you to have something."

"What?" she asked, hoping he didn't hear the breathiness of her voice. Her brain was still stuck on his mouth exploring her body.

He grabbed her palm and turned it upright. Something cool and metallic fell against her skin. She traced it with her fingers. "It's for protection," he said, his tone deep and solemn.

Marks had been etched into the face. "What does it say?"

"*Forged in righteousness.*"

Emotion welled within her. Honestly, she didn't get the significance of the inscription, but the gesture was beautiful. "Thank you."

"Here, let me." He lifted the necklace and she offered him her back, pulling her hair into a handheld ponytail. His fingertips skimming the back of her neck tickled and fueled her arousal. "Done," he rasped, his breath ghosting over her skin. She turned back to him. "To work, it needs to be worn against your bare skin. Like this." He slipped it under her shirt and the metal fell against the skin of her chest, cool and heavy. "Against your skin, it will prevent magic being used against you. Okay?"

She nodded, his seriousness beckoning hers.

He tugged it out and laid it atop her shirt again. "But, for what we're doing next, I need it off your skin. Which leads me to a question."

Something about the tone of his voice was odd, hesitant. "Uh, sure."

"Do you trust me?"

"What does that have—"

"Please. Just tell me."

She searched his face. His eyes were absolutely blazing at her, that intense light again playing around them, seemingly coming from them. "Yes," she said.

"I don't have a car."

"I know. You have a truck."

"Wha— Oh. No. I don't have a truck, either."

"You drove one here yesterday. And what does this have to do with how I wear my necklace?"

He tugged his fingers through his hair and groaned. Man, how she'd die to do that. Just once. "Never mind about the truck. I need the necklace off your skin so I can do this." His hand clasped hers.

Suddenly, the world disappeared. Laney screamed as light and color exploded all around her.

∞∞

"Are you sure about this?" Megan asked. "I don't really know what I'm doing."

Boreas crossed his arms and nodded. "Do it."

"This is crazy." She stepped to his side.

"Maybe. But it is also time. If I want to participate in your world, I need to look the part." With everything going on, being at Owen and Megan's wasn't even a question. He wouldn't leave them unprotected. He'd made that mistake once before. Never again. He tugged the towel tighter around his shoulders and shifted in the chair.

"I can't believe I'm doing this," she said, taking a long lock of his hair in hand. "You can't be mad at me if it doesn't turn out."

He chuckled. "Fear not."

"Sure, easy for you to say. Here goes nothing." She lifted the scissors and cut off a length of his hair. "Oh, my God." Megan held the long white strand so he could see it.

"Excellent. Continue."

She dropped the hair to the kitchen floor. Speaking no further, she worked around his head. Each cut of his hair left him feeling lighter, freer.

His thoughts turned to Ori. Orethyia. His Athenian princess. From the first time he'd seen her dancing on the banks of the Illissus, he'd wanted her. And she'd wanted him in return. They'd run away, angering her father, who spread rumors that Boreas had abducted her. Ori paid the stories no mind and insisted he not do so, either.

Years later, her death came as such a shock. At her father's invitation, she'd returned to visit him. Boreas had wanted to accompany her, but she'd begged him to let her attend her first reunion with her father alone. She'd feared that Boreas's presence would antagonize him. Finally, Boreas had relented.

The greatest mistake of his life.

King Erechteus had slain her for disobeying and humiliating him before his people, for honoring a god above her father. Only the fact that the king fell at Poseidon's hand in a war not long after prevented Boreas from exacting his own revenge.

Upon the sight of his beloved's body, her face frozen in a pale mask of death, Boreas's hair had turned immediately and irrevocably white, a physical badge of his shock and grief.

Afterward, he cared for nothing but their children and his job as Supreme God of the North Wind and Winter. He paid no mind to his appearance. He made no effort to soothe his heart with new love, even eons after the fact. He worried not about trivial needs like happiness and companionship.

And then Owen, the son he'd adopted long, long ago, met Megan. Megan's love had restored Owen to the world, returned his humanity, and gave him a blood family he'd never before possessed.

And their joy had thrown into stark relief everything Boreas had given up on.

But he could fix that. Now was as good a time as any. No. For Owen, Megan, and Teddy, now was *the* time to rejoin the living.

Not to mention, Tabitha…

He sighed. One change at a time.

"You okay?" Megan asked.

"I am fine." Or would be.

"Beard, too?" She stepped in front of him.

He smiled. "Beard, too."

She shook her head. "Okay. I'll cut it short and then we'll use the clippers."

"Good."

"I still can't believe I'm doing this," she said, tugging at a hank of hair on his cheek.

"Well, I cannot believe I've waited so long to have it done."

She paused and met his gaze. Her eyes were glassy with unshed tears. "You look so much younger already."

"Yes?" He arched an eyebrow. "Do not cry or you will be unable to see where you are cutting."

Dabbing her eye, she gave a watery laugh. "Okay." She finished trimming his beard.

Boreas ran his hand over his head, his face. He smiled.

Megan traded the scissors for a pair of clippers. With slow upward strokes, she ran the clippers through his hair. "I don't know if I'm getting this exactly even."

"Worry not."

"Owen is going to flip out when he sees you."

"Yes." Boreas grinned, imagining everyone's reaction.

She ran her fingers through the top of his hair. "I'll leave it longer on top. It's a style."

He chuckled. "If you say so."

After a few moments, she stepped in front of him again. She made a few more passes, then lowered the clippers to her side. "Just the beard now. Do you want to—"

He stood up and rubbed his jaw. "You know what? I want a clean shave."

"Owen has razors and shaving cream in the bathroom."

He squeezed her arm. "Thank you, Megan."

"Um, Boreas?"

"Yes?"

Her gaze ran over his robes. "If you're trying to fit in, it might be time to update the clothes, too."

He looked himself over and nodded. "Indeed." He thought of the clothing his brothers wore and willed the change. His fur robe gave way to a pair of blue jeans and a light gray long-sleeved T-shirt.

Megan gasped. "Holy wow."

Had he done something wrong? He looked himself over again, not seeing anything amiss. "What is it?" Was the denim supposed to be this stiff?

"You look so different." She met his gaze. "So *good*."

"Oh. Good. Well, okay, then."

"There's just one thing." She smiled and pointed at his feet. "You should probably try to keep those on the floor."

Boreas had so long ago given up on any pretense of humanity, he usually paid little attention to the conventions of the physical world. "Right." He settled himself upon the floor, standing just as a man would. "So." He held out his arms. "How do I look?"

Her smile was slow but bright. "Very handsome."

Footsteps jogged up the basement stairs. "Shall we see what Owen thinks?"

She nodded, a big grin shaping her pretty face. "Hey, Owen? Can you come here a minute?"

Boreas faced the passage from the living room into the kitchen. He threw Megan a wink.

Owen came through the doorway. "What's up, angel—" He did a double take and froze. His mismatched eyes narrowed on Boreas's face. Shock transformed his expression a moment later. "By the gods! Boreas?"

Good humor flowed through him. Since Owen's marriage and Teddy's birth, it was an emotion with which he'd been becoming more and more familiar. "Ha! You did not recognize me right away."

His mouth dropped open and he appeared to struggle for words. "What…why…?"

"With all the time I spend here, I need to fit in better with this world. And I was overdue for a change."

Owen nodded, his gaze shifting to his wife, nearly bouncing with excitement. "Aw, angel. Did you do this?" He crossed the room and took her in his arms. She nodded against his chest. Intense satisfaction at their happiness filled Boreas's heart. "You did good," he whispered.

"Well, I still require a shave."

Owen stepped in front of him. "I am glad you're here," he said, holding out his hand.

Boreas grasped the offered hand and pulled Owen into his arms. "As I am glad to be here, son."

And now that his physical appearance was no longer a liability, he could play an even bigger role in guarding this precious family of his. He might've failed Ori, but it was a mistake he'd never make again.

Chapter Thirteen

Chrys! Chrys! Laney screamed, barraged from every angle by blinding light and color. No. Not *blinding*. Because she could see it. Every bit of it.

She slammed back into her body, swayed, fell into something hard and warm. *What the hell just happened?*

"Laney, what's the matter? What's happening?" Chrys's voice, deep and strained.

She threw herself around him, emotion overwhelming her, and labored to restrain the sobs threatening to tear up her throat. It had been the better part of ten years since she'd last seen light and color so vividly, so fully, coming at her from every angle.

He spoke in that language she didn't understand, then, finally, his arms settled around her. He pulled her in tight, one hand petting her hair in slow, soothing strokes. "Shh, you're okay. I've got you."

No matter how hard she tried, she couldn't get her breathing to even out or her heart to stop pounding. She was shaking so hard she didn't think she'd stay on her feet if Chrys wasn't holding her.

"Can you tell me what just happened?" he rasped against her hair.

"I...I...what did you do wh-when you took my h-hand?" she managed, her limited vision filled with his unique aura from standing up against him. The near blindness was so familiar, so much a part of her. That glimpse of sight... So unexpected, it had been as terrifying as it was awesome.

He pulled back and cupped her face in his big, warm palm. His thumb stroked her cheek, catching tears she didn't realize had spilled. For a long moment, she felt examined. She inhaled a calming breath and leaned her face into his hand.

"Come here," he said. He led her to the bed and tugged her down beside him. "I'm sorry. I should've explained it. I just...I suck at this. I never do this."

"Do what?" she whispered, trying to focus on his face.

He tucked a strand of hair behind her ear. Goosebumps erupted on her arms as he treated her to a series of soft, affectionate touches. "Get...involved. Reveal stuff about myself."

His words had her heart thumping for a new reason. "Involved" was a good thing, right? "Involved" meant she wasn't the only one affected by whatever was going on between them.

He leaned his forehead against hers. Laney sucked in a breath. Something about the moment felt weighted with a significance she didn't understand. And, was he shaking?

She debated for less than a second, then gave in to the urge she'd felt since the first time they'd met. She reached up and caressed his hair. Oh, God, it was thick and soft. Her fingers ran through the golden strands, her nails lightly scratching his scalp.

He released a halting breath and swallowed hard, light seeming to concentrate around his eyes again. "I pulled you into the elements with me. Out of the physical world and into the wind. That's what happened when I touched you."

For a long moment, Laney tried to absorb the meaning of his words. *Into the elements?* "How?" She stroked his hair harder, loving the feel of it against her sensitive fingers.

He shuddered. "It's just part of me, part of my nature. But we don't have to—"

"I could see," she whispered.

He lifted his head from hers and, from the way the light shifted and focused, she knew his eyes were right in front of hers. "Are you saying you could—"

"Totally see. As in"—she shook her head, amazement and more than a little fear flowing through her—"no more blindness."

"Almighty Zeus. Are you okay? Did it hurt?"

"No. No, it didn't hurt. It just scared the shit out of me." She gave a small laugh despite the way her head was spinning. "It was incredible."

"I…I don't know what to say."

Laney's heart squeezed, and her chest filled with the pressure of her competing emotions. Total wonder at the return of something she thought she'd never again have, even if for only a moment. Sadness at the thought of being reminded of exactly what she didn't and couldn't have. Anticipation of doing it again, seeing it again.

Screw the fear. This was a "dare to know" moment if she'd

ever had one. It might hurt like hell to be plunged back into the dark again, but in the meantime, she was embracing this amazing, magical opportunity to see the world in all of its full, bright, glorious detail. "I'm ready now." She nodded. "I want to try again."

"Are you sure?"

"Please?" she whispered. "I can do it."

For a long moment, he didn't respond. Finally, he grasped her hand and laced his fingers through hers. "When we shift, just think your words. I will be able to hear you. If it's too much, just say so, and I'll pull us right back out. You will be totally safe."

She nodded. "Okay."

"At first, we'll stay right here. If you can…see, just take a moment to study your surroundings. Get grounded in your sight. Does that make sense?"

"Yes." The pressure in her chest shifted, now filled in part with intense gratitude for his compassion and thoughtfulness. His concern for her was clear in his words, his touch.

"Here we go," he said in a low voice.

She sucked in a harsh breath as they shifted. Her soul trembled.

Talk to me, Laney.

She heard his voice, just as he'd said she would, but the return of her vision was so monumental, so overwhelming, that she couldn't divert one iota of attention from soaking in the details of the world around her. It was just her room, but it was *her room*. Her bed with its molded headboard and purple comforter. Her shelf of trophies and ribbons from her high school equestrian club. The evening sunlight pouring through the sheer lavender curtains and throwing rainbow prisms off of the crystal teardrop hanging in the window. A million shapes and colors flooded her brain, bolstering her memories and restocking her imagination.

Laney?

I'm okay. I'm...better than okay. It was, perhaps, the most amazing moment of her life.

What does it look like?

Just like I remembered, only more. *More colorful, more detailed, more...alive. So, now what do we do? How do we get where we need to go?*

I'll guide us. It won't take long.

It could take forever, as far as she was concerned. *All right. I'm good to go.*

The next thing she knew, she was looking down on the roof of her house. She squealed.

I've got you.

I'm okay, I'm okay. Oh, my God. She scanned all around, and her awareness fell upon the setting sun. She gasped. Somehow, that incredible emotional pressure filled her, even in this form. *The sun. I haven't been able to really see it in years.*

I'll help you see anything you want to see.

She would've sworn he brushed her face. But how could that be? She looked around, to the barn and the fields beyond. *Sappho!*

Yes. Slowly, they moved over the house, the yard, and toward the barn. The horses were grazing in the field.

Oh! She's even more beautiful than I'd remembered. The Friesian's black hair normally made it difficult to see her details. But now, Laney could see the whole of just how gorgeous and majestic she was. For a long moment, she lingered.

She visited each of the other horses and committed to memory their colors and markings and mannerisms. Chrys brought her to Rolly last.

What happened to him? Chrys asked.

Someone shot him a couple weeks ago. You wouldn't believe some of the things people do to horses. Growing up, my grandfather was involved with rescue organizations. He always said, "If you're not part of the solution, you're part of the problem." So I kept up his work after he died. When I heard about Rolly, I couldn't resist.

The Appaloosa shook its head and stomped.

You never cease to amaze me. Before she could answer, he spoke again, *I have never liked to see something hurting.* He pulled her around to the surgical wound on the horse's lower belly. *And there's no reason this guy has to.*

What do you...

The question fell away as Chrys's presence beside her seemed to change, focus, narrow. A warm wind blew around them, *from* them. She gasped as, before her eyes, Rolly's wound started to change, too.

Are you doing that? That's amazing.

For several long moments, he didn't answer, but the steady healing—the kind that would've happened over the next couple weeks—continued right before her until all that remained was a scar. The horse nickered and trotted off a few paces as if trying out his new healthfulness.

When Chrys's voice came, it was low and soft. *If I can't heal you, I'll heal something you love.*

Emotion overwhelmed Laney. He'd *healed* him, healed the thing she'd always loved most in the world. Another Kant quote came to mind: "We can judge the heart of a man by how he treats animals." And by that measure, Chrys had proven himself in spades. *Thank you*, she managed. *I can't believe you just did that, but thank you.*

As if the gift of her sight wasn't enough…

If Laney had been in her body, she was sure her heart would've grown too large for her chest.

∞

Chrysander was on full-out sensory overload.

First, there'd been Laney's desperate embrace in her bedroom. He'd forced himself not to pull away. She'd needed him, and he'd wanted to be strong enough to be there for her in any way—in *every* way. When was the last time someone had hugged him? He couldn't even recall the last time someone's hands had surrounded or held him. The normal breath-stealing panic had been there, but he'd focused on Laney, on her warmth, on the comfort she seemed to receive from his touch.

Then, she'd dragged her fingers through his hair. Electricity had shot through his nervous system, skittered down his spine, and settled into the sudden steel of his cock. He always blocked a lover's grasp from his face or his neck or his hair. It was too intimate, too familiar. But ever since he'd curled himself around her on the barn floor and realized what she'd risked to tend to his wounds, Laney Summerlyn had slowly but surely been slipping around defenses he'd built up eons ago.

Now, her absolute wonder at the return of her sight in this form… It slayed him. He hadn't even thought such a thing might be possible. That he could do this for her, give this to her, and that she trusted him to share this experience with her—it might've been the most meaningful thing Chrysander Notos had ever been a part of.

He hadn't planned on the detour to heal her horse, but hearing her talk about rescuing horses, and thinking of what she'd done for him as he'd laid injured in his sacred animal form, he suddenly *had* to do something else, just for her. The incredible gratitude that flowed through their intertwined energy? It was the greatest, most unexpected reward.

We should head out to meet my family now, if you're ready?

Yes. I think I am.

Chrys willed them up, up above the fields, but low enough that Laney could still study all over which they passed. As they chased the westward-moving sun, Chrys swooped down to race along a train, sailed just over the slow-moving waters of the Potomac River, and weaved in and among the buildings of Washington, D.C. As they flew, Laney exclaimed, laughed, gasped. He anticipated each reaction, honored that she shared them so freely. When she asked if he could take her to see this or that more closely, he couldn't have denied her if he'd wanted to. Which he didn't. Each and every detour was for Laney's benefit and pleasure.

Chrys would've gone anywhere. He wanted her to see everything. And he wanted to be at her side when she saw it.

And, gods, how the gratitude and the joy and the absolute delight poured off her. He'd never felt more touched—nor derived more comfort and satisfaction from such closeness with another being—as he did while they soared through the darkening summer sky toward his brethren's home.

After all the pain he'd caused, after all the conflict and discord his very *existence* had wrought, learning he had the capacity to create something so good and so pure and so righteous threatened to remake him at the most fundamental level.

And it was all because of Laney.

As her energy twirled and twisted with his on the wind, Chrys wasn't sure he would ever truly feel content without her warmth and courage and strength at his side.

It was a sobering thought, given who he was and the current crisis, not to mention that tolerating one hug was a helluva long way from proving able to provide the kind of emotional and physical support Laney required—no, *deserved*.

He took a moment to pull himself together, regret filling his gut at what he needed to tell her. *We're almost there.*

All right. Isn't it all so beautiful? I mean, I knew it was. But I just didn't remember it quite like this.

Chrys pictured her face. *Almost too beautiful for words.*

He navigated them toward the neighborhood and brought them in along the cozy street of well-kept houses on which Owen and Megan lived. Knowing Laney would need a moment to collect herself when they returned to their bodies, he circled into Owen's backyard and brought them down under the cover of an old tree with broad, sprawling branches.

You might be disoriented for a few minutes, but I'll take care of you.

I know you will.

Four simple words. Her trust shot straight to the center of his being, opened his defenses to her a little wider.

And then they were corporeal again.

Laney sucked in a gasping breath. Her fingers dug into

his biceps when she swayed. "I think I need to sit down," she rasped.

He guided her to her knees, so they knelt facing one another. "How are you?"

"I don't know yet." She ground the heels of her hands into her eyes, resting her forehead in her palms.

Watching her, Chrys's gut tightened. Worry clawed through his chest. *Had it been too much?*

Her shoulders shook. Intense emotion rolled off her and slammed into him. And then she launched herself at him, the movement so sudden and unexpected that Chrys lost his balance and toppled backward. She landed on his chest and crawled up his body. Kisses rained down on his neck and face. Her hands plowed into his hair.

Pinned down. He was pinned down. He grunted, every muscle in his body rigid with anticipation over whether his fight-or-flight response would win out.

And then her words sank into his consciousness.

"Thank you, thank you, thank you." A litany of gratitude spilled from her lips and covered him in kisses and caresses that punctuated the outpouring of her affection.

Chrys's mind froze, waited, debated. Then he groaned, his body demanding things his mind was fighting against. Taking her in his arms, he rolled them in the soft grass. His fingers found her hair. His lips found her lips. His body settled into the cradle of her thighs.

"Chrys," she rasped around the edge of a kiss, her hands still grasping and tugging at his hair. "Thank you…for everything."

He mentally body-checked his anxiety, and threw himself into kissing her so deeply, so completely, so thoroughly, that he forgot all the rest of the shit going on in his head. Just forgot the hell out of it.

And, was it just him, or did the sounds of her pleasure increase the more aggressive he got?

The question blazed through his blood and had his cock punching at his jeans. So little separated him from her intense heat. And he was so fucking tempted to will the clothing away and slide home.

An awareness of energy slid through his mind. Just as Chrys's brain came back online, a voice called out from the back porch. "Hey, when you two lovebirds are done out there, we'll be waiting for you."

CHAPTER FOURTEEN

"Omigod!" Heat flooded her cheeks. What the hell was she thinking, jumping Chrys with his whole family just inside? And they were all gods, too. Like humiliating yourself in front of other humans wasn't bad enough.

"Go to hell, Z." Chrys stroked the side of her face. "Ignore him. He's an asshole."

"I heard that."

She choked on a laugh, the good humor in Chrys's voice easing her discomfort.

"You have any brothers?"

"No," she managed.

"Lucky," he groused.

"*Chrysander.*"

"We'll come in when we're good and ready, you dig?" For a long moment, his lips hovered just shy of hers. And then he kissed her. Soft and slow. "You've honored me, Laney Summerlyn," he said in a low voice, just for her. As if his earlier actions hadn't done enough to warm her heart, his words touched her further. A sudden burst of wind swirled around them. He groaned, his forehead falling atop hers. "I'm sorry. He's not going to leave us alone."

Disappointment had no more begun warring with embarrassment when they were suddenly on their feet again. "Holy crap! Give a girl some warning, would ya?"

He kissed her cheek. "I'll try. It's kinda second nature to me. Come on."

"Wait." His heat and light paused in front of her. "Do I look okay?" She smoothed her hands over her hair.

"By the gods, you could never look *just* okay. You are a beautiful woman. And they will love you."

She blew out a breath, nerves tossing her stomach. "Okay. You'll have to guide me, though. I don't have my cane, and everything here will be unfamiliar."

"So, how do I—"

"Just hold your arm straight down and walk normal. I'll hold on and follow. Let me know if we come to any steps or doors or obstacles I need to step over." She moved to his side and took hold of his bicep just above the elbow.

"A lot of flat grass and then three steps at the porch."

"Okay," she said, walking a half step behind him. Scanning her gaze over their path, Laney attempted to paint a picture of where they were for herself. She pushed away the disappointment that she couldn't see the way she had moments ago. "Who lives here?"

"My nephew Owen and his wife Megan. And their son, Teddy."

"Owen's the snow god?"

"Yeah."

"And is Megan a god, too? Er, a goddess?"

"Nope."

"Oh." So, a god could be with a human? Could have children with a human? *Cart before horse much, Laney?* "And, uh, who else will be here?"

"Just my brothers, Boreas and Zephyros."

"Right."

"Okay. Three steps up. There's a handrail."

Laney found the metal rail, forgetting until she attempted the first step about her stitches. She gasped and paused. "Stitches," she managed.

Next thing she knew, she'd blinked in and out of the elements again, the momentary explosion of color revealing what he'd done.

"Problem solved," he said.

She couldn't help but chuckle.

"Z," Chrys said.

"Chrys. Laney."

"Hi," she said, her gaze finding Zeph's blue aura next to Chrys's golden one.

"Been here long?" Chrys asked.

"No. Just got here when I harassed you."

Chrys muttered something in that language she didn't understand and the wind gusted out of nowhere.

Zephyros laughed. "Come on in. We have business to attend to and we don't have all night."

In the distance, thunder rumbled. Laney lifted her gaze to the sky. Great. Just what she needed. A storm when she was someplace she didn't know.

"You okay?" Chrys whispered as he guided her forward. She nodded, nerves returning. "Okay, the door opens to the right. There's a small step up...now."

Laney cleared the doorway. The screen door and inner door closed behind her.

"Small mud room, then kitchen, then living room after that."

"Thank you," she squeezed his arm and worked to assemble a picture for herself. The dim room they entered opened into a brighter, larger space. The change in the lighting momentarily stole the rest of her sight. Ahead, Zeph exchanged pleasantries with a woman.

"Where's Ella?" the female voice asked.

"Be here any minute."

"Good. Chrys," the woman's voice exclaimed. "I've missed you being here all the time, eating my food."

"Well, there's no time like the present." He chuckled. For a moment, he seemed to lean away, but not so much that Laney had to drop his arm. "Good to see you. That baby ready to come out and meet his uncle yet?"

Laney scanned her gaze over the woman. Blond hair. Big smile. No glowing aura.

"Bite your tongue, Chrysander Notos. I might be big as a house, but this kid can stay put for another month or two."

There was a pause just long enough to feel awkward. Thunder cracked in the distance, but closer than before. "Megan, this is Laney Summerlyn. Laney, Megan."

Laney extended her hand. "Hi, Megan."

A cool hand slipped into hers. "Welcome, Laney. It's nice to meet you. Why don't you all head into the living room. Owen and Boreas are in there." Something about the tone of her voice changed. She sounded...excited?

"This way," Chrys said to her.

Zeph's heavy footsteps went ahead of them, then suddenly

stopped. Next to her, Chrys drew a sharp breath.

"Good gods!" Zeph's footsteps continued into the room. Stopped again. "Boreas?" A weighted pause filled the room. "Welcome back, brother," Zeph said, his tone different — more serious, almost relief-filled.

"Thank you, Zephyros," a deep voice said. More formal than the others. His aura was a bright white. Next to him, another god, with a softer white light, stood.

"Dude," Chrys said, still next to her. "You got a makeover."

Everyone laughed.

Laney tried to follow the conversation, attempted to visually piece together who was who, but because of the number of glowing auras in the room and her general unfamiliarity, she was uncomfortably ungrounded.

"I'll be right back," Chrys said. She forced a smile and nodded. "Da-yum, B. You are totally rocking the twenty-first century." Laughter and teasing followed.

Someone slipped in next to her. "My father-in-law completely changed his appearance," Megan whispered. "They're just seeing it for the first time."

Laney smiled, genuinely this time, Megan's kindness easing the awkwardness. "How drastic of a change?"

"From long hair and beard and, uh, outdated clothes, to short hair, shaved face, and new clothes."

"They sound happy."

"Yeah." From Megan's tone, Laney knew she was smiling. A crying sounded out from somewhere in the house. Upstairs? "Oh, darn. I'm sorry. That's Teddy. I better go get him."

The men all offered apologies for the rowdiness of their reunion as Megan crossed the room and made her way up a set of steps on the far side, from the sounds of it. Rain pattered against the windows and, outside, the winds gusted.

A moment later, another god—a woman, by the voice— entered the room, a new round of greetings and exclamations erupting over the surprise Boreas had presented.

Unsure of the layout of the room, Laney was momentarily trapped by her disability. Thunder rolled across the sky like a growl, until it sounded from right above them. She couldn't recall the last time she'd felt this out of place, this out of control. She hugged herself and wondered if it was a mistake to have come.

৪০৫৪

Chrysander turned from the group to find Laney standing where he'd left her. But...she appeared different, like she'd shrunk into herself. He bit out an ancient curse and crossed the room. "I'm sorry, Laney. Come meet everyone."

"Maybe you should just take me home. I don't—"

"I would really like you here. With me." *Way to go, Notos. Thoughtless, much?* He cupped his hand around her neck, massaged the tense muscles he felt there. The strangely intriguing desire to strip her down and treat her whole body similarly surged through him. The image was immediately appealing and so damn sexy.

"So you can protect me."

Responses competed for air time, but Chrys dismissed all the rationalizations for the truth. "Because I *want* you to be here."

Finally, she nodded.

"Here. Take my arm." Relief flooded through him when

she did. "Everyone," he said in a raised voice. "I'd like to introduce you to Laney Summerlyn."

One by one, Chrys said their names. Laney seemed to let her gaze rest on each person, almost like she was studying them. With this many people, would she be able to keep them all straight? If the gods all appeared to have auras to her, maybe that would help.

Chrys frowned, hating the idea that she would feel even a little uncomfortable. "Hold on a second. I have an idea." He took her hands. "You trust me?"

She gave a small, uncertain laugh. "Sure." He pulled her into the elements. The room appeared around them, along with its four inhabitants. Make that six—Megan descended the stairs with Ted in her arms.

This might make it a little easier. Sorry I didn't think of it sooner.

You did this so I could see them.

Yeah. He glanced to the men, all of whom were aware of what he was doing. The approval was palpable in the room.

Chrys ignored their attention and introduced her to them again.

He tried to see them as she might.

Zephyros, with his flaring blue eyes and short brown hair, stood close to Ella, a pretty woman with brown hair and eyes. The pair couldn't stop touching one another, and it was easy to see the affection between them. Not surprising after everything they had gone through to be together. An unfamiliar pang of envy rolled through his being.

In the center of the semi-circle stood his oldest brother, now ruggedly handsome with gray eyes that flashed to silver and short, spiky hair. Given the youthfulness of his face, Chrys wondered if the pure white of his hair surprised her. It was certainly incongruous, and the transformation was definitely something he never thought would happen. Seeing Boreas like this again was a moment Chrys would never forget. And he could tell from the emotion that had overcome Zeph when his brothers had exchanged greetings that it was the very same for him.

Next, he reintroduced Owen, with his dark eyes that were actually two different colors, a fact that his long hair sometimes hid. And completing the group was the very pregnant Megan, whose blond waves Teddy gripped in his fist. With an arm around her shoulders, Owen pulled the pair into his side and kissed them, the baby first, then Megan. And Chrys's unfamiliar envy got that much more familiar.

Thank you so much, she said to him. *I can't tell you how much this helps. It was very thoughtful.*

I'm sorry I made you uncomfortable. It won't happen again. At least, I'll try my damnedest.

"I don't mean to rush you," Zeph said, "but we should begin."

Boreas nodded. "Yes. Before the storm rages out of control."

Chrys returned them to corporeality. It was time to say what needed to be said. Long past time, actually. He guided Laney over to an armchair, and she sat. He remained by her side as everyone found a seat wherever they could. Overhead, thunder cracked and rumbled. Another reason to get on with it.

In the Realm of the Gods it was a different story, but here on Earth, the longer multiple Cardinal Anemoi congregated in one place, the more the elements from their respective realms would clash and collide. Should they stay together long enough, what seemed a typical summer storm would escalate into a devastating maelstrom that would spare nothing and no one.

They had twenty, thirty minutes. Tops.

Which meant he needed to face the shitstorm he knew would erupt when he revealed why he'd been incapable of subduing Eurus all summer.

As if to underscore the point, thunder crashed so explosively the windows rattled and the house shook.

"All right, Chrys. Let's hear it. What in the name of Hades has been going on between you and Eurus?"

The question hung in the air for a long moment. Chrys debated whether to start at the beginning or just come right on out with the doozy of a revelation he'd been sitting on most of the summer.

Fuck it. Shit, meet fan.

Feeling Laney's warmth near him, he met Owen's eyes, then each of his brothers'. "Eurus has Father's firestone ring."

Chapter Fifteen

Zephyros jumped to his feet. "What did you say?" Save Megan, everyone else joined him. Five pair of eyes cast their critical judgment upon him. The air in the room took on an electrical quality.

"You heard me. Eurus has the firestone ring." Every muscle in Chrys's body went rigid, bracing for whatever they threw at him. He'd deserve every bit of it.

"What in the seventh circle of hell are you talking about?" Zeph growled.

"Wait. That gaudy thing with the wings?"

All eyes whipped to Ella. "How do you know that?" Boreas asked.

She paled. "That night. On the bridge. He wore it then." She didn't need to explain further. Everyone understood implicitly that she referred to the night Eurus had killed her human form by throwing her off the tallest tower of the Chesapeake Bay Bridge. Chrys hated that he'd made her relive even a moment of that night.

Zeph materialized right in front of him. "By Zeus and all the gods," he hissed. "Why have you withheld this from us? That was the end of March!" For a long moment, lightning illuminated the world outside the windows as if it were day.

Behind Zeph, Ella gasped. "I didn't know it was significant. I'm sorry."

He returned to her side and took her face in her hands. "You have no cause to apologize, love. You had no reason to know. Unlike *him*." Fierce blue light slashed from Z's eyes. Thunder clapped and rolled, the loud rumble going on so long it seemed it might never stop.

"He's right," Chrys said. Their disapproval sat like a jagged block of ice in his gut.

Teddy whined and fussed in Megan's arms. "I think I'll take him upstairs," Megan said in a small voice. Owen helped her up and kissed her cheek, his intense, strange eyes following her like he was torn between joining her and remaining. Dark light flared from his gaze when it cut back to Chrys. "Go on," he said.

Chrys blew out a breath. "I didn't know right away. That night, I went after Eurus. For a long stretch of days, I could not find him." Chyrs had assumed he'd holed up at his ancient citadel in the eastern extreme of the Realm of the Gods—it was a place the brothers had always avoided because Eurus's ability to bestow misfortune and unluckiness was strongest there. "In the meantime, things were touch and go with Ella. So I hung at your place and decided that, if all else failed, I'd resolve it once and for all when I came into my season upon the summer solstice."

"I'm still waiting to hear something that justifies sitting on this revelation, little brother," Zeph said.

"At first I went after him with both barrels blazing. Unsuccessfully. I figured his besting me stemmed from desperation, that he knew he was fighting for his godhood. And then I switched tactics and tried to reason with him." Zeph bit out a curse in the ancient language. Undeterred, Chrys pushed on. "The first time we conversed, I saw the ring."

"That was still nearly three months ago. Damn it all to Hades!" Wind pounded against the side of the house, a preternatural freight train of sound.

"Look, *now* it's crystal fucking clear I made the wrong decision. But at the time, I thought I could handle it. It was my season. I was by far the strongest of any of us. If not me, then who? One of the Olympians? I feared going to them might've put Father's head on the chopping block, too, for not confessing the loss of the ring." He'd tried to protect everyone's interests, and ended up failing right down the line.

"Zephyros, the bandages Father wore that night at the Acheron. You asked him what happened and he brushed it off," Boreas said.

"Good gods, you're right. How in the hell could Eurus have bested Aeolus? When would he have ever had the chance?"

"Eurus was hurt, too," Ella said, as if thinking out loud. Zephyros turned to her. She drew a line down her face with her finger. "That night, he had some sort of a mark or cut. Even in the dark, I could make it out."

Chrys had become well familiar with Eurus's disfigurement, but, for the longest time, not with how he'd come by it. Not until the night he'd crashed through Laney's roof, that is. "Yes. She's right. And I think I have a good idea how it happened." Debating only a moment, he pulled off his shirt.

Gasps sounded out around the room. Fuck, did he really look that bad?

He gave himself a quick onceover. Enormous, uneven twisting scars above his right pec, a slashing whip mark on his left arm, a minefield of bruises and assorted smaller scars. His back wasn't much better. Okay, so he wasn't doing any underwear modeling or winning any beauty pageants, that was for damn sure. What would Laney make of his scars?

Chrys traced the deep scar on his forearm. "This is what appears on Eurus's face."

"You were *whipped*," Zeph said, voice full of outrage. The lights flickered once, twice, but held. "And...stabbed? Is this from the night you crashed through Laney's barn roof?" Chrys nodded. "Fucking hell, you are lucky to have survived." After a moment, Z pointed at Chrys's arm. "I wear those marks on my back, as you well know. How would Eurus have gotten whipped in the face? Father has his faults, but he would never have done that."

Chrysander had asked himself that question before. His mind conjured the image of Zephyros kneeling in the Hall of the Gods last spring, his naked back bared and waiting. He'd endured seven lashes at their father's hand for infractions involving the use of divine power in the human realm. Chrys had thought the charges were a whole lot of bullshit. Eurus's crimes had been far greater. So Chrys had asked their father why he wasn't going after—

"Shit, that's it," he said. "He planned to punish Eurus after you. Somehow, Eurus got that ring off of Father, but not without a fight—one that resulted in the injury on his face."

"Aeolus must answer for this," Zeph said, shaking his head. "We should find him, now—"

"Good luck with that," Chrys said.

"What do you mean?" Boreas asked.

"In between getting my ass kicked for three months, I've been searching for Aeolus. Unsuccessfully."

Boreas frowned, silver light flashing from his eyes. "Do you think Eurus has him?"

"I don't think so," Chrys said. "He'd be crowing that shit to the heavens if so."

"We'll find him. And he *will* answer for his role in this." Zeph glared. "But that doesn't explain why *you* didn't say something before the situation went critical."

Chrys tugged his shirt back on. "I didn't want any of the rest of you getting your asses kicked — or worse. Not with new families counting on you. Me? I have a whole lotta nothing to lose."

The words were out of his mouth before he'd thought to say them, and he immediately wanted to reel them back in. He didn't need to be baring his pathetic sob story on top of everything else.

A long pause left the declaration hanging there, one the thunderous cacophony all around them did little to fill. Boreas tilted his head. "*Chrysander.*"

The reproach in the way he'd said his name made it damn difficult to hold his brother's sad silver gaze.

Tentative fingers landed on his back and arm. He flinched, but calm followed as Laney slipped her fingers into his, then just stood there. Silently. Her forehead leaning slightly against his bicep.

She was standing by his side.

Awe settled into every cell in his body. That she'd taken a stand with him, for him. That she cared enough to...what? To show that she cared? Yes, at least that. And that her touch, far from eliciting the usual anxiety-filled downward spiral, released some of the tension in his muscles, some of the ache crushing his heart.

When had *that* ever before happened? Foreign emotion swelled uncomfortably in his chest.

He gave her hand a squeeze and swallowed hard. "I thought I could handle it," he said in a low voice. "I should have been able to handle him. He should've let me make this right so he didn't have to die." Voicing the word lodged a knot in his throat. His brother was going to die. Almost unavoidable now. And he was going to own a part of that, any way you sliced it.

"Jesus Christ, Chrysander. Eurus lost the capacity to know what was right a long time ago. Maybe eons ago. You cannot do that which is impossible," Zeph said, his tone more restrained now, his words echoing what Laney had said earlier in the evening.

"It is admirable that you have not wanted to give up on him," Boreas said. "I am the oldest of the four of us and have always felt responsible on some level for not doing better by him. I should've done more to intervene in Father's treatment of Eurus. It was never the boy's fault that our mother died in childbirth. But Aeolus was blinded by his grief, and Eurus was a convenient target. He didn't deserve it. Any of it. But, more and more, I find myself agreeing with Zephyros."

Chrys cut his gaze to B. "It wasn't your fault—"

"Nor was it *yours*," Boreas said, nailing him with a stern, unrelenting stare, one that communicated that his older brother intuited some shit Chrys would just as soon keep private.

Laney didn't know what the hell was going on. Truly, her head was spinning so fast it might fly right off her shoulders. Between the argument, the raging storm, and the power flickering, she had one nerve left. Maybe. If she was lucky. Pair that with the strange sense of foreboding she'd been feeling as she listened to their conversation, and she was damn near adrift in confusion.

But there was one thing she did know—Chrys needed her support.

In her mind's eye, she pictured him as a lone island stranded in the midst of vast wastes of unfriendly sea, and she hated the analogy. Hated all the anger and aggression the others were throwing at him. Honestly, she didn't understand the situation enough to know if he was in the right or the wrong, but she did understand the separating feeling of standing out from the rest. She did understand loneliness. And she sure understood loyalty, too.

Trembling with equal parts uncertainty and sympathy, she'd debated going to him. She didn't want to intrude, or embarrass herself by tripping or stumbling. And then something Chrys had said had stolen her breath: *I have a whole lotta nothing to lose.*

She was out of her seat without making a conscious decision to do so, her hands reaching out toward the unusual heat that always seemed to surround him until they found his hard body. The thought that he'd been sacrificing himself for the others and that he believed no one would miss him if he'd died, that he was expendable… Her very soul revolted against those ideas until emotion strangled her throat and pressed against her chest.

When she'd curled her hand into his, for a moment, he'd tensed. But then his arm had relaxed and he'd pulled her in more tightly against him. Deep satisfaction had roared through her alongside white hot fear at the idea of him being killed. *I'm here for you, Chrys. Do you hear me? I'm here.*

If she hadn't already suspected it before, the thought of losing him, the thought that he might've died before he ever fell into her life, brought into stark relief that she was developing feelings for the god she held in her hands. Not just lust. Not just curiosity. But scary, messy, probably-a-bad-idea *feelings*.

Thunder detonated above the house, like bombs were going off all around them. Reeling from the emotional revelation, Laney flinched into Chrys's side.

"You okay?" he whispered.

She nodded against his arm, not wanting to burden him with worrying about her.

"We're almost out of time," Owen said. "The storm rages too fiercely."

"Yes," Boreas said. "We need a plan." As Laney looked toward Boreas, his aura suddenly warped and flashed. For a moment, it disappeared completely. Laney blinked and the effect went away. What the hell was that? Had she really seen it, or were her eyes playing tricks on her?

"Find and confront Aeolus," Owen offered.

Everyone agreed. She continued to study Boreas, but whatever had happened didn't occur again. She'd been straining to see everything she could since they'd arrived. Her eye was just fatigued. In truth, she had the beginnings of a headache.

"There is something else," Chrys said, his voice sounding uncomfortable, regretful. "We need to find out who was behind Tisiphone's visit to Laney's house this morning. I was thinking that, well...that maybe Ella could talk to Mars and see if the Olympians—"

"I'll do it," Ella said.

"I do not want Ella in the middle of this," Zeph said at the same time, his aura flashing purple. Thunder and lightning blasted the world and blackness swallowed them. The power had been knocked out. Only the fact that Laney could make out the gods' lighted auras kept her from flipping out.

For a moment afterward, it was silent except for the baby's cries upstairs. Owen excused himself to go help Megan, and then there were a series of small sounds Laney couldn't interpret. Finally, Ella said, "I'm already in the middle of it, Zeph. And you're not the one who put me there. Nor Chrys. Eurus has dragged me into this time and time again. I *need* to play a role in solving this problem, once and for all."

"But, Ella—"

"I *need* to, Zeph."

Admiration rolled through Laney at Ella's courage and determination.

"Damnit," Zeph bit out. "I understand. I do." He sighed. "So be it."

"Thank you, Ella." Chrys's respect for her was clear in his tone. "I've also learned from Apheliotes that Eurus keeps his son Alastor imprisoned."

"What?" Zeph asked. "What in the hell is wrong with our brother's head?"

"I don't know the why of it," Chrys said. "But if such treatment is common, it strikes me we might have allies in at

least one of his sons. Apheliotes has agreed to find out what
he can." As he laid out the skeleton of a plan, pride warmed
Laney's heart and helped beat back her fear. Competent,
smart, strategic—it was an incredibly sexy combination.
Paired with his physical beauty, it was downright lethal.

"Given this news, with Alastor, maybe. With Devlin? Not
damn likely. That apple didn't fall nearly far enough away
from the tree," Zeph muttered.

"But it is possible," Boreas said. "And worth exploring.
Anything else? I fear we must part now."

Chrys hesitated, then dropped Laney's hand. "Just this."

"What is that?" Boreas asked.

Laney struggled to figure out what they were talking
about. The others came closer, and she realized they'd come
to examine something in Chrys's possession.

"Cool blade, but what about it?" Zeph asked.

Tracing her vision to Chrys's hands, she gathered small
glimpses of the vicious-looking knife he held.

"I paid Hephaestus a visit. Seems this dagger possesses
some useful anti-god mojo of the Underworld type."

That strange sense of déjà vu came over Laney again, but
she couldn't pinpoint why.

"Good Gods," Boreas muttered.

"That is the best fucking news I've heard all day," Zeph
said. "What'd you have to do to get his help?"

"Let's just say I caught him in a generous mood."

"Well, thank the gods for minor miracles," Zeph said.

"Yeah," Chrys said, his tone serious and intense. "And
Eurus isn't going to have a clue what hit him."

Despite Chrys's confidence, Laney couldn't help but
worry about him and the risk he was about to undertake. If

anything happened to him, well, she didn't know what she'd be able to do. But she'd give anything to help keep him safe.

CHAPTER SIXTEEN

As the weather continued to deteriorate, the gods exchanged rushed good-byes and departed, Boreas first, then Zeph and Ella. Within minutes, the storm ratcheted down in intensity, making it somewhat easier for Laney to breathe.

Chrys's light appeared right in front of her. "Thank you."

"For what?" she asked, longing for his touch again.

"For being here. And for supporting me."

She gave a small shrug. "I didn't like the way they were talking to you." Thunder rumbled and she hugged herself. "And I didn't like the idea that you felt that no one would care if you were gone." More words, scarier words, lodged in her throat. She forced them out. "I'd care."

"Laney, I can't—"

"Don't. Okay? I get it. Just…don't."

He sighed. "We should go. The storm won't dissipate until I leave."

She frowned. "What do you mean?"

"The weather is part of what I am, part of what all of my

brothers are. We control and influence it with our energy. But when we all get together, it becomes bigger than any of us individually. So the best remedy is our departure."

For a moment, she felt like he spoke a foreign language. "So, wait. This horrible storm…are you saying *you* caused it?" Her scalp prickled.

"To an extent. This one was so bad because three of the four Anemoi were together at once, something we generally avoid because the concentration of our energies causes…well, this."

Laney tried to wrap her mind around the idea that this man possessed the power to create something that absolutely terrified her. "Why not meet…wherever you're from, then?"

"Humans aren't permitted in the Realm of the Gods. Which would've meant you and Megan couldn't come with us."

"Oh. What would happen if all four of you were in one place?"

"Nothing good," he said. And though she was curious, maybe she didn't really want to know. This storm had already been enough to scare her out of her mind. At least she didn't have to go out in it. Except… Her stomach plummeted. "To go home, we have to go out into this storm, don't we?"

"Yeah, but since we'll be—"

"Oh, God," she said, hugging herself again.

His heat moved closer. "What's wrong?"

She shook her head, not wanting to admit it. But, given what they had to do, how could she not? "You're going to laugh."

"I won't."

She chuffed out half a laugh. "You will, trust me."

His knuckles dragged down her cheek. She leaned into the touch and let the words fly. "I'm scared of storms."

"You're…"

"Yeah." It was quiet, but some kind of tension rolled off him. She arched an eyebrow. "You're laughing, aren't you?"

"No," he choked out, voice filled with humor. "It is rather ironic, though."

"Shut up. Stupid god. It's not funny." She pressed her lips together to hold back the smile that threatened and whipped out her hand. She managed to smack him in the stomach. *Holy crap!* He was a freaking wall of muscle.

Laughter spilled out of him and he grabbed her hand, held it. "Don't worry, Laney. You'll be safe. I promise. You'll be a part of the elements, so they won't hurt you."

She sighed. "I just…I don't know. I have a weird feeling." Suddenly, she didn't want to go home. Blackness filled her vision, like she was standing in the dark. She blinked and the light returned.

"I won't let anything happen to you."

She was being silly. What choice did she have? It wasn't like she could walk back to the Eastern Shore. The night's weirdness was just getting to her. "Okay."

"Ready to blow this popsicle stand?"

She chuckled. "They have popsicles stands in…wherever you're from?"

"The Realm of the Gods."

"The Realm… Right."

He grabbed her hand. "No, but they totally should. Popsicles are awesome."

Light and color filled her vision, telling her he'd pulled them into the elements again. The shift hadn't seemed as jarring, as explosive, this time. Thank God.

They went up into the sky, and though the rain and wind were all around them, *were them*, it was just as Chrys had said. The wind didn't buffet her, because she was the wind. The rain didn't batter her, because she was the rain. The thunder and lightning didn't scare her, because she knew exactly when they'd occur. A tremendous thrill roared through her. That she got to experience this, that he'd made her see the beauty in something that had long terrified her, that he'd shared it with her at all.

This is amazing, Chrys, being a part of this, being a part of something bigger than yourself. Thank you for bringing me with you tonight. Thank you for...getting involved. Even if he'd only done it out of obligation or duty, this moment, this night, this whole time since she'd first laid eyes on him was something to be cherished forever.

Warmth surrounded her, like he was hugging her. Words came to her, in that odd language she'd sometimes heard him speak, but not in the way they normally communicated. It was like the words were on the wind. Something about the sound of them flooded longing through her being. And heat.

Overwhelmed with everything she was feeling, everything she'd experienced this night, Laney didn't speak again. Instead, she just soaked in every bit of the splendor of the nighttime world. After all, this was the world she'd been without the longest. Her night vision had been the first to go. Normally, she was completely blind in the dark. Now, she could see that the night wasn't black, but was painted with a palette of blues and greys and purples that possessed its own beauty.

And Chrys had made it all possible. Gratitude joined the wonder flooding through her.

Who knew when she'd get to do this again? If ever. She didn't want to miss a minute of their trip.

By the time they passed over the Chesapeake Bay, the storm was gone. The moon rose high in the sky, gifting Laney with a whole other vision of night. One that was as romantic as it was mysterious. For a long moment, she reveled in the sight, in the warm caress of the winds blowing through and over her. She imagined the sensation was Chrys's fingers. Heat streaked over her, as if answering her yearning.

At the edge of her consciousness, intense sadness slinked back and forth and threatened to swamp her. How she missed seeing the world around her. What she wouldn't give to have her sight returned to her. She'd said she didn't wish for the return of her vision. But in a moment like this, how could she not? These experiences with Chrys were amazing, yes, but also a special form of torment because, when they got home, she'd be mostly blind again. And she'd feel the loss more acutely than she had in a long, long time.

Enough. The joy and opportunity of the moment were far worth whatever pain might follow.

The landscape below them turned familiar. *We're almost there*, she said.

Yes.

They came in over the cottage construction site, then the pastures, and the barn and house came into view. It was a beautiful setting. She'd always loved it here. It was the only place she'd ever thought of as home.

Now, Chrys was going to be there with her. At least for a while. How was that going to work? Did he sleep as a human did? Would he want to sleep with her?

And would she let him if he did?

A warm gust surrounded and caressed her. And Laney knew the answer to that question.

You might feel disoriented again. I'll help you through it.

She knew he would. And, anyway, last time she'd felt less disoriented—although that was there, too—than overwhelmed with gratitude. And lust for him. Now, she knew it was more than lust. As much as she wanted this man, this god, she also cared for him. Just how much? The night had been such a jumble of emotions, she couldn't really define what she was feeling. But there was no question that Chrys appealed to more than just her body.

The house came closer, closer, and then they were inside. The open living room surrounded them, and suddenly she was in her body again. She gasped and swayed. *Okay, definitely disoriented*, she thought. Hands caught her and held her steady.

"Breathe through it. I've got you."

She concentrated on her breathing, on matching hers to his. Except…his was fast, shallow…ragged? His golden light filled her vision, but she forced herself to focus. Finally, part of his face came into view, but the darkness threw too many shadows.

"Can we turn on some lights?" Somewhere, Finn shook, then he grunted as if stretching after a nap.

"Yes."

Every light in the room illuminated.

Laney flinched, her gaze cutting from one lamp to the next as her vision adjusted. "Well, that's…handy."

"It's all just energy." Heat rolled off Chrys's big body. His voice was tight, gravelly.

Maybe so, but it was a magnificent display of power, too.

Arousal flowed through her veins, concentrating in the full weight of her breasts, the tingle of her puckered nipples, and the ache of her center. She leaned in, wanting to kiss him. Needing to.

He slipped her necklace back under her shirt. "Since we're done traveling for the evening, you can wear this against your skin again." His fingers lingered on her skin.

"Okay," she said, his touch heating her blood. Did he realize what he was doing to her? "You know, I never thanked you for Rolly. In person, that is. I know it's silly, but I care about those horses like they're my kids."

He dragged his fingers along the collar of her shirt. "It's not silly. And you're welcome. It was the least I could do."

She released a shaky breath. "Animals never judge, you know? They love unconditionally. I don't know. I've just always had a soft spot for them…" And seeing him treat an injured animal so kindly? It wasn't just that Chrys was hot and sexy and powerful, she *liked* who he was, as a person. God. Whatever.

"Laney?" he said in a raspy voice.

"Yes?" she whispered.

"You're incredibly sexy when you talk about the things you love."

The room did a little spinny thing around her. "I am?"

His heat moved around her, until she felt him along the length of her back. He pushed her hair over one shoulder. "Yes," he said, his breath ghosting over her skin. "Sharing the wind with you was…" His lips dragged over the sensitive spot behind her ear and he exhaled roughly. "It was an honor."

She tilted her head, opening to him and nearly dizzy with

anticipation. She'd been wanting him for days. Dreaming of what that might be like.

Strong arms surrounded her. Large hands splayed across her stomach. Slowly, Chrys moved his hands upward, dragging her shirt with the movement. He cupped her breasts.

Breathing hard, Laney fell back against his chest. His erection pressed into her lower back. The evidence that he was as affected as she was momentarily stole her breath. A hot thrill shuddered through her. She arched, grinding against his firm flesh behind her and pushing her breasts into his massaging grip.

A tingle ran down her scalp and neck. Uncomfortable. Alarming. She pulled herself upright and waded through the haze of lust.

A shadow shifted. No. A light. A black light that deadened everything around it. "Chrys?"

Maniacal laughter sounded out of the darkness. "Did the three of you really think you could gather unnoticed?" A man's voice tsked. "I must say, I'm so glad I left her alone before. Because now you get to see each other die."

"Get down!" Chrys grabbed Laney just as the black light flared. Suddenly, a light as brilliant as the sun flashed, stealing her remaining sight.

"No!" she screamed, jumping in front of Chrys. Electricity like a thousand pins and needles slammed into her, surrounded her, sought to penetrate and lay her heart to rest. Paralyzed, she gasped and fought to drag in oxygen. But she couldn't…she couldn't…

And then the world went utterly black.

৪৩৮

"Laney!" Chrys yelled. *Oh, no. No! Gods, have mercy*.

For the space of a breath, the whip of lightning engulfed Laney's whole being, holding her body stiffly aloft, arms strapped at her sides.

Chrys lunged for her, and the blaze disappeared as suddenly as it had appeared. Laney's unconscious body fell into Chrys's outstretched arms. He crumpled with her to the floor. The attack of energy had knocked all the lights out, and now the dark appeared pitch black in the wake of the brilliant illumination.

"Oh, gods. Laney? Can you hear me?" Chest filled with crushing, icy dread, Chrys gently rolled her off him and cradled her too-still, too-hot form in his arms. Muscles lifeless. Mouth lax. He tilted his face toward the heavens. "Eurus! Hear me! My word! My vow! I will fucking kill you if it takes my last breath!" he roared, thunder crashing overhead. But there was no reply. Eurus had gone as quickly as he'd come, a hit and run of pure, malicious evil.

"Please," he rasped, pressing his hand over her heart.

The rapid-fire rhythm revealed the stress of the attack, but it was proof of life that would've brought him to his knees if he hadn't already been on the floor. At her throat, Hephaestus's amulet glowed. Chrys would never be able to repay that god for the life-saving gift.

"Laney. Wake up. Come back to me." He stroked his hand over her feverish forehead.

Every particle of his being screamed for vengeance, demanded he pursue his brother to the ends of the earth. Further. He had the infernal dagger. By the gods, he would have his revenge. For Laney, for Ella, for all the others Eurus had hurt.

But not tonight. No matter how his psyche screamed its outrage, his soul was tethered to the woman lying in his arms. Everything else be damned, his duty lay right here.

What those feelings truly meant, he didn't allow himself to explore.

Heaving a deep, shaky breath, Chrys pressed kisses to her cheek. She'd cared for him. She'd stood by him. She'd *protected* him. One moment, the lightning whipped toward Chrys's chest. The next, Laney flew in front of the conflagration. Why had she sacrificed herself for him? What had she been thinking? And, now, she fought for her life.

How *dare* Eurus lay hands on this woman? She was his and his alone.

Chrys froze. Where the hell had that come from?

She wasn't his. If this night proved anything, it was that Chrys did not deserve Laney Summerlyn. If he could not even protect her, he didn't have the right to be in her presence at all. And that was on top of a myriad of other reasons why he didn't deserve her and could never have her. His fucked-up wiring regarding touching. His need to control. The war—for that's what this now was—that raged around him.

Needing to see her more clearly, he willed on the lights and dragged gentle fingertips over her cheek. Her shirt and shorts were badly singed. Sweat beaded over her red, puffy skin. And, good gods, was she on the verge of blistering?

Enough! She needs you!

Too hot. He had to bring her temperature down. Fast.

Without a moment's debate, Chrys willed all of their clothing away. The more of him that touched her, the faster he could syphon the heat from her body.

He moved to cover her, and hated himself a little more—

if that was possible—for having to push through the ancient anxiety that gripped him as he anticipated all that skin-on-skin contact.

His chest settled on her chest. His hips on her hips. His legs covered and surrounded hers.

Scorching. She was absolutely, intoxicatingly on fire. It would've been mind-numbingly arousing if he didn't know the threat the heat posed to her well-being. Still, blood filled his cock and turned it to steel between them. He gritted his teeth, unable to control his body's natural reaction to the temperature.

Breathing deeply, he concentrated on pulling the heat into himself.

Please let this work. Gods, maybe the amulet hadn't protected her after all.

He absorbed what he could. And then he took more. He would take whatever he had to. For her.

Chrys pulled the energy in until it turned volcanic inside him. Restraining that amount of power had him shaking so hard he feared hurting her. He locked his jaw and muscled through the burn, intent upon his life not to fail at this one thing.

Come on, Laney! Come back to me.

Damn his brother to the eternal fields of punishment! And damn himself! This. This was the scenario he'd feared that night he'd yielded to her pleas to stay, to talk. Gods only knew what had prompted Eurus's return to Summerlyn, but no doubt his interest had been piqued to find Chrys's energy more prominent than it had been before.

Eurus might've yielded the whip, but this attack—and, dear gods, its consequences—lay at Chrys's feet. What a fool he'd been to think he could be the source of Laney's joy he'd felt as he sailed with her on the wind. He had *always* been a source of destruction. Damnit, that shit went way back, to Chrys's childhood, to when ancient peoples feared him for the crop-destroying capabilities his storms possessed.

But, man, while guilt would *always* eat at a part of him for Eurus's death, another part—a baser part—would revel in his blood and dance on his fucking bones.

Laney whimpered and her body came to life beneath him, flinching and tensing.

Relief and hope flared. But as she continued to fight beneath him, he groaned, too, her movement agonizing against his over-sensitized skin and swollen cock.

Cooler. She was cooler. Not normal, but not endangered. Thank the gods.

Her eyelids flickered. Struggled. Opened. Gorgeous blue stared up at him for a long moment, unfocused and unseeing.

"Chrys," she gasped, her voice raw. "Oh, Chrys." Tears welled and spilled down her temples into her hair.

The physical expression of her pain sliced into him until he could hardly bear it. But he would. Because he deserved it. And because she deserved his strength.

"Y-you…o-ok-okay?" she asked, adrenaline and shock giving her the shakes.

Me? He frowned. Surely, the dark hum of the overloaded energy vibrating through him made him mishear her. She couldn't possibly be asking about—

"W-was so…so…sc-scared for…you."

"Jesus, Laney, you infuriatingly brave, fearless woman. I am fine. Except for my heart, which stopped when he struck you. Except for my soul, which was nearly extinguished when

I thought you dead. I am fine, because of you. But you—"
Foreign, overwhelming emotion lodged in his throat, choked
off the words that tried to form. Words communicating
desires he had no business wanting, declaring feelings he
didn't understand and didn't believe himself capable of,
anyway.

"Back," she said.

"What?" he managed.

"My…" She whimpered and arched under his weight.
"So hot. H-hurts."

Chrys wrenched up off her. Though her skin still bore a
pink flush, the swollen red was gone. And despite everything,
she was achingly beautiful, perfectly formed, utterly
desirable. He raked his gaze up to hers. "Your back burns?"

Eyes wide and panicked, she nodded.

"I'll fix it, Laney. I promise."

Grateful for the soft carpet, he eased her onto her
stomach. From neck to heels, her body bore the same distress
he'd removed from her front side. It was like the lightning
had seared her outside, but hadn't been able to penetrate
within.

"I'll fix it," he whispered again, once more covering her
body with his. "Gods," he gritted out as his chest pressed
against her back and his rock hard cock nestled between the
soft cheeks of her behind. Her arms lay above her shoulders,
and when he covered them with his own, she lifted her hands
and laced their fingers together.

Focus. Focus only on taking in the heat.

He tried. He really fucking tried. But she was squirming
and shuddering and tormenting him with hot, unrelenting
friction.

Almighty Zeus, one shift of his hips and he'd be in her...

Thunder rumbled overhead. Winds whipped through the trees surrounding the house. Rain fell in loud, fat drops. He couldn't hold back energy this immense. It must release. Damnit all to Hades, he didn't want to hurt her further.

But he was so close to the edge of his control.

Cooler. She's cooler. He'd quelled the blaze. "Laney, is it... is it better?" he asked, tremors making it difficult to speak.

She moaned. "Yes."

"I...I have to—" He swallowed hard. "For just a few minutes, I have to go."

"What? No!" Despite the hoarseness, the strength of her protest anchored him. "S-stay. Need...you."

He dropped his face to her hair. Oh, a mistake. The appealing natural scent of warm citrus infused him, fueling his frantic arousal, making him want more, *demand* more.

She arched, grinding her soft ass against his cock.

One hand flew to her hip, gripping, clutching, restraining. "Be still. I have the barest hold on myself right now." He hated how terse his words sounded, but couldn't hold back. The energy had him jacked up 'til he was nearly instinct alone.

Get up, get up, get up, he told himself over and over, but he couldn't gain control over his own base desires. *Get in her, get in her, get in her.*

"No," he growled. He pushed himself up, his body howling in protest until he felt as if two sides of himself warred with one another.

Laney gasped. "Don't go." She pushed up on her elbows and looked over her shoulder. Her eyes had gone a blazing cobalt, wide, expressive, and fiery with a desire he didn't know if he could resist.

CHAPTER SEVENTEEN

"Don't look at me that way, Laney. I'm so damn close to lifting your hips and burying myself inside you that I'm afraid to move."

Heat roared through her, but this time it wasn't from whatever had attacked her. It was from her pounding desire for the god currently kneeling behind her.

He was safe. And she was okay. Mostly okay, anyway. And he'd done that for her. He'd taken care of her, just as he promised.

She didn't know what had happened in the moments after she saw that awful black light, but she did know they were damn lucky to be alive. And that made Laney not want to waste another moment. There'd be time for explanations later. Now, she wanted him. She wanted him wanting her.

"Chrys," she croaked, her throat sore and parched. "Don't be afraid. I'm not." Shoving away her nerves, she pushed up onto her hands and knees, the carpet soft underneath. She stopped just shy of grinding herself into what she *knew* from how he'd laid on her moments before was a massive erection. Adrenaline roared through her until the room spun. His thighs straddling her calves were all she knew, all she could feel.

Rough hands settled on her hips. "Don't. Move." He spat out a curse in that odd language. "Jesus, woman. I'm trying not to hurt you here."

She started to turn to him, wanting him to see the sincerity and trust in her face and eyes. Next thing she knew, he'd halted her movement by pinning her wrists against her lower back in one of his big fists. Fear and lust shot through in equal measure. She spoke over her shoulder, "You wouldn't hurt me, Chrys. You healed me. Again."

He tugged her upper body back against his chest, forcing her to arch against him. "You don't understand what's about to happen here," he whispered, his voice low and gritty. "I don't make love. I don't do soft and romantic. I fuck. I dominate. And I restrain my lovers because I can't stand to be touched. Sure, I get my partners off good, but then I walk out the door. So, whatever fantasy about us you've got playing in your head right now is whole solar systems away from my ugly reality."

For a long moment, Laney was sure her heart stopped. And then it took off at a full-out gallop that left her breathless. No one had *ever* talked to her that way. He was just trying to scare her away. Had to be. And, truth be told, she was a little scared. But she was also wetter for him than she'd ever been for another man. Right at this moment, she couldn't really think about why his tight grip, rough tone, and coarse words set her body on fire, but there it was. Her nipples puckered. The emptiness between her legs ached. After what'd happened, she *needed* to connect with him, in every way. Arousal flowed so thick through her blood, she'd take him any way she could have him.

In that moment, she *yearned* for him, her body, her heart, her soul.

Laney tilted her face up toward his, his warm glow filling her vision, her nose tracing along the hard angle of his jaw. "I want you however I can have you, Chrysander. I trust you." And after what they'd just survived, she needed him, she needed the physical proof they'd made it through. Together.

He blew out a halting breath. "You shouldn't. Right now, you shouldn't. The healing…I am overloaded with energy right now. I can't…I don't think I can hold back." His words rasped with arousal and need and pain—all three touched her down deep.

"Then don't. I'm not fragile. I won't break." She dug for courage. "Don't believe me? Feel between my legs. That's what you're doing to me." She kissed his jaw, once, twice.

For a long moment, he didn't seem to respond, and then the light in the room flared, the air took on a tingly, electrical quality, and Chrys's muscles tightened everywhere they touched.

With a groan, he claimed her mouth with a possessive, invasive kiss she felt in every nerve ending. His hand gripped her jaw and forced her to arch further to accommodate the demands of his kiss. His tongue stroked and explored and took her mouth, stealing her breath until dizziness threatened. He wrenched back, breathing hard. "Last chance, Laney."

"I'm yours," she whispered. At least, she wanted to be. If he would have her. If he would take her, as he'd threatened.

If he'd fulfill the dark promise of passion he'd made.

In an instant, he pushed her away until she was upright on her knees. Still holding her wrists behind her back, he urged her upper body forward, forcing her rear out. The unexpected movement threw her off balance. She thought she'd fall, but she hung by Chrys's grip on her wrists.

His heat radiated against her backside. He dragged the head of his cock through her wetness, then pushed into her entrance.

The sensation of fullness was immediate, and he was barely inside her. Laney moaned, so desperately excited her skin seemed to tingle. Gripping her hip with his free hand, he withdrew and thrust again, and again, and then he fully seated his cock inside her, the hair on his thighs tickling her rear.

He paused, and the lights in the room flared, the brilliant white visible even with her poor vision. But she couldn't think on the meaning of it because the pressure within her was so deliciously intense. And maddening, too. Laney was just about to beg him to move when he ground out a curse in that foreign language and pulled out. Then slammed right back in.

Laney gasped and threw her head back.

He stroked into her again and again, the barely controlled full-withdrawal-and-thrust rhythm stealing her breath and blanking her mind of everything except him. His hips snapped against her bottom and his grip tightened on her wrists. She longed to touch him, to skim her sensitive fingertips over every inch of him, to dig her nails in his back, but *not* being able to forced every bit of her attention to the incredible dragging friction of his hard, thick length pumping in and out of her. Add her blindness on top of it all, and his cock literally became the center of her world.

His hold on her wrists tightened until it was nearly painful. The lights flared again. Nearby, something popped—a lightbulb? The sprinkling sound of glass followed. "I'm sorry," Chrys grunted. "I've got to release some of this or I'll hurt you." Another bulb popped, then another. From outside, a sharp wind suddenly rattled the windowpanes.

"Whatever you need," she rasped as his hard thrusts quickened.

"You feel so fucking good," he said, voice full of gravel, punctuating his declaration with hammering strokes. Another bulb exploded, closer this time.

She gasped. "So do you." She fisted and unfisted her hands in his grip, partly from the numbness settling into her fingertips, partly an outlet for the erotic energy flowing through her body.

Chrys grabbed her hair and wound it around his fist, forcing her to arch. She moaned as the change in her position had him hitting new places inside her. He was completely in control of her body. And she could say with complete certainty that she loved it.

Glass shattered again, and Laney's eyes flew open. The room had almost no electrical light now, though Chrys's aura shown so brightly, its yellow glow illuminated most of the room.

Chrys released her hair and stroked his fingers down her spine, once, twice. The third time, he caressed all the way to where her cheeks separated. His palm settled there, just above her crack, his fingers spanning her lower back, his thumb extended downward. The pad of his thumb paused over her rear opening.

Laney whined as instinctive fear and desperate, forbidden

curiosity swirled within her stomach. She shoved the fear away. He wouldn't hurt her. He wouldn't do anything she didn't want. But did she want this? No one had ever even touched her there. But she couldn't deny how much that one simple movement of his finger had ratcheted up her arousal and made her juices flow.

"Shh." He dragged his thumb over the opening, exerting a foreign pressure against the tight pucker with each pass.

"Chrys," she whimpered, her mind in chaos over how damn good it felt.

"I want to take you *everywhere*. Over and over."

He might not have done romantic, but he certainly did erotic. His words shot straight to her clit, and her body lurched toward an orgasm that promised to be bigger than she could possibly handle. Never before had sensation felt so intense, had she felt so out of control, had another person felt so *in* control of not just her body, but her mind and her heart.

Suddenly, his hand returned to her hip and his pace increased. A series of fast, frenetic strokes that rubbed the head of his cock against a place inside her that had her keening low in her throat. The sound joined the rapid, wet *slapping* of his skin against hers and the mumbled curses that spilled from his lips. Somewhere, more lights exploded. A strange humming buzz filled the air. The room smelled hot of electricity and summer and sex. Her shoulders started to ache from the demanding pull of her body toward his, but she wouldn't have changed anything about their lovemaking for all the world. Even if he refused to call it that.

Laney's heart squeezed. The physical intensity between them combined with their earlier emotional connection to shove her feelings further down a path she probably shouldn't go. She was falling for him. She knew it. It was likely going to

cost her. When he left—and he would leave, she knew that—
her small, isolated life was going to feel that much smaller,
that much lonelier. But that didn't change what she was
starting to feel.

The pain, the pleasure, the overload of sensation and
emotion of every kind—she wasn't sure she'd ever felt more
alive.

"Jesus," he groaned, and a blast of thunder cracked above
the house. Laney cried out.

Chrys tugged her wrists hard enough to force her up
onto her knees and back against his chest. The position had
her nearly sitting on his damp thighs, which hammered up
into her in slower, harder, precise strokes that felt so much
deeper. His breath rasped in her ear, mixed in with a series of
low grunts and curses. She reveled in the sound of his desire,
in the press of more of his skin against more of hers, and
thrilled at how amazingly *hot* he felt. Feverish, even.

In a hot hand, he cupped one of her breasts, jutting out
because of how she was arched against him. He squeezed
and massaged one, then the other. As she watched, he rolled
her nipples between his fingers, tight enough that she caught
her breath before releasing a long moan, but not so tight that
it hurt. Then he skimmed his palm down her belly, leaving
a trail of heat in his wake. She quivered in anticipation. His
fingers curled between her legs.

"You're going to come for me," he growled.

"Yes," she rasped, the command helping to ensure it
would happen sooner rather than later.

He stroked her clit, his nails occasionally scraping the
sensitive flesh and shoving her arousal higher. His hand
moved faster, harder. She moaned, gasped, held her breath.

She was so close, so close.

"Now, Laney." He pinched and rolled her clit between his thumb and finger.

The third tug brought her orgasm slamming into her. She cried out, her head thrashing on Chrys's shoulder, her body convulsing. His fingers still moved, dragging out her pleasure until it was hard to breathe.

"Damn, that was gorgeous," he said, pressing a rough kiss to her ear.

The praise made her heart squeeze, but she couldn't respond. Her muscles rebelled, refusing to hold up her weight. She went limp against him. He wrapped an arm around her chest and they fell forward onto her stomach, his muscular form atop her, his thighs going to the outside of hers. Their sweat added a slick friction to his thrusts.

He released her wrists and pushed up onto his arms, moving within the tightness the new position created. Fast. Hard. Driving. Chasing. Thunder rumbled low and long, growing louder and more intense. He grabbed her hips and yanked her body back to meet his demanding thrusts.

"So good, Chrys," she managed. "I knew it would be."

"Fuck," he groaned. Then he withdrew completely. Glass exploded and thunder splintered the nighttime air as hot, liquid stripes fell across her back.

He came on her.

The thought released a wanton satisfaction throughout her tired body. She literally wore his desire on her skin. But why had he— *Holy crap, Laney!* Never once had she thought of protection. Gratitude had tears pricking the backs of her eyes. How many times had he said he'd take care of her? And he had, again.

Leaning over her, he pressed a kiss to her cheek. "Stay here. I'll be right back."

As if she could move.

∞∞∞

Chrys returned a moment later with a warm washcloth in his hand. She hadn't moved an inch. Sleepy blue eyes peered up at him and Laney gave a small, crooked smile. "Hi," she whispered.

"Hi," he said.

He straddled her thighs and reached out. But then he drew back and just soaked in the image of this beautiful, brave, trusting woman lying naked on the floor, painted with his seed. He'd come so close to losing control with her. Excess energy still rippled through him, making him tremble, stirring up the wind outside. Glass littered the floor in every direction, like someone had sprinkled glitter all around them.

She'd very likely saved his life tonight, and it wasn't the first time she'd risked herself for him. Tending to him when he'd fallen through her roof, terrified of the storm that raged around her but determined to help a creature in need. Hell, she'd even stepped in front of him when Zephyros had appeared in her room that day. Why did she keep doing it?

And how could he let her continue?

The question had a ready answer: he couldn't. He needed to leave. He needed to find another way to protect her.

Immediately, every part of him rebelled at the idea. His brain ruled out the possibility that anyone else was better suited. His body demanded more of hers—her heart, her tight slickness, her touch. And Almighty Zeus if that last one wasn't a head-spinner.

His heart... *Aw, damnit all to Hades.* His heart fucking *ached* at the idea of leaving her.

Had he...? No. *No.* What he felt was guilt that he'd caused her harm, over and over, and regret that he'd intruded upon the quiet, ordered life she led. Disgust with himself for endangering her when he should've just stayed the hell away in the first place.

It wasn't the first time he'd fucked everything up for someone, and it probably wouldn't be the last. And wasn't that a real slap in the ass.

Laney shivered, refocusing Chrys's attention on her.

The wet cloth he held had cooled, so he balled it within his fists and infused it with his natural warmth. Then he cleaned her off everywhere he'd soiled her. She hummed, a sound full of relaxed pleasure, and a little smile played around the corner of her lips. Her obvious trust and faith in him was like a knife impaling his chest. He was greedy for it, but that didn't mean he deserved it. And he didn't. He set the rag aside.

Calling heat to his hands again, Chrys massaged Laney's shoulders.

"Feels good," she mumbled, eyes closed, lips curved in a small smile. "Masseuse could be a fallback job, if you ever need one."

"Good to know," he managed.

He watched his hands move over her soft skin. He'd been rough with her. Too rough. He'd called on every ounce of restraint he'd ever possessed, but with all that energy overloading him, there was only so much he could hold back. Not to mention how fucking *good* it felt to be inside her. Not only had she accepted every demand he'd made of her body, but her enjoyment of it seemed to match his. It wasn't the act that some of his lovers put on for him. With her, there was no agenda, no favor seeking, no notch carving. Just pure, honest arousal and real, uninhibited pleasure. So he wanted to do everything he could to take away the pain she'd likely feel in the morning from the way he'd used her.

Pain that he'd caused. Go figure.

He massaged her neck, her shoulders, her upper back. By the time he'd moved on to her arms, her slow, steady breaths told him she'd fallen asleep.

He worked down her limbs, gently kneading and caressing. His gaze zeroed in on the redness on her right wrist.

Thunder cracked low in the sky.

He'd fucking marked her. By morning, the red stripes of his fingers would bruise. As if her skin didn't already bear enough evidence of his destructiveness.

Speaking of which…

He swung his leg so he knelt beside her. Crisscrossed black stitches still ran down the back of her thigh and calf, her bandages gone when he'd dispensed with her clothing.

The cuts, though, were almost entirely healed. From when he'd laid atop her and drew off her heat? His energy had certainly been potent enough.

She hadn't wanted the cuts healed. She'd had perfectly good, human reasons for her position. But now that it had begun, he would complete it. Eurus's attack changed things. Yes, she had the amulet, but still, given everything, she shouldn't be injured. Not now.

The thought made him wonder if her blindness was correctable. He didn't possess that level of healing power, to be sure. And he wasn't sure if Zeph did, either. Hephaestus? Maybe. Zeph's father-in-law, Mars? Almost certainly. He tucked the question away for another time.

Leaning down, he willed the stitches on her calf away and released a healing stream of his warmth over what remained of the wound. This close to her, the scent of her sex made it difficult to *not* want to take his time, linger, explore. Gods, she smelled so damn good. He would've liked nothing more than to spend a whole night with his face buried between her legs, worshipping her and drinking her down.

Shaking off the fantasy, he sat up and observed his handiwork. Scars remained, but at least she would be able to walk without pain.

But now what to do? He had to go after Eurus. He had to find his father. He had to get far, far away from Laney Summerlyn.

He couldn't leave her unprotected, and he couldn't leave her here, which meant he also had to violate her demand to be allowed to stay here through all this. *Damnit.*

There weren't many great options, and certainly none that didn't tear at a part of his soul. With regret pressing on his chest and making it hard to breathe, he reclothed them both, her in the pajamas he'd seen her wear before, since her clothes had been ruined in the attack. He rose and surveyed the room, which looked like a freaking war zone. Given what had happened, it wasn't far from the truth.

He commanded the South Wind to come forth. It swirled through the space and pushed the shards into neat piles. One at a time, he marshaled the wind to scoop them up, carry them across the room, and dump them into the kitchen trash. Last thing he wanted was for her to cut a foot on broken glass after she returned home. *Without him*, his brain added.

Ignoring the sinking feeling closing in on him, Chrys scooped her into his arms, adjusted her amulet, and did the only thing he could think of that made any sense—for both of them.

CHAPTER EIGHTEEN

Laney woke up on a moan, her bones, her joints, even her skin aching. Lifting her eyelids took more energy than she had, so for a long moment, she didn't bother to make the effort.

Exhaustion weighed on her like a lead blanket. She tugged the covers over her shoulder and turned to her side.

She gasped and pushed onto an elbow. "Chrys?" She frowned. Everything was…wrong.

Somewhere, a clock ticked.

The blanket balled in her fist was thick and chunky—an afghan?

Light streaked across her field of vision, followed by the soft murmur of an engine outside. A passing car?

Problem was, she didn't own a ticking clock, a crocheted afghan, or a house that sat by a street.

As odd, she wasn't dressed in the same clothes she'd worn earlier. Instead, she had on the pajamas she'd slept in last night.

Her heart hammered so hard she felt the beat's echo

under every inch of her skin. *Where the hell am I? And what the hell is going on?*

"Chrys?" she called, dread filling her stomach. Nothing. No answer. Just the torture of the ticking amid the silence. "Chrys!" She swung her legs off the bed. But she was totally blind, no idea where she was or what the room looked like, the darkness stealing what little vision she had. Tears sprung to her eyes.

Had whatever—or whoever—attacked her come back to finish the job? If so, why was she still alive? And what had happened to Chrys?

Panic bubbled up her throat. *Please let him be okay.* She choked down the fear. Until she got her bearings, she had to hold it together.

Wood floor underfoot, she sank to her knees. Crawling was safer than walking blind. If she could find a lamp or a light switch, she could begin to figure out what the hell was going on. Hopefully.

Swinging her hand proved that the coast was clear, at least to start. She felt around for a night table and eventually found one. Walking her hands up the front, she prayed she'd find a lamp.

Her fist hit glass. Something clanked, splashed, and then crashed to the floor. Laney squealed at the unexpected noise and jerked back.

Footsteps thumped nearby. Laney froze, listening. The door to her room rattled, opened. Light poured through the opening, blinding her, but the sharp contrast between the dark and light did nothing to help her see. Dreadful anticipation shivered over her skin. She flew back against the bed.

"Are you okay?"

She choked on a scream. "Who are you?"

"It's Megan Winters. We met last night. You're at my house."

As Laney's brain struggled to process this information, a male voice called from the direction of the door. "Is everything okay?"

Megan sighed. "Not really. But, yes."

"Why am I here?" she managed, her vocal chords strained by her panic. No response. "Megan?"

"Here. Let me help you up." Fingers touched the back of her hand. She flinched, but then clasped hands with the woman and rose to her feet. "Chrys thought you'd be safer here. Please tell me he discussed this with you."

"Uh, no. Last time I talked to Chrys—" Heat flooded her face as memories of the sex they'd had paraded through her mind's eye. "No, he didn't." She sagged against the bed's edge and hugged herself. Blood still pounded under her skin, and the flood of adrenaline left her shaky. "What time is it?"

"About four in the morning, I think."

"I…" She swallowed, so many questions competing for air time she wasn't sure which to give voice to. Why had Chrys left her here? Where was he? When was he coming back? And what was going to happen when Seth discovered her gone in the morning?

As she calmed, she became aware of the light filling the room. She scanned her vision around for a moment. The details of the room's décor remained foggy, but at least she could confirm that the woman talking to her was the same one she'd seen when Chrys had pulled her into the elements.

Megan's voice interrupted the confusion of her thoughts.

"I'm sorry. Will it help at all to know that the next time I see Chrysander, I'm going to kill him?"

She managed a smile. "Maybe. Yeah." The humor slid off her face. "I can't stay here. I have to go home."

"Do you know what happened last night?" Megan asked.

A lot of things happened last night. Holy crap, her head was spinning over it all. She smoothed her hands down her front, over her pajamas. Why had he brought her here in these? She dropped her hands into her lap. "Which part?"

"After you got home."

The memory of that dead, black light passed before her mind's eye. Her scalp prickled. "We were attacked. In my house. But that's all I know."

"Mind if I sit down?" Laney shook her head, and the mattress shifted as Megan sat on the foot of the bed. "Chrys said it was his brother, Eurus. That Eurus tried to kill him but you got hit instead. The past six months, a feud has erupted and escalated among the Anemoi, the three you've met against Eurus. Last spring, he killed Zeph's wife. From what they say, it's not the first time he's killed. Something's happened that makes him more powerful than he should be. Chrys went with his brothers to figure out what to do. He didn't want to leave you alone."

Laney rubbed her forehead. "I appreciate the explanation, I do. But I…"

She pressed her fingers to her lips. Chrys should be the one telling her this. They'd made love, or had sex, or whatever he would call it. At the very least, that should've earned her a conversation, some basic common courtesy, not being dumped a hundred miles from home in a stranger's house in the middle of the night. She didn't know whether to feel humiliation that he'd dumped her off like a child who needed babysitting or be grateful that he was trying to take care of her, even if he'd gone about it all wrong. He should've asked her— She gasped and rubbed the back of her right leg.

"What's wrong?"

No bandages. No stitches. No cuts. He'd healed her. "I cut my leg and had stitches. It's all gone."

"He healed you."

Pressing her lips together and bottling up her mounting anger, she nodded. She'd told him *not* to heal her. How the hell was she going to explain her miraculous recuperation to the doctor? To Seth?

Seth. He was going to be so worried when he realized she wasn't at the house. What would he think? What would he do? She groaned and dropped her head into her hand, a throb squeezing her skull. Not now. She couldn't begin to deal with that problem on top of everything else.

Not safe here.

The thought crashed into her brain like someone forcefully implanted it. A montage of a thunderous rumble and flames and unapproachable heat ran through her head.

She wrenched up, her skin erupting in goose bumps. Something bad was going to happen here, she was suddenly sure of it. She forced a deep breath. The weirdness of the night was just getting to her, that was all. And no wonder. In the last twelve hours, she'd traveled through the air, been attacked by a deranged god, been healed by a god she was falling for, had sex for the first time in four years—no, had *amazingly mind-blowing* sex, and woken up sore, confused, and scared in a stranger's house. It would be odd if she *didn't* feel strange, after all that.

But one part of that foreboding thought stuck with her. "If I'm not safe, then that means Chrys is worried Eurus will come after me again. And if that's true, I shouldn't be here, endangering you and your family as well."

"I appreciate the thought, but the guys stationed some of the ordinal Anemoi here while they were doing whatever it is they had to do. And my husband's here. You shouldn't be alone, not with all this going on."

Problem was, she felt horribly alone. Chrys was gone. They hadn't had a chance to talk after everything that had happened in her living room. Where did they even stand? *I get my partners off good, but then I walk out the door.* If she believed him, they stood exactly nowhere. Her shoulders slumped. "What's 'ordinal?'" she asked, hoping to divert her spiraling thoughts.

"Oh, I don't know how much Chrys explained to you about—"

"Assume it wasn't much." Her spirits plummeted at the admission. Aside from that first night he'd lain in her bed and answered her questions about how he ended up on the floor of her barn, he hadn't really shared much about himself. Rolly's healing came to mind. Okay, she *had* learned a lot about him as a person, but not the specifics of his life and his family and his world.

"Well, there are four cardinal Anemoi, each in charge of a different wind—north, south, east, and west—and season. And there are four ordinal Anemoi, the intermediate winds, like northwest, southwest, southeast, and northeast—three of whom are downstairs right now. And then there are eight inter-ordinal Anemoi, in charge of the half-winds, like north-northwest."

"Interesting family tree."

Megan chuckled. "Yeah. Takes a bit to wrap your head around, doesn't it?"

"I'll say. Most days, I never leave my farm. I do my freelance writing, ride my horses, and help manage the farm. An exciting day for me involves shopping in Salisbury or a day trip to the beach. Now all of a sudden I might be in love with a—" Her face went hot and she wanted to disappear through the floor. Or into thin air. Since she now knew that was possible. She twisted her hands in her lap. "Please forget I said that."

"Said what?" Megan paused. "You know what would make this night better? Coffee. And maybe some cookies. Or some ice cream. My neighbor keeps bringing over new flavors of homemade ice cream. What d'ya say?"

Laney released a shaky breath. She wanted to hug Megan for the hard right turn in the topic. "I don't want to keep you up all night."

"It's fine. Teddy sleeps great, but he's up with the sun. I doubt I'd go back to sleep before he started fussing anyway. Come on, don't make me snack alone."

She gave a small smile. "Okay, then, why not." Anything was better than sitting here by herself and wondering what the hell had happened to her life. And what would happen next.

∞

"Where the hell could he be?" Zeph asked.

Chrys didn't have an answer. For two days, he and his brothers had searched non-stop for Aeolus. His villa on the Aegean Sea, his citadel in the Realm of the Gods, each of their divine estates. Boreas had gone to the Underworld to make sure their father hadn't somehow ended up there, while Zeph and Ella confirmed with a very displeased Mars that the Olympians didn't have him, either. Standing on the bluffs overlooking the deep blue Aegean, they'd come full circle and were no further ahead than when they started.

How is Laney doing? Chrys bit out a curse. No matter how hard he threw himself into the search, he couldn't get Laney—or his guilt and regret at dumping her at Owen's without a word—out of his mind.

No. The mistake had been putting her in harm's way. Not leaving sooner. Giving in to his blood-pounding desire for her.

His body tightened. Damnit all to hell. What more did he want? What more did he truly think he could have? And at what cost?

Love 'em and leave 'em. His specialty.

Enough. Focus on the damn job at hand. Chrys blew out a hard breath. "What other places hold significance for him?" He traded glances with his brothers. The sun couldn't set on another day without them finding him.

"And why has he gone so deep underground?" Zeph asked. "We're wasting time."

"Underground," Boreas murmured, scrubbing his hand over his stubble-lined jaw. "What if…"

"What?" Zeph stepped closer as Boreas looked to the west, where the evening sun hung low in the sky.

Underground. Chrys turned the word around in his mind and followed his oldest brother's gaze. Memories best forgotten sucked him several millennia into the past. To the youth of the Anemoi. To their father's effort to control the turmoil they unleashed over heavens, land, and sea. To Zeus's edict to rein in the power of the Anemoi or face the Olympian's wrath.

Aeolus had imprisoned them in a cavern far beneath the sea at the edge of the known world. A place the ancients called Calpe. Today, the world referred to the location as the Rock of Gibraltar.

"That would be some messed-up shit right there," Chrys said. Out of nowhere, clouds gathered and the winds kicked up.

"But hiding there would make a certain twisted sense, wouldn't it?" Zeph asked. "If he doesn't want to be found, he knows it's the last place any of us would ever willingly go."

Damn straight. Aeolus had kept them locked up for a year. Something about the below-sea chamber prevented their transforming into their elemental states, and so they'd been trapped and powerless. Their roars for freedom helped establish the ancients' fear of traveling past the strait into the open ocean, beyond which, they believed, nothing existed. At least, nothing good.

During their incarceration, Aeolus had forcibly taken blood from each of the Anemoi and syphoned off a small part of their elemental natures. And had laced both into a ring that gave him control over them for all time.

The firestone.

After he made the ring, Aeolus released them from their prison at Calpe, but they'd never truly been free again.

And now Eurus had the ring.

"Well, I guess we're going whether we want to or not." Chrys glared to the west as the sky darkened.

"Indeed," Boreas said. "We have to give it a look, so let's

get this over with."

They traded glances and nodded, resolve bonding them. One by one, they shifted into their elemental forms and took to the air. Over 1,600 miles separated Aeolus's Greek citadel and the rock formation that jutted off the southwestern tip of Europe on the Iberian Peninsula. They couldn't get there soon enough, as far as Chrys was concerned.

Within an hour, the massive limestone cliffs appeared on the horizon. The closer they got, the more apparent the enormous scale of the rock became, rising over a quarter mile above the churning sea. Hundreds of caves and crags and caverns made up the internal structure of Gibraltar. If their suspicions were on target, within one of the most remote caverns, one not accessible to humans, they would find their father and get their answers.

And it was about time. Less than a dozen days remained until the equinox. With each passing day, the end of Chrys's season—and the beginning of Eurus's—approached.

When Gibraltar loomed before them, they plummeted toward the Mediterranean. A cave sat almost at sea level on the east-facing side. Their pathway to hell.

Home, sweet, home, Chrys thought.

They shot within.

At the periphery of perception, divine energy beckoned. Triumph roared through Chrys's psyche. Aeolus was here. Fucking finally something was going their way.

They twisted and turned, threading an ever-narrowing needle as the caverns and tunnels gave way to steep crags and narrow, eroded passages through which water trickled. The air grew cooler, danker, more stale the further they descended.

But that was of little consequence. What mattered was the growing strength of their father's energy signature. They were getting close.

Do you feel that? Zeph asked.

Chrys concentrated. And immediately picked up on what had captured his brother's attention. More than one energy signature radiated among the rock walls.

Two. No, three, Boreas said. *Take care.*

Getting closer did little to clarify what they were flying into. Somehow, the signatures were dulled and warped, perceptible but unreadable.

They came through a final crevice into a long rectangular space framed by jagged stalactites and stalagmites. Not the same space in which they'd been imprisoned, at least—

Movement. Shouts. A flash of lightning exploded through the cavern. A figure shifted into the elements, the energy vaguely familiar but not someone Chrys could identify.

The stranger bolted from the space. Who was it? What did they have to do with his father being here, of all places? Only one way to find out. Chrys turned in pursuit.

"Chrysander, stay." His father's voice echoed off the rock.

Resentment crawling down his spine, Chrys materialized right in front of his father, Boreas and Zeph right behind him.

"Who was that?" Chrys growled. He took in his father's appearance. Tall and broad, the supreme storm god wore his commanding presence as if it were a second skin, which made it especially odd that Aeolus could currently give Chrys a run for his money in the battered-and-bruised department. "And what the hell happened to you?"

"And when were you planning to tell us about your ring?" Zeph said, pointing at Aeolus's unadorned hand.

"Do they ever stop talking?" Someone stepped out of the deep shadows. Tisiphone.

Damn caves. He hadn't even sensed her. What in the hell was she doing here?

She strolled up and took a position to Aeolus's right. Black snakes writhed upon her head. Two twined around her neck and arms.

Zeph glared, the blue light of his gaze shifting from her face to their father's. "*You're* the one who sent her? And you accused *me* of misusing divine power in the human realm. You sent a fucking Fury among people."

Not just any people. Laney. The danger she'd been in was like a chunk of ice in his gut.

The snakes hissed and the sound reverberated around the room.

"You will address her with respect," Aeolus said, controlled anger seeping through the words. "She has offered her help and I have accepted. Seeing how Chrysander has failed to handle Eurus, we should be grateful for the assistance."

Heat roared through Chrys's veins, casting off an electrical charge into the air. Around the perimeter of the cavern, trapped gases sparked. "Yeah, well, maybe if you'd shared the little nugget of joy that Eurus managed to get the goddamned firestone from you, I'd have had a better idea what the hell I was up against." The sharp bite of his voice echoed off the rock formations.

Uncertainty flashed through Aeolus's green eyes. Tension crackled between the father and sons. Finally, Aeolus's massive shoulders sagged. "Yes."

"That is all you have to say?" Boreas asked. "For the love of Zeus. You created this whole situation. You could at least have more to say for yourself."

Aeolus gave his eldest son a once-over, his gaze lingering for a moment. If he had an opinion about Boreas's new appearance, he didn't voice it. "I am well aware of my shortcomings, Boreas. But I think our focus should remain on how to solve the current problem, rather than assigning blame for how it came to be. There will be plenty of time for that later, if we're lucky."

Boreas stared at him a long moment, the silver in his eyes flaring. He offered a tight nod. "Fair enough."

"Does that mean you have a plan?" Chrys asked, the cool dampness of the cave sending a shudder through him. A few degrees colder, and he'd be having a problem in here.

He gestured to Tisiphone. "We are working on a plan."

Chrys frowned. Why the hell had Aeolus allied with a Fury? She and her two sisters might've been avenging goddesses, but they were also servants of Hades. And he could be one devious bastard.

Her lips twisted upward in a wicked smile. "Your trust is so heartwarming, Notos." She stroked the snake at her neck.

"Why should I give it?"

"Because she is on our side," Aeolus said. "Eurus has committed so many murders—"

"Homicide. Filicide. Attempted fratricide. Attempted patricide." She ticked off the clipped words on spindly fingers and shook her head. "It is past time he *pays*. Justice demands it." The snakes on her head writhed in a wave.

Eurus's crimes were many. About that, Tisiphone was absolutely right. Ella's horrific murder last spring. The suspicious circumstances surrounding the death of Eurus's youngest son, Farren, ages ago. The attack that left their father without the firestone ring.

The image of Eurus wielding the lance of lightning over his own chest flashed through Chrys's mind. Yes, even the attacks on himself, including the one that could've claimed Laney. Chrys ground his teeth together. These were only the tip of the iceberg of Eurus's transgressions.

Chrys looked at Tisiphone anew. Fierce outrage sharpened the already stark features of her face. "So you're here solely to right these wrongs?"

She nailed him with her black eyes. "Punishing crimes of murder and avenging the dead, these are my purpose."

"Why now?" Zeph asked. "Eurus's crimes are not new."

"That is true," she said. She and Aeolus exchanged a glance. What was their deal? "But they are more egregious. More frequent. And more destructive than ever before."

Aeolus raised his right arm, bringing his hand—minus the last two fingers—into view. He fisted and unfisted his remaining digits. Chrys stared, shocked to see his father maimed. One more crime for which Eurus had to pay.

The silence grew awkward. "So, what's the plan?" Chrys asked, needing the conversation to move along. The cold was sinking into his muscles and joints. "We were thinking of trying to gain the alliance of Eurus's son, Alastor. And I have this." He materialized the dagger in his hand.

"Leave the sons to me," Aeolus commanded.

At the same time, Tisiphone hissed and jerked backward. "Where did you get that?"

Chrys traded glances with his brothers. He spun the blade in his grip. "From a friend. It's made of infernal iron—"

"I *know* of what it is made," she said. "It's mined in Tartarus and laces the cave system below us. And it can temporarily paralyze or neutralize a god. Or worse."

It was nearby infernal iron that screwed with their powers in here? The cavern in which Aeolus had held them sat further underground—no wonder he'd been able to confine them. The walls were a virtual cage of the power-stealing iron. Well, now he had a way to use it to his advantage. He eyed the blade and nodded. "Yes. A little odds-evener, as it were."

"Why do you wish us away from the sons?" Boreas interjected. "Chrysander already has Apheliotes seeing where they stand. It is a sound plan."

Aeolus's eyes flared green. "Call him back."

Chrys caught the blade's grip in his palm and frowned. "That ship sailed. Aphel left for the East this morning."

"By the gods, Chrysander. You'll ruin everything." Aeolus's voice boomed through the cavern.

Dread slinked in icy tentacles through his gut. "What the hell am I missing?"

Aeolus spun on his heel and paced away, cursing under his breath in the ancient language. Tisiphone turned, watching him.

For the first time, Chrys paid attention to the god's clothing. Not the normal luxurious robes he wore when presiding over one of the ceremonial halls on his estates. Not the tunics often worn among the gods in the divine realm. Loose black pants. Form-fitting black shirt. Hair pulled back by a leather cord and damp with sweat…

"Wait a second. Wait just a goddamned second." On anyone else, he would've sworn it was workout gear. The disappearing energy signature. The flash of light just as they'd entered the cavern. The pieces of the puzzle clicked together in Chrys's brain. "You were fighting someone when we came."

Aeolus hesitated a fraction of a step in his pacing. That tell affirmed Chrys's suspicions. "Who was it? Who was here when we arrived?"

Aeolus turned. For a long moment, he met Tisiphone's gaze. She gave a nearly imperceptible nod. He drew himself up to his full height. "Not fighting. Training."

"Who?" Chrys asked, fighting back a shiver.

"Eurus's son, Devlin."

CHAPTER NINETEEN

"Tell me where you are right now," Seth growled through the phone.

Laney scanned her gaze over her borrowed bedroom. It was the third time she'd talked to him since her "disappearance" two days before, but he was no calmer now than he'd been the first time. "I can't, but don't worry—"

"*Don't worry?* You left the farm without any notice. Your purse, your phone, your house keys—they're all still here. And yet I'm supposed to believe you're just fine? You haven't traveled by yourself since before your grandfather died."

Guilt washed acid into her stomach. Of course he was right. And she heard, too, what he hadn't said—it wasn't just that she hadn't traveled by herself, it was that she hadn't gone anywhere without *him*. Between the deterioration of her vision and the rural location of the farm, she really was trapped without someone to drive her. And Seth was always there for her.

"I'm sorry," she managed. She shifted positions on her bed.

"But you're not going to tell me."

She shook her head, unable to turn him down for the millionth time. "Please trust me. I know I'm asking a lot, but I'll be home soon."

"Trust *you?* How about you trust *me* to help you with whatever's going on. We've been friends for forever. It's my job—as your friend, as your farm manager, as the man who made a promise to your grandfather—to watch out for you. If you're not going to tell me what I need to know to do that, for whatever reason, I'm calling the police."

Tension roared down the line despite the silence. Had they ever been this at odds with one another? There was only one way to fix it. She held her breath for a long moment, then let the words fly. "I'm in Fairfax, Virginia."

He didn't respond right away. "Where?" he said, tone full of barely restrained anger.

Shoulders falling, she gave him the address.

"I'm coming to get you."

Her scalp prickled and her stomach seemed to take flight. "No, don't. I—"

"This isn't up for debate."

"But—"

"Stay put, Laney. I mean it. I'll be there as soon as I can." The line went dead.

She gaped at the phone. "Holy crap," she whispered to herself. How the hell was she going to explain all this to Seth? The walls of the room closed in on her at the thought. She had to get out of there, just get some fresh air to clear her head and help her figure out what to do.

Laney eased off the bed and smoothed her hands over her borrowed T-shirt. Luckily, a few of Megan's pre-

pregnancy summer clothes had fit well enough to get by for a few days. She sighed and counted the paces to the bedroom door. In the two days she'd been there, she'd thrown herself into pacing out the distance between things so she could move around as independently as possible and not be any greater burden on the couple than she already was.

Six steps to the door. Knob on the left. Eight steps down the hall to the top of the staircase. Thirteen steps down to a landing at the bottom, turn left, and two more steps to the living room floor.

She crossed the living room to the kitchen. Empty. Thankful not to have run into anyone, Laney made her way to the mud room that led to the back door.

She kicked something and froze, throwing her hands out in case she tripped. Something bounced. A ball? Maybe one of Teddy's toys?

Ahead of her, the light brightened. The back door.

A few more paces, and she was opening it, stepping out onto the brick porch. The sunlight stole her remaining vision, as it always did. No matter. Chrys had told her there were three steps. She felt for the iron railing and found it.

When she reached the grass, she stopped and allowed her sight to adjust. Underfoot, green came into focus. Laney stood there for a long moment and scanned her vision over the yard. Longer than it was wide, there didn't appear to be any obstacles that would trip her up.

The glare remained too bright to locate what she was looking for at this distance, so Laney set out carefully, counting the number of steps she took so she could make her way back to the porch. After twenty paces, she paused and scanned again. To her left. There it was.

The tree under which she and Chrys had materialized after that first miraculous journey through the wind. After he'd gifted her with that amazing, whole view of the world. Under that tree, she'd kissed him.

Heat washed over her skin that had nothing to do with the midday sun.

She made her way toward the sprawling branches, hunching to ensure she didn't hit her head on an unseen low-hanger. When she reached the trunk, she pressed her hand flat to the bark. Rough and craggy, she pushed her finger under a piece and pulled it away. Then she sat, her back to the tree, her knees pulled up in front of her.

Closing her eyes, she let her head fall back as she breathed in a deep, invigorating gulp of fresh air. Already, just being out of doors lifted some of the weight from her shoulders, made it easier to breathe. She hated being a burden. She hated uncertainty. And she especially hated the feeling of helplessness. As nice as Megan and Owen were—and she truly did like them—she didn't belong here.

But Chrys does.

True. But that was hardly relevant if they weren't together.

In her head, she heard the strained rasp of his voice. *I walk out the door.*

She fingered the heavy amulet that hung around her neck. Whatever power it held worked. She bore no side effects from her attack.

Oh, which was the truth of Chrys? The man who says he always leaves his lovers, or the man who promised to take care of her?

And why, after a lifetime of insisting on her independence,

on her ability to take care of herself, did she hope with all her heart the latter was the real Chrys?

Because you're falling in love with him.

She thunked her head against the tree. Hard to believe it hadn't even been two weeks since Chrysander Notos had fallen into her life. How could she be falling so hard for someone she'd known for such a short time? For someone she knew so little about, and who knew so little about her? She thought about Seth, who knew almost everything there was to know. She didn't believe two people had to be *that* well acquainted to fall in love, but did she really feel that strongly for Chrys? If so, given his little speech, she was probably so, so screwed.

The breeze ruffled her hair, and Laney tucked a few wayward strands behind her ear. Random memories of the time they'd spent together ran through her mind. But they were no more helpful in sorting out what to believe. For every instance she recalled of his intense brand of care and consideration, there existed an example of him pulling away or leaving.

Why was he always pulling away?

I restrain my lovers because I can't stand to be touched.

Laney's throat tightened at the memory. Twin reactions coursed through her. Arousal stirred as she recalled every restraining grip, dominant hold, and commanding word from their lovemaking. But deep concern dampened the pleasure. Because she'd heard the pain behind the admission, behind his description of his "ugly reality."

Pressure squeezed her chest. Not once had she ever fully seen Chrys, but that didn't keep her from knowing he was a beautiful, beautiful man. Inside and out. Nothing about him was ugly. Not to her. Not even the rough sex he'd warned her away from.

She tried to recall all the times he'd pulled away…

Their first kiss, when she'd grabbed his back. In her bedroom doorway after her shower. Before she'd ended up against the door, she'd tried to wrap her arms around his neck, but he'd pushed her hands away and pinned her. He'd been totally into her until…until she wrapped her leg around his.

Her heart kicked up in her chest. Now that she was looking for the signs, she found them everywhere. In the flinches and muscle ticks and tension when she touched him. In the way his breath caught. In the way he apologized every time he pulled away.

Oh, Chrys.

The more she'd thought about their night together, the more she knew to the very core of her that his sexual dominance resonated with her in a way she never would've expected. Maybe it was the novelty of it, or the edginess, or the rough way he handled her—like she wasn't fragile or damaged, but strong enough to take what he needed to give her. But as much as she knew she could accept that part of him, her arms ached to hold him. Her fingers tingled with the desire to trace over his face, to explore every inch of his body.

Neither of which he would want.

Which didn't really matter if he didn't want *her*, now did it?

Laney groaned. Her head was one big circle of confusion. And, in a couple of hours, Seth was going to be here to add to the mix. Her only saving grace was he was going to have to wade through D.C.'s horrid rush hour traffic, which would hopefully give her a few more hours to figure out how to explain the impossible without him hauling her off to the nearest psych ward.

She let herself enjoy the warm breeze for a few more moments, then pushed herself up. She didn't want Megan to get up from her nap and worry about where she'd gone.

Counting out her paces again, she headed back the way she came.

Damnit. She swung her arms in a careful circuit, but couldn't find the railing. She must've veered off her original path, but the glare of the sun after sitting in the shade made it impossible to see.

Shielding her hand over her eyes, she waited for them to adjust, that uncomfortable feeling of being out of place settling back into her shoulders.

"Are you okay there? Can I help you?" a woman's voice called from off to the left. "I'm Tabitha, Megan's neighbor."

Laney cringed internally. No doubt she looked ridiculous standing in the yard utterly lost, yet probably mere feet from the door. She forced a smile. "I've, uh, gotten myself a bit turned around." She gestured to her face. "I'm almost blind and still learning where everything is here."

"Well, don't you worry about a thing." Her voice neared. "Any friend of the Winters is a friend of mine. How can I best help get you back inside?"

Sincerity rang through her words, putting Laney more at ease. "If you'll let me take your elbow, I can follow you in."

"One elbow, coming right up." Tabitha stepped to her side and Laney took her arm.

"I smell roses."

The other woman chuckled as she slowly led her across

the lawn. "I was pruning. Warm as it's been, some of my repeat bloomers might just have one more flowering in them."

"Yeah? What color are they?"

Tabitha hesitated, as if the question caught her off guard. "Two are the palest, softest pink. One is white with just a hint of goldenrod along the petals' edges. I've got several shades of red—one almost maroon, it's so dark, another that's bordering on fuchsia, and two that are the classic rose red. And then there are my absolute favorite—they have bright, canary buds that can't help but make you smile."

The woman's words had the same effect. "You described them beautifully, like an artist, or a writer."

"That is sweet of you to say. I paint, so I've always appreciated color." They paused. "Here are the steps."

"Perfect. Thank you. I can find my way from here." She gripped the iron. "I'm Laney, by the way."

"Very nice to meet you." Tabitha stepped away. "Do you like ice cream?"

Laney chuckled. "Do you ever find someone who answers that question in the negative?"

She laughed, a pleasant, open sound. "Not living next to Owen, I don't. I think that man would live on ice cream if he could. I've made up a few more flavors and was going to bring some over for them to try, but tell me which you prefer and I'll make sure I bring some of that special. I have orange chocolate chip, mint, strawberry, and coffee."

"Yes, please."

"Uh, which?"

Laney grinned. "Any or all."

"My kinda gal. All right. Tell Megan I'll be over."

Laney nodded, still smiling at the force of nature that was their neighbor. The brief conversation made her realize she missed having girlfriends, people she could chat to about everything or just nothing at all. She had Seth, of course, but it wasn't the same. He'd talk about the horses or the farm or her medical care until the cows came home. He was the only person in the world who could share stories about her grandfather, and who understood just how important those memories were to her. But the books she was reading, her feelings and fears, men? Not so much. "Thanks again, Tabitha."

"You bet," she said, her voice moving away. "See you later."

She felt around for the doorknob and found it. Amazing how a bit of kindness from a stranger could lift your spirits.

The thought made her pause. Megan and Owen had offered that, too, hadn't they? They'd been nothing but kind and helpful and understanding since she'd arrived. And not only that—Megan was so easy to talk to. She really listened, and she was funny, and she was the only person on earth she could talk to about the whole supernatural god thing.

Get it together, Laney. Time to stop moping and start appreciating. She hated the weakness of feeling sorry for herself. Done. Enough. Over.

For now, it was time to accept the situation and make the best of it. When Seth arrived, she'd figure out what to say. And when Chrys returned—she refused to believe it could be an "if"—she'd get the clarity she needed on where they stood, and go home to nurse her broken heart if that's the way the cookie crumbled.

Until then, she'd enjoy the new friends she was making. And the homemade ice cream wouldn't hurt, either.

‫〰‬

For a long moment, their father's revelation hung in the darkness. Then all hell broke loose.

Zeph faced off with Aeolus. "Devlin? What the hell are you thinking?"

"You've let *him* know what's going on, but not us?" Boreas asked.

The collective tension gave the air a sizzling, electrical quality. Chrys tugged his hair out of his face. "How do you even know you can trust him?" This whole situation was getting more complicated by the minute.

"Enough!" Aeolus glared at Zeph, who finally eased off a step. "He is strong. He is on the inside. And we need his help."

Zeph planted his hands on his hips. "But he's too close to his father. He's not trustworthy."

"There's no love lost between them, I can assure you."

"Not liking his father isn't the same as not being loyal to him, for whatever reason. And it's not the same as being free of his influence."

Chrys nodded at Zeph. "And Aphel says while Eurus keeps Alastor imprisoned, Devlin is free because he's doing his father's bidding." A thought slammed into his brain. "Son of a bitch. Devlin's part of the reason the weather's been so chaotic all summer. A storm or a destructive wind would arise, and I'd go thinking I'd find Eurus, only to come up empty-handed. It was clear divine energy was present, but I didn't recognize it." He held his hands out. "Until now. That same energy signature is all over this room, which means it was Devlin all along. Jesus, he's been actively working with

Eurus all this time."

"Why did you think contacting Alastor would ruin whatever plans you're making?" Boreas asked, a deep frown on his face.

"Because Eurus must believe you distrust his sons, especially Devlin. When you encounter one another in battle, Eurus must believe it."

Zeph scoffed. "No problem there, since we *don't* trust him."

Boreas held out a hand. "What is it you're training Devlin to do?"

Aeolus held Chrys's gaze as he spoke. "As long as Eurus possesses the ring, the three of you are disadvantaged. Even without the ring, I am at least his equal, if not stronger, but there's only one of me." Chrys gestured for him to continue. "I'm training Devlin in my powers. I'm training him to become my equal."

Outside, thunder cracked, strong enough to rumble the rock around them. A whirlwind whipped through the cavern. Two stalactites crashed to the floor in a spray of limestone.

"You're. Doing. What?" Zeph asked, voice seething.

"Did you even *hear* what I just said?" Chrys asked, white-hot adrenaline sending tremors through his body. Or maybe that was just the cold.

"How is such a thing even possible? He is *not* your equal," Boreas said. "He is the son of the weakest Anemoi."

"But he will be his equal. He almost is." Tisiphone stepped in front of Aeolus, placing her body between them.

"How?" Chrys and Zeph asked at the same time. When Aeolus hesitated, Chrys pushed. "The less you tell us, the more vulnerable you make us. What are we talking about here?"

"I've amplified his native powers by having him drink of the Styx, and we've cultivated powers resembling mine by having him drink of the Phlegethon."

Chrys dug his fingers into his temples, his brain balking at the magnitude of recklessness Aeolus was describing. Two of the five infernal waterways, the Styx was the river of hatred and the Phlegethon the river of fire. As she resided in the Underworld, Tisiphone's contribution to the plan was at least clear now. But by the gods, it was the equivalent of putting Devlin on rage steroids and handing him a flamethrower. "Almighty Zeus, Father. That's not a Hail Mary, that's the fucking nuclear option."

Aeolus's green eyes blazed. "He will master it. He nearly has. And as he's been finding ways to sneak off here for two months and keep our secret all this time, I believe he has more than proven his trustworthiness. And he has the greatest access to Eurus, including in the Eastern divine realm, where Eurus considers himself safe from all of us."

Zeph glared. "But how do you know he hasn't already told Eurus what you're doing here? How do you know Eurus isn't permitting it? He could be playing both sides, and you'd never know."

"Eurus would never allow his son to become more powerful. And Devlin holds a grudge against his father that is a mile deep and twice as wide. He wouldn't jeopardize the chance to take him down once and for all."

"Be that as it may," Boreas said. "That doesn't mean he's loyal to *you*, either."

"Indeed," Aeolus said. "But instinct tells me he is. Trust me."

Zeph scoffed and jabbed a finger toward their father's

hand. "That would be easier if the recent history of deception didn't exist."

"Perhaps. But what is your alternative? This thing is done."

His words hung in the air between them, their truth incontrovertible.

"So it is," Boreas said. "Now what?"

"I continue to train Devlin for at least a few more days. A week at most. Then we set a trap and lure Eurus out. Between me, Devlin, and now you with the infernal dagger, we have the means to take him down."

Zeph shook his head. "Am I the only one who sees this has catastrophe written all over it?"

Chrys nodded, the cold making it harder to breathe. "Maybe. Probably. But Father's right. What's done is done. We'll get one shot at this, so we just need to do it and do it right."

"Agreed," Boreas said. "But here's my question. How are you going to lure him? What's the bait?"

Aeolus met each of their gazes, then glanced at Tisiphone. Heaving a long breath, he looked back at his sons. "Me."

CHAPTER TWENTY

Chrysander saw a resignation in his father's eyes he didn't like, but all they had were a bunch of shit options.

"Now, you should depart," Aeolus said. "The rock and iron shield our energy, but don't block it completely. If a storm hasn't already kicked up, it soon will."

Tisiphone stepped to his side. "Same time?"

"Yes." He seemed to hesitate, but then he turned to her, took her in his arms, and kissed her.

Well, hello. His brothers' expressions bore the same surprise he felt. Since his mother left long, long ago, his father had never done more than scratch the occasional itch. No more wives. Nothing you could call a relationship. Like father, like son. But the lingering kiss spoke of something deeper, something more meaningful.

They pulled apart. "Be careful," he said.

She nodded, then looked their way and winked. "Close your mouths before you catch a fly."

Aeolus smiled. Chrys arched an eyebrow at the unusual

display.

Tisiphone took to the back of the cave and disappeared. Since the caves possessed deposits of infernal iron, there clearly was a connecting tunnel that allowed her passage to the Underworld. Aeolus's use of this place might've been twisted, but it was equally brilliant.

"Where will you go?" Boreas asked.

"Nowhere. I'm staying here."

Chrys nodded. "When should we next meet?"

"Week from today. If Devlin appears ready sooner, I'll send for you."

They all agreed, then awkwardness settled into the spaces between them.

"Okay, well," Zeph said.

"A week, then," Boreas said. "I'll, uh, leave first. I'm going back to Owen's." He met Chrys's gaze.

Chrys's gut clenched. A shudder tore through him. Laney. Guess it was time to face the music. "I'll meet you back there."

Boreas nodded, then shifted into the elements. His energy shot from the room.

"I'm going home. Stay in touch," Zeph said to Chrys. He gave Aeolus a tight nod, and followed after Boreas.

Chrys looked, really looked, at his father. Exhaustion carved lines into the other man's face. "Need anything?"

Aeolus shook his head.

"Well, I'm outta here, too."

"Wait." Aeolus stepped closer, and Chrys braced. His father's hand settled onto his shoulder, and he forced his body to tolerate the contact. "I wronged you, earlier. This isn't your fault. Not any of it."

Surprise stole his response. He could probably count on

one hand the number of times his father had admitted he was wrong.

"Not *any* of it, Chrysander. Do you hear me?"

He swallowed, hard, appreciating the words even if he couldn't fully believe them. But still, he said, "Yes."

"Good." Aeolus dropped his hand. "Go, before the cold harms you further."

"See you in a week." Chrys disappeared into the elements.

He backtracked through the crevices and crags and caverns, anticipating the comforting Mediterranean warmth surrounding him. Already the air was warmer...so why was an icy feeling of dread crawling down his spine? He extended his consciousness, specifically opening himself to read other energy signatures. Below, his father remained as he'd left him. Ahead... Alarm. Aggression. Desperation. But it was like watching a screen filled with static. The damn rock obscured the full picture of what he was flying into.

Whatever it was, though, wasn't good.

Chrys poured on the full force of his godhood, working his way through ever-larger spaces, until he shot out the sea-level cave door through which they'd entered Gibraltar.

Screech, screech, screeeeeeech!

What in the hell?

The rough sea tossed and crashed. Gusting winds blew spray into the air. And three enormous birds circled and dove in the tumultuous, night sky above him.

Chrys shot up. The birds swooped and dive-bombed. Lightning split the sky. He slammed on the brakes and reared back.

Not birds. *Oh, shit a fucking brick.* Harpies. The heads of women with long, colorful hair atop the bodies of birds with thick-barreled chests, broad wingspans, and sharp talons.

They were shrieking and circling and clawing at one space of air.

Boreas.

His brother flashed in and out of the elements as the preternatural assault continued, his shirt shredded, along with the skin underneath. Damnit all to hell. What kind of dumb bad luck was it to run into them *now*? Vicious and cruel, Harpies were known for abducting and torturing. If they got their claws into Boreas, it was going to be game over.

Zephyros's energy torpedoed into one of the beasts, knocking it across the dark sky. The assault distracted the other two just long enough for Boreas to shoot up and away.

The beasts quickly regrouped and searched out their target. Chrys swung wide around their flight pattern to reach Boreas. Where had the one Zeph hit gone? Chrys scanned in a three-sixty.

There. On the peak of Gibraltar. The lame Harpy scrambled to gain purchase. Further down the ridge stood another figure, a hooded cloak whipping around him in the wind.

Not so fast, big brother, you'll spoil my fun.

Eurus! Chrysander spun, feeling his brother's energy but unable to pinpoint it with so many divine beings in the storm-beaten sky at once. All he knew is that Eurus's voice came from above him, not from the direction of the unknown observer.

Boreas loosed a blood-curdling scream.

Chrys shot upward and ran into a current of superheated air. Bastard was using the South Wind—*his wind*—against Boreas. They couldn't get that fucking ring back fast enough. Holding steady in the steaming flow, Chrys concentrated on attracting every bit of the air into himself. Splintering thunder cracked overhead.

Behind him, Boreas groaned.

B? B? You okay, man? No answer. *Zephyros, get Father! Go!*

Zeph's energy whipped past him, scattering the Harpies as they made for Boreas again. Slashing rain erupted from the swirling clouds.

The South Wind stopped blowing, freeing Chrys to look for Boreas. They had to get him out of here.

In a cacophony of flapping wings and screeching birdcalls, one of the Harpies dive-bombed Chrys. They could perceive him in all his forms, and he just barely avoided a haircut of the ripped-out-of-your-skull variety. He whipped around and... *No!* Pounding thunder made the very air vibrate.

One of the Harpies had its claws deep in Boreas's bloody bicep. The other swooped in on great spread wings to grab his free arm.

Over my dead body.

Chrys shot out over the sea, rippling into corporeal form, infernal dagger in hand.

That can be arranged, Eurus sneered.

Out of nowhere, icy air lashed at his body, created a frigid turbulence that fought his forward motion. Chrys pushed through it, drawing on the overload of South Wind heat he'd imbibed moments before. It countered the attacking North Wind, allowed Chrys to come up fast behind the Harpy that already had Boreas in its clutches.

Chrys reared back his arm just as the bird turned its feminine head. He swung the dagger in a vicious slash, opening up a bright, red gaping wound in its throat. The Harpy issued a gurgling screech and flailed, but didn't drop his brother.

A blast of North Wind knocked him back. Chrys cloaked himself in more of the South. But the sub-zero air surrounding him would wear through his reserves quickly. Just where he was, the rain froze and ice pelted him, cutting and bruising his face and arms.

He launched himself at the bird-woman again. It thrust its wing out to protect its core, so Chrys jammed the blade through the feathers and used the leverage to pull himself up the Harpy's big body.

With an outraged screech, it dropped Boreas, leaving him dangling by one arm in the other Harpy's clutch.

That's right, you screeching bitch.

He tugged the blade free, lunged for its neck, and aimed hard and fast for its chest.

Eurus materialized right in front of him, arms outreached to block the blow.

The dagger sliced full and deep across the palm of Eurus's hand and plunged into the Harpy's chest. His brother roared in pained outrage; the bird screeched in agony.

Eurus lunged at him. Pain exploded across Chrys's cheekbone. The blow knocked him back, forcing him to pull the knife free, but the job was done.

A wall of frigidity rammed into him. Then another. From every angle, the blistering North Wind battered him until he was in a freefall with no idea which way was up. He could do nothing, nothing but grip the dagger with all his might. He couldn't lose it.

Commotion erupted above him. Lightning flashed. Thunder

boomed in deep cracks. The remaining Harpy screeched. The cavalry had arrived. He was vaguely aware of Zeph's and Aeolus's voices.

He slammed into the churching black water.

Time slowed to a crawl as the impact reverberated through every part of him. The sea might as well have been cement for how much it cushioned his fall.

The height from which he fell drove him under. Waves rolled and crested overhead.

The cold stole his breath, made his muscles seize, and his joints threaten to snap.

Extreme heat, Chrys could do all day long. The cold, though? That was a complete show-stopper. Do not pass go. Do not collect $200.

His skin, his lungs, his eyes—everything burned.

Something seized his neck. Chrys gasped, sucking in great mouthfuls of cold sea water.

Jesus, not like this. Don't let it end like this.

Cold. Alone. So many regrets.

Consciousness flickered.

Not yet. Not before I can... In a flash, Laney's beautiful face, her dark hair, her deep blue eyes, all came to mind. He struggled to hold on to the image, onto why it mattered.

But he couldn't. He couldn't. It faded, and Laney was gone, and so was everything else.

৪০৫৩

Laney pushed away her empty ice cream bowl and rubbed her stomach. "So good, Tabitha. Thank you." She glanced at the clock. Ninety minutes had passed since she'd talked to Seth. Depending on rush-hour traffic, he'd be here within two to three hours. *God, let the Beltway be a parking lot.* She needed every minute to figure out how to explain the situation.

"Can I have more of the orange?" Owen asked.

Everyone chuckled. It was his second serving of seconds.

"What?" he asked.

"All yours. Makes me happy to see," Tabitha said.

She'd come over about an hour before, and Megan had whipped up a quick and hearty salad with crisp lettuce, chunky vegetables, sweet fruit, and grilled chicken. Summer in a bowl. The four of them had chatted while they ate, Teddy eating and playing at Megan's side, and the fun, free-flowing conversation set Laney more at ease. For the first time since she'd woken up scared in the middle of the night, she felt comfortable, like these people were friends.

"So, Laney," Megan said. "What kinds of things do you write — What is it, Owen?"

Laney frowned and tried to scan their faces, unsure what she'd missed.

His spoon clanked and he jerked into a standing position, judging by the movement of the white light around him. "I'm very sorry, Tabitha. This is rude and unexplainable, but you should go."

"What?" she said.

"Owen?" Megan asked again.

Laney's stomach rolled. The quiet alarm in Owen's voice, so different from his usual easy-going demeanor, told her something was very wrong. "It's okay," he said. "Damn, too late."

What was happening? Did it have something to do with

Chrys?

An image slammed into her mind: the god they called Boreas, prostrate on the ground, Owen, Megan, others kneeling around him, Zeph pressing on his chest. She gasped as the scene disappeared as quickly as it came.

Out of nowhere, a commotion erupted in the living room. Men's voices. Groans. *Oh, God.* Owen's light darted across the room. Footsteps followed.

A hand grasped hers. "Do you have any idea what's going on?" Tabitha asked.

What the hell was she supposed to say? In truth, no, not really. And what she did know would make her sound crazy. "Uh…"

"Come on," she said, urging Laney up.

"I think we should give them some space," Laney hedged. Surely Tabitha didn't know what Owen, Boreas, and the others were. Owen had ordered her to leave for a reason. Obviously his senses had alerted him to the appearance of his magical family.

Tabitha tugged her up. "Sounds like someone's hurt."

Fear tightened Laney's throat. "I know."

"You know something."

Finally, Laney nodded. "Owen's family. They're…different."

"I'll take care of Boreas. Help Chrys," a male voice ordered. Zephyros?

Why does Chrys need help? Every fiber of Laney's body demanded to know what was going on. Indecision pulled Laney in two directions. But Owen was right, with his family already here and having appeared out of thin air, it was too late to shield Tabitha from knowing more than she should. "Please guide me in?"

She wrapped Laney's hand around her arm. They crossed the room and passed through the doorway. "Oh, my God," Tabitha said.

Heart beating a mile a minute, Laney scanned her vision over the sudden crowd of people—gods, by all the divine auras—who suddenly filled the room. Zeph leaned over Boreas, who was sprawled on the floor. Owen and Megan were at his side, Teddy's fussing ratcheting into a full-out cry.

"Stay here a minute. I'm going to grab Teddy," Tabitha said.

Laney nodded, still searching for Chrys. Men—gods—she didn't know stood at the windows. One pushed by her and moved to the back door, judging by the sound of his footsteps. Thunder rumbled overhead and she gasped.

Where was Chrys? Between the number of people, the rush of voices, Teddy's cries, and the storm brewing outside, both her vision and her hearing struggled to make sense of it all. Why couldn't she at least find the golden glow she normally saw around him?

"Let me have him, Megan."

"What? Oh, God, Tabitha, I'm so sorry you have to see this."

"Don't worry about that now. I'll take care of him. Should I call 9-1-1?"

"No," a chorus of voices responded.

"We need to get him warm," a man's voice said. Who were they talking about? And where was Chrys? "Find as many blankets as you can."

"Go with Ted," Owen urged. Wind gusted against the side of the house.

"No, I'm not leaving Boreas."

The sound of the baby's cry neared. "Come on, Laney," Tabitha said.

The depth of her disorientation tempted her to flee. But she couldn't, not without knowing... "No. I— Do you see a blond-haired man?"

"Uh." She paused, as if looking. "On the floor, by the stairs, but—"

"Is the path clear between here and there?"

"I really think you should—"

"Please."

"Stay to the right, but there's a chair sticking out in the corner." The one she'd sat in at the meeting the other night. Tabitha's description was just enough to orient her in the room, even if the specifics were vague.

She crossed the space, passing first by Boreas and those helping him. Déjà vu had her pausing near them. This was just like that weird thing she'd seen at the table. A premonition? Instinct? Yeah.

"You're killing me with kindness, Zephyros," Boreas gritted out.

His voice captured her attention, and she stared down at the small grouping. Between Boreas's white and Zeph's blue, a soft yellow glow trailed over the older man's body. What in the world?

"Yeah, well, when I'm done you can pay me back."

Boreas laugh-grunted. "Do not make me laugh right now."

Laney forced herself away and zeroed in on a brilliant silver aura with flashes of gold throughout. Sprawled on the floor in front of the owner of that unique light lay Chrys, his aura so pale it was no wonder she hadn't perceived it from across the room. He was shivering and mumbling, fragments of words only occasionally discernible.

She sank to her knees on the carpet near his head and reached out a hand. "Chrys?"

"Keep back," a deep voice ordered.

Laney jerked away. She scanned her vision over the huge god at Chrys's side dressed all in black, long brown hair pulled back.

"He has a knife and is delirious. We don't need another injury."

Emotion squeezed her throat. She nodded and dropped her gaze to Chrys. She yearned to touch him, to prove that he was here, to let him know she was there for him. "What's wrong with him?"

The god ignored her. "His energy is all over you."

Heat roared over her face, but as the full meaning of his words sank in, a fierce satisfaction filled her. "Good."

She got the distinct feeling he was observing her. When she looked up, she saw that she was right. She found his gaze. His eyes were a brilliant green, so like… He and Chrys were related. She was sure of it. But it was a conversation for another time.

Footsteps pounded down the stairs, and stopped just before the bottom. "Here are blankets."

"Good, set them there and help me hold him down so we can disarm him. He won't let the dagger go." Thunder boomed ominously nearby.

Hold him down… She gasped. "No! You can't." She leaned in closer, careful not to touch him. "Chrys, it's Laney. Can you hear me?" His head jerked toward her. "Chrys, come on, wake up. Can you hear me?"

"You're Laney?" the huge god asked. "He's been saying

your name."

He has? Pressure filled her chest until she thought it might burst.

She focused on his face. So pale. Blue tinged his lips. "Chrys—"

"Laney," he groaned. His eyelids heaved open once, twice, but sagged closed again. "La…."

"I'm here. You're at Owen's. Everyone's here."

He whispered something she couldn't make out. His eyelids opened wider this time, and his teeth chattered. He moaned, a huge shudder wracking through him.

"What's happening?" she asked. Rain pounded out a beat on the windows.

"It's akin to severe hypothermia."

"We have to warm him." She rested the back of her hand against his forehead. So cool, too cool. She was so used to his unusual warmth that he actually felt cold to her.

He groaned and pushed his face against her hand.

Oh, he sought her touch! "He won't hurt me," she whispered. Instinct had her speaking the words, but the truth of them coursed through every cell in her body. "He won't." She crowded in closer and cradled his face in her hands. So cold. "Open your eyes. Chrys. Listen to my voice and open them."

He obeyed, but his eyes struggled to focus. "La…"

"Yes. Listen. We need to help you. You're holding a knife. Give it to—" She looked over a shoulder at the god beside her.

"Aeolus. I'm his father."

Oooh. She couldn't even process that tidbit right now. "Give the knife to your father."

"No."

"Chrys—"

"No, y-you."

"What?" He was so out of it. What if he didn't get better? Was that even a possibility for someone like him?

"You…knife. In c-case."

Her heart squeezed. He wanted her to have it? "Okay, okay," she said, worry and love for him nearly overwhelming her. *Love?* She shook her head and forced herself to concentrate. "Which hand holds the knife?" she asked his father.

He didn't answer right away.

"I'm nearly blind. Which hand?"

"Right."

"I'm going to take the knife now. Chrys? Okay?"

"You."

"Yes, me." She crawled around his other side so she could touch him as little as possible. Last thing she wanted was to increase his discomfort. Dragging her fingers down his right arm, she half expected him to flinch or pull away, but he didn't. Finally, her hand reached his, curled in a tight, shaking fist around the grip of the dagger. "Let go. I'll take it." Just when she was sure he wouldn't, his hand slowly turned and his fingers went lax. She felt for the grip and grabbed it.

Holy crap, it was heavy. Far heavier than it looked. And icy in her hands. But she'd told him she'd take it, and he wanted her to have it.

"Bring the blankets," Aeolus said.

She leaned away from his chest as his father and the other men spread blankets over Chrys. Drawing close to his face, she whispered, "You're going to be okay. You hear me?"

His head lolled toward her. "S-so-rry."

"Shh."

"Sor-ry."

"Hey. All you need to worry about right now is getting better." Unable to resist, she pressed a kiss to his forehead. *I love you.* The thought came unbidden, spiking Laney's heart rate even further, but she just couldn't sit and analyze it now.

Chrys tossed aside the covers and pulled her against him, his arms bands of steel around her back.

Laney gasped at the unexpected move, but then nearly melted into him. He was just doing it for warmth, she knew that. But it was so like the hugs she'd yearned to be able to give him that she couldn't care.

Except he was so cold. Shivers wracked through him.

"Chrysander, you need the blankets," his father said.

"He's freezing. If he needs this, just cover us both." She pushed herself atop him, careful to keep the knife away from his body, wrapped her free hand under his big shoulders, and nestled her face against his neck.

He groaned and pulled her in tighter, like he was trying to climb inside her skin. And if she could've done that for him, she would've. How many times had he healed her? Just once, to have the power to do this for him. She would do anything.

Heavy layers of blankets draped across her back, covering them both.

Dampness seeped through her clothing. His was wet… and a big part of the cold she felt. She lifted her head to Aeolus. "His clothes are wet. We should get them off him." She willed the threatening embarrassment at the statement away.

"You love him."

Competing reactions surged through her. Hesitation to admit it was true. Embarrassment at his *father* asking this, and in front of his entire family—not that they appeared to be paying any attention. And, if she did, fear of him not thinking her good enough. His pause when she'd revealed her disability hadn't escaped her notice. None of which mattered right now. Only Chrys did. And she was prepared to give him whatever he needed to survive this.

"Yes, I do, but—" She gasped.

His clothes disappeared. And so did hers.

"Your heat will help him," he said in a low voice. "Fear not. We will keep you covered. Watch over them," he said to another god. "I will go restrain the storms."

She buried her face in Chrys's neck, not understanding everything going on around her, but also not caring. It took only a moment for her self-consciousness to fade, for everything else to fade away, until there was just the two of them. He needed her, and she'd do anything for him.

"I've got you, Chrys. I'll take care of you," she murmured. For however long she could. For however long he'd let her.

CHAPTER TWENTY-ONE

Chrys couldn't stop shivering. Aches throbbed through his joints. His jaw was stiff. Even his teeth hurt.

So cold. The kind of cold that got inside you and never left.

Except… The more he pushed through the fog of pain, the more he sensed a warmth. And, maybe he was dreaming, but he swore he could smell Laney's warm, sweet scent. He forced the twenty-pound weights that were his eyelids open. "Laney?" he rasped.

She lifted her head. "I'm here." Her hand skated up and stroked the side of his face, his hair.

Confusion swamped him. Where were they? Who was shouting? And why was Laney on top of him?

Panic loomed in the distance as the meaning of that last question sank in. She covered him from neck to shins. But though it threatened, the panic didn't come. All he felt was relief, comfort, gratitude. A sign of just how desperate his condition, no doubt.

He became aware again of her hand petting his hair and forced his eyes to focus on her pretty face. Worry furrowed her brow even as her lips shaped into a small smile.

Almighty Zeus, he thought he'd never see her again.

"Hi," he managed to say.

Her smile brightened. "Hi."

A series of images flickered through his mind, but he couldn't make them stick long enough to make sense of them. "What happened?"

"I don't know the details, but it seems there was some kind of attack. And you're way too cold. They said you needed heat. But I know you don't like, um, to be touched, so I'll get up if you—"

"Stay." He swallowed the lump that took up residence in his throat. No judgment. No drama. It was like she just...got him. "I need you." *And I want you.* Even if he didn't deserve her. Selfish bastard that he was, that didn't mean he could give her up. At least not right now. Not with his power drained so achingly low, not with the cold emptiness crawling through every part of him. And fuck if using her this way didn't make him the world's biggest asshole.

She nodded, still stroking his hair. "I will. Just close your eyes and rest."

Her gentle touch soothed him and lured his eyes closed. "Stay," he mumbled.

"Okay," she whispered, and tucked her face into the nook of his neck.

•❧•

Voices seeped into his awareness. Chrys tried to resist them, but before he knew it, he was dragged into consciousness.

"...don't think it's w-working." Laney's voice.

"Maybe a hot bath?" someone said. Owen?

"He'll draw the heat out of bath water in minutes," another male voice said. It was too much to keep up with. He willed himself back under again. If he could just sleep...

"Do y-you have an electric b-blanket?" Laney asked.

"I still say he needs the Acheron," someone said.

"I agree with Boreas. The risk is too great. We're stronger together. If today proved nothing else, it proved that. He wouldn't be alive if he'd been alone."

Boreas was okay? He tried to ask, but couldn't form the words.

The conversation continued, and one thing kept Chrys from giving in to the bone-deep desire to fade away, to just escape the pain of the agonizing cold. Laney's voice. Except something was wrong with it.

"We have t-to do s-something. I'm not enough."

He frowned at that idea and forced his eyes open. Owen's living room took shape around him. Laney's soft, warm body still covered his, though she'd shifted to rest her face against the other side of his neck. And she was... shivering.

At first he wasn't sure, because he couldn't stop shaking. His muscles were nearly screaming from the constant tremors. But...she was, too. *That* was why her voice sounded wrong. Her teeth were chattering.

No. He'd caused her enough pain. Damnit, he just couldn't stop, could he?

He swallowed hard, forcing moisture into his mouth. "Get...get her off me. Get her off," he said louder.

For a moment, she went still. But then shudders wracked through her again.

"Now. She needs to get off me."

"Okay," she said in an odd voice. "Just give me a second. I, um, I don't have... I'm not dressed."

Not dressed? How in the hell? He concentrated on the feel of her body, the feel of her body on his. Sure enough, they were both as naked as the day their gods made them. The thought shot arousal through him, even if he was in absolutely no condition to act on it. His hands skimmed over her back. Jesus, she was freezing. The realization killed the pleasure he'd felt a moment before.

"Megan, could you m-maybe help me? Do you have a robe or something? Another blanket?"

"Yes." Footsteps skirted around them and made their way up the stairs.

Chrys rolled his head to the side. Despite hearing the other voices, he had been so focused on Laney he hadn't really paid enough attention.

It was a freaking packed house. Owen, Livos, and a number of the other lesser Anemoi. Except for a few clearly acting as sentries at the windows, they were all staring at him and Laney.

His Laney. Who was naked. In the middle of a room-full of males. With only a blanket separating her body from their eyes.

His arms tightened around her. Aggression and possessiveness tore through him so fierce it brought his cock to life.

Laney sucked in a breath, her stomach muscles tensing against his length.

What a goddamned piece of shit he was. Like it wasn't bad

enough he used her this way. Now he had to make it worse by getting off on it. "Everyone get the fuck out of here so she can get up."

Except for the sentries, who kept their attention focused solely on the windows, the room cleared. Footsteps sounded on the stairs again.

"Here you go," Megan said, pressing a fuzzy pink robe into Laney's hand. "Do you want help?"

"No. Thanks," she said in a small voice. When Megan left the room, she lifted her upper body off of his chest and attempted to slip into the robe while still under the covers. From throat to belly, her skin was red from the prolonged exposure to his cold. Sonofabitch.

She sat up further as she pushed her second arm into the robe. The change in position pressed the beautifully hot place between her legs into his groin.

He groaned.

"Sorry," she whispered. Her hands fumbled to secure the robe around her. She looked over her shoulders, as if making sure no one would see her. Then she slipped off him.

Immediately, he missed the feel of her, her heat, her closeness. It was like she'd taken everything good and right in the world with her. But her health and comfort were more important.

Clutching the robe at her throat, she arranged the covers over him, tucking them in tight around his neck and shoulders. "I'll leave your knife right here next to you."

His knife? The dagger. A vague memory of giving it to her shimmered through his mind's eye. "You keep it."

She frowned, but didn't look at his face. She didn't meet his eyes. Maybe it was unintentional? But then she scooted away, far away it seemed, and pushed herself into a sitting position on the bottom step, the blade resting in her lap. Shaking, she pulled the robe closed over her legs. Still not looking at him, or talking. Worry shaped her expression, but there was something else there, too…

I'm not enough.

He frowned. No. That wasn't it, was it? Because it was so the other way around. But the more he thought about it, the more he saw hurt in the set of her shoulders, in the downward cast of her eyes, in the tremble of her lips…

"Laney—"

"Don't say anything." She shook her head. "Conserve your energy. Just concentrate on getting better. That's all that matters." Using the end post of the bannister, she pulled herself up. "I'm gonna go change now."

"But, Laney, I didn't mean to hurt your feelings. I just—"

"I know. Really. Just rest." She turned and made her way up the steps.

For a long moment, Chrys watched her go. With every step she took away from him, something deep inside him cried out, demanded he open his mouth and give voice to the desire careening through him. Not just for her body, or her heat, but for her, the woman. Laney.

He kept his mouth shut.

When she was out of sight, he dropped his head back to the floor and closed his eyes. It was better this way. His life was a disaster on every level. And she deserved far, far better.

∞

Boreas sat at the kitchen table and ate his fifth heaping serving of ice cream. Tabitha's ice cream. He now understood Owen's obsession with the stuff. Not only was it delicious, but the ingested cold was restorative.

Tabitha sat across the table from him, his grandson asleep in her lap, quietly watching. He regretted that she'd gotten caught in the middle of their chaos, even as he enjoyed her company and the smell of fragrant flowers on her skin. "I am sorry you had to see all this," he said.

Her mouth opened and closed and she shrugged. "I'm not exactly sure what I'm seeing. A half hour ago, you were literally shredded. And now you're...not. How is that possible?"

"The less you know, the better."

She looked down as Teddy nestled into her. "Maybe. But I already know enough to know we're not in Kansas anymore."

Boreas frowned. "Kansas?"

Intelligent brown eyes dragged over his face, as if studying him. A foreign heat rose inside him. "You don't know the reference?"

He shook his head. "Should I?"

"Curiouser and curiouser."

"What is?"

"You don't get that one either, do you?"

He swallowed his last bite of strawberry ice cream, studying her in return. "I am failing some test right now, yes?"

She shrugged. "I'm just trying to figure you out."

His body stirred at the idea. He settled his spoon in the empty bowl, crossed his arms over his chest, and met her inquisitive gaze. "I like the sound of that."

A lovely pink arose on her cheeks. "Oh." Her gaze flickered to his lips.

He gave in to a small smile, but it fell just as quickly as the conversation drifted in from the living room. Everyone else was in there, now debating how to heal Chrysander's hypothermia.

His gut clenched. As if he weren't indebted to his youngest brother enough for saving his life, Chrysander's condition was his fault. He wanted to help, but because their winds and their natures were extreme opposites, he was the last god that could be of any use in improving his situation.

He loathed this feeling of uselessness, of helplessness.

But with every swallow of the ice cream, strength and power had returned to him. Thank the gods Zephyros had the ability to heal the kinds of wounds which had torn apart his body. It made the decision to return to Owen and Megan's easy—a decision upon which Boreas had insisted in case Eurus decided to attack his son's family. And it also gave them the ability to stick together, which Aeolus's presence made possible—he had the ability to quell the storms that would've normally erupted when multiple Anemoi gathered in one place. Given Eurus's madness, his apparent alliance with the Harpies, and Devlin's treachery, they needed the strength in numbers.

Devlin. When Boreas had first emerged from Gibraltar, he'd seen him, standing on the edge of the cliff. The boy's eyes flashed black, the same kind of deadness that inhabited his malevolent brother's gaze, and watched as the Harpies swooped in and attacked from behind.

Zephyros's instincts had apparently been right on the money where Eurus's eldest son was concerned.

Had Devlin been playing Aeolus all along?

Who could say? It hardly mattered now. Even though Father still argued that the situation might not have been what it appeared, it was a risk they couldn't take.

Which left them exactly nowhere.

Owen entered the kitchen, followed by a number of the others. "How are you?" he asked, his mismatched eyes serious.

"I will be fine. Worry not."

He shrugged one big shoulder. "Can't be helped."

Boreas nodded. "Yes." He looked at the group assembled around the room. Except for Zephyros, who had gone to collect his wife, and their shared subordinate Skiron, god of the Northwest Wind, almost all of the Anemoi were here—a highly unusual occurrence. "What is going on?"

"Chrys is still"—Owen glanced at Tabitha—"struggling to get warm. Laney's now freezing, herself."

Boreas's gaze dropped to the table, to the empty bowl… Wait. "Something hot. Is he conscious enough to drink uh, uh…" He struggled to name an appropriate drink.

"Hot chocolate? Hot tea?" Tabitha offered.

"Yes, precisely." He stared an extra moment at the woman he'd admired from afar all these long months. Trapped in the middle of an impossible situation, she'd kept her cool and helped his family. As if he needed more reasons to find her appealing. He gave her a smile.

Owen nodded. "It's worth a try."

Megan walked into the kitchen. "What is?"

His son turned to her. "Could you make Chrys something hot to drink? A lot of it?"

She squeezed his hand. "Of course."

"Or—" Tabitha pressed her fingers to her lips. "I don't want to interfere."

"Not at all. What is it?" Boreas asked.

"If what he needs is a way to get really warm, really fast, I have a hot tub."

CHAPTER TWENTY-TWO

"Ready to go?" Boreas asked, crouched at his side.

Chrys looked up at his oldest brother, more filled with relief at his survival than he could articulate. He gave a tight nod.

To his right, footsteps padded down the stairs. "What's going on?"

Laney.

Chrys turned his head. She stood on the landing in a T-shirt and shorts, the dagger in her hand. Gods, she was so damn beautiful. His chest ached with it, with his desire for her. He wanted to wrap himself around her and never let her go.

The yearning was totally foreign, but that didn't make it any less real. His brain was too fogged to know exactly what to make of it, though.

"Tabitha has a hot tub next door. We're going to try using that to heat Chrys up," Boreas said.

She nodded. "That's a good idea."

"Would you like to come, Laney?" Boreas asked.

Chrys studied her, nearly holding his breath to see what she'd say.

"That's okay. I don't want to be in the way."

Chrys frowned. She'd just risked herself for him. Again. No one had ever so frequently and selflessly been there for him the way she had these past couple weeks. He could *never* think of her as "in the way." The idea revolted his soul.

Her lip quivered and she hugged herself with her free hand.

"You're still cold," he said, the realization releasing his protective instincts. "Come. You need the heat, too."

When she didn't respond, Boreas said, "He is right. Come down and hold out your hand."

He looked to his brother. "Give her a minute to adjust. Her sight returns when she's in the elements. It's a little jarring."

Boreas studied him a moment, his gaze too wise, too knowing for comfort. "Okay."

Slowly, Laney descended to the bottom. She extended her left hand, palm down. "What do I do with this?" She raised the knife in her right.

Chrys pushed out from under the covers. "I'll take it," he said, accepting the dagger. "And move your necklace so it doesn't touch your skin."

She pulled it so it lay on top of her shirt.

"Ready?" Boreas asked. They both nodded. "Sorry I'm the only one here to do this, Chrysander. Father is busy holding off storms, and Zephyros has not yet returned."

In his current condition, Boreas's touch was likely to be uncomfortable, but he shook his head. He'd take an eternity of discomfort to know his brother was safe. "I'm glad you're here, you dig?"

Boreas took their hands. His northern touch was a white-hot bite on Chrys's still-icy skin. He gritted his teeth as they shifted into the elements. But the distance they traveled was short and the torment was over in an instant.

He crouched naked next to the in-ground tub, the water bubbling and throwing off the most fantastic steam. Except for a soft ring of lights underneath the water, darkness surrounded him. How long had he been out of it?

He looked to his right and left. Alone. "B, what are you doing?" Why hadn't they—

His brother and Laney appeared beside him.

Laney's expression was emotional, awed. "Thank you," she whispered to Boreas.

For what?

Boreas nodded and turned to Chrys. "You need help in?"

"I'll be fine," he said, ignoring the muscle fatigue and aching shivers he couldn't control. "Get out of here before you melt."

He arched an eyebrow. "We have this property surrounded now, too. Take as long as you want. Summon me if you need anything." He disappeared.

Laney slipped her amulet back under her shirt.

"What did you thank him for?"

Her gaze lifted to his, a blush painting her cheeks. She licked her lips. "He held on to me…so I could look at you, so I could see you."

The emotion in her voice wrapped around his heart. He thought of the night of the meeting, when he'd pulled her into the elements so she could put faces to all the voices she was hearing. She'd seen them all, except him, beyond what her limited vision allowed. "No doubt I look like shit," he said, struggling against the seriousness of the moment.

She shook her head. "You're gorgeous. Although, I already knew that."

He frowned, unsure how to respond to the yearning in her startlingly blue eyes, slipped into the tub, and groaned.

Hail to Zeus and all the Olympians. It was pure, glorious heaven. The heat was life-giving, restoring, and soothed his cold-ravaged body so thoroughly all he could do was *feel*. He let himself sink under completely, the rolling hot water providing the all-encompassing warmth the blankets had not.

Laney's voice sounded as if from a distance. She splashed into the water. Her hand hit his arm and then she grabbed at his shoulders, pulling him up. "Chrys!"

He broke the surface and sucked in a gulp of air. Whirling, he searched out the source of her alarm. "What?"

"I thought—" She pressed her fist to her mouth.

What? He replayed the last few moments. He got in, went under— Oh. "You thought...I was drowning?" His gaze dragged over her T-shirt. Her nipples pushed enticingly against the wet material. She'd waded in with all her clothes on. Trying to protect him.

Laney nodded, her expression full of concern...and something else. Something he didn't want to examine too closely. Because damn if it didn't make him want a whole lot of things he really shouldn't want, not if he was to do right by her.

"I'm fine." Taking her hand, he guided her to one of the benches along the side. "Sit. The water will warm you." He almost urged her to take her wet clothes off, but thought better of it. Already, the hot water was filling him with strength, restoring his power, sending delicious heat flowing through his veins. The steam carried her warm citrus scent. He breathed it in, wanting more of it, more of her. His cock came to life. Before he did something stupid and selfish, he turned, crossed to the opposite side, and sank onto his own bench.

A wet *slap* made him look up.

Oh, damn.

Laney had taken off her shorts and tossed them on the wooden planking. As he watched, she pulled her shirt over her head, revealing her bare breasts underneath. Water beaded and ran down her skin as she reached to deposit the clothing behind her. The underwater lights cast an intriguing pattern of highlights and shadows over her body, one that made him want to explore all the dark parts with his fingers, and tongue.

Clearly, he felt more himself already.

"I'm glad I can see the light you give off. Between the dark, the glare of the spa lights, and the steam, I can't see anything else."

Can't see? She'd charged sight unseen into the water after him? "How did you know I'd gone under?" he asked, trying to hold back the anger building in his chest. Why? Why did she keep risking herself for him?

"Your aura got dimmer for a moment. And then you didn't respond when I said your name." Her breath caught. "When you first got back to Megan and Owen's, your aura was so faint I couldn't find you."

The compassion. The protectiveness toward him. The affection so plain on her face. It was all too much.

"Stop it, Laney. Just stop." He hated the gruffness of his words, but couldn't control it.

Her jaw dropped open. "What?"

"Stop…" He tugged his fingers through his wet hair. *Tempting me to give in. Tormenting me with things I can never have but want so desperately I can't breathe.* Desire and regret lodged a knot in his throat.

A range of emotions played over her face. Hurt. Rejection. Anger.

Determination.

Laney pushed into the center of the pool. He sat up straight in his seat, his back coming hard against the tub's side.

"What do you want me to stop doing, Chrysander? Huh?" She waded closer and stopped right in front of him. "Do you want me to stop caring? Do you want me to stop worrying about you when, for the third time since we've met, your brother has tried to kill you? And nearly succeeded? Do you want me to stop thinking about making love with you? About how good you felt inside me?"

"*Stop*," he said again, bracing his hands against the walls to restrain the urges her words were letting loose, heartfelt urges that warred with every bit of his common sense.

She pushed closer, her legs skimming the insides of his spread thighs. "I can't stop. I wouldn't want to even if I could. I lo—"

He lunged for her and claimed her in a devouring, soul-stirring kiss. He knew what was about to come out of her mouth, because she was wearing the emotion on her face, in her eyes. He just couldn't hear it. He wasn't ready for it. He might never be ready for it because he wanted to hear the words so damn bad.

Laney moaned into the kiss. Cradling her face, he drew her in closer, plundered her mouth thoroughly and deeply with his tongue. He poured every bit of suppressed longing into the kiss until she was swaying, jostled by the flowing, bubbling water. She stumbled and threw her arms out for balance. But what she didn't do was try to touch him.

As if he didn't already care more than he should, at that moment he felt what only could be called love for Laney Summerlyn.

She pulled her lips free and gasped. "I want you. So much."

Arousal, need, desire stormed through him until his body was strung tight, a battle between what was right and what he wanted raging within.

Gently, she removed his hands from her face. She brushed by him and he frowned. She was leaving. Her loss was like a sucker punch to the gut, but it was for the best. No matter that she was taking his whole world with her.

Laney climbed onto the bench. "You want me, too. I know you do. I don't even have to see you to know it. I feel it."

The words, so different from what he expected, sent his brain scrambling.

As he watched, Laney spread her knees on the bench and braced her hands against the tub's edge. She looked over her shoulder. "Take what you want."

Her body drew him like a magnet. And then finally, *finally*, he surrendered to what they both wanted.

Hunching himself around her, Chrys pressed his back to her front. His cock slid between her thighs, so very close to her incredible velvet heat. He covered her hands with his against the edge of the spa. "What are you doing to me,

Laney?" he rasped.

She turned her face against his. "Loving you," she whispered.

The words slayed him.

She loved him. This smart, brave, sexy-as-all-hell woman loved him.

He couldn't wait another moment.

Pressing against her lower back, he forced her to arch and grind her rear into his groin. He tilted his hips, dragging the head of his cock against her heat, and drove home.

He filled her in one long stroke.

They both cried out. Chrys held her face and captured her lips, wanting to claim the sound of her pleasure, along with everything else. He broke free as his cock withdrew, then he slipped into an easy, languorous rhythm that allowed him to feel every inch of her tight channel. He used his hands to pin hers to the tub's edge, forcing their upper bodies together as his hips tilted and thrust. It was pure, sensual torture to not drive hard and fast. But this one time, he felt himself wanting to cherish, needing to savor.

She moaned, a high-pitched sound so full of pleasure. Under his hands, hers gripped and flexed. "Oh, God. Faster. Move faster."

He dragged his teeth down her neck, then softly bit the tendon that sloped into her shoulder. "No. Just feel this. Just feel me in you."

"Unnh, do that again."

He almost didn't hear her plea over the roar of the jets. "Do what?"

"With your teeth."

Aw, hell. Holding back his arousal had him gritting his teeth. "You want me to bite you, Laney?" She nodded. "Where?"

"Everywhere."

"Yeah," he whispered against the soft, wet skin of her neck. Still fucking her in excruciatingly good, slow strokes, he nibbled her there, biting her harder along that tendon, on her ear lobe, on the tendon behind her ear. Her approving moans shot right to his balls, making it harder and harder to take things slow.

"Can I ask you a question?" she rasped.

"Now?" He couldn't help but smile. "Fire away." Chrys caressed one hand over her front. Around the curves of her breasts, stroking over her nipples, drawing teasing circles lower and lower over her belly. She gasped and flinched. "You were saying?"

Laney let out a breathy chuckle. His fingers slipped between her legs, finding and circling the hard nub of her clit, and she moaned. "I want to make sure I do what you like."

The sentiment was as sweet as it was sexy. "You already are."

"No, I mean, if I wanted to, um, to go down on you, could I touch your…"

Holy fuck. Arousal kicked him in the back. He pounded into her harder, and swirled his fingers over her clit faster. "My what, Laney? Say it."

"Cock. Could I touch your cock?"

"Jesus. You've been thinking about touching my cock?" Maybe, just maybe, he could be ready for her to try touching him everywhere. And his cock was sure as hell a good place to start.

She nodded and moaned. "And taking it in my mouth."

"I would fucking love that, Laney. The touching and the sucking." He dropped his forehead against her back and forced his hips to still. It was too good. He couldn't make it last. But not before she found her pleasure. "You're going to come for me. And while you're doing it, you're going to tell me what else you've been thinking about." An idea in mind, he pushed her forward and a little to the left. "Spread your legs wider."

She gasped. "Chrys!"

He grinned. "You're going to spill everything that's going on in that pretty head of yours while that jet pounds your clit with hot water. Fuck me while you get off on the jet, Laney."

She ground her hips forward, thrusting her clit into the rush of water, then pressed back, impaling herself on his cock. She trembled and moaned and every bit of it was the most mind-blowing torture.

"Talk."

"O-okay. Um, it's hard to think."

He scraped his teeth on her neck again. "Good."

"Well, I…I wonder if you went down on me, if I could touch your hair." She moaned louder, her movements becoming faster, less even. "Your hair is soft. It makes me want to fist my hands in it. So I just need to know if I could do that."

He loved the contrast between his sweet Laney and the no-holds-barred Laney who came out during sex. "You think about pulling my hair while I'm eating your pussy?"

"God, *yes*."

"Come. Come right now."

Her hips jerked and pressed against the jetting water. Her walls tightened and clenched, and then she was crying out and milking him until he was biting the inside of his cheek to fight back his own orgasm. "That was fucking phenomenal. More."

Breathing hard, she sagged against the tub's edge. "I can't. I think I'm gonna pass out."

He pulled her up, setting her hips in front of the jet again. "Maybe you will, but not yet. I'm not done with you. Tell me more."

He stroked her clit as the water pounded, using his fingers to open her lips to the pulsing water. She shrieked and writhed and shook against him.

Laney slipped the hand he wasn't holding behind her back and slid her middle finger to the top of her crack. "I…I…was thinking about when you touched me here."

Each admission was more sensually devastating than the last. "You liked that?" She nodded, panting hard. "Has anyone ever touched you there? Has anyone ever taken you there?"

"Nooo," she moaned, thrusting against the jet.

"Would you like to be touched there?" She nodded again. "Now?"

"Please."

The need in that one word nearly had him emptying his balls. She was the sweetest fucking temptation he'd ever encountered, and though he wasn't ready to confront how she really made him feel, he wasn't obtuse enough to think she wasn't very, very special to him. And always would be.

"Hand back on the wall," he growled. The speed of her compliance put another nail in the coffin of his restraint. Standing behind her, he kept his strokes slow and dragged his hand from her front around to her back. He squeezed her beautiful ass, separating the cheeks and revealing her rear opening. He stroked two fingers over the tight pucker, reveling in the moan the light caresses unleashed, and then he pushed one finger in, just a little.

"Oh, my God." Her hips jerked, almost dislodging him from her pussy.

Chrys held the tip of his finger still, giving her a chance to get used to the feel of his intimate invasion there. Suddenly, she pushed back, impaling herself on his dick in her pussy and his finger in her ass.

In her arousal, her actions, her words, she was so honest and open and just fucking fearless. He found it sexy and appealing and admirable. He pushed his finger in further and then withdrew, fucking her with his finger while he—

"Omigod, I'm coming." Her passages went tight, tight, tighter, and then she was spasming around him and moaning and crying his name.

It was all he could take.

He pulled his finger free, gripped her hips, and said, "Hold on tight."

Every ounce of desire let loose as Chrys came at her with a series of hard, fast, shallow strokes.

"I shouldn't come in you because we don't have protection," he growled. "But I fucking want to." And he did. He *really* did. And damn if that desire didn't warrant some close consideration. But not now.

She unleashed an answering moan. "Come on me."

"Oh, gods, Laney." His brain shorted as the orgasm hit him in the back.

Suddenly, she pulled away and spun on the bench. Chrys almost lost his balance but then she grabbed his ass, hauled him up to her, and claimed his cock with her mouth right at the bubbling waterline.

He buried his hands in her hair and lost himself. Absolutely lost himself to this mortal woman. She sucked and licked and moaned around him as he came until he couldn't see, couldn't hear, couldn't breathe. The only thing he knew, the only thing he could feel, was his Laney holding him up, drinking him down, and accepting him in every single way.

Their connection—the way they fit together, the way they complemented one another, the fundamental feeling of rightness he felt when he was with her—he couldn't deny it any longer.

Whatever happened. Whatever was right or wrong. Whether the world woke up in the morning or was going to bed for the very last time. He loved Laney Summerlyn to the very center of his being.

The fierceness of the feeling simply wouldn't be denied.

Gently, she dropped him from her mouth and sat back in the bench. She peered up at him with the most ridiculously adorable innocent smile. "Hey, this jet works good on the back, too," she said.

He burst out in laughter, full-out belly laughter like he hadn't felt in, *gods*, months. At least. Bracing his hands on either side of her head, he leaned down and kissed her. He pulled back but kept his face close. "You know, you only asked about touching my cock, not my ass."

Her face was already flush from the sex and the steam, but he would've bet money that she'd blushed, too.

"I improvised. Sorry."

He grinned. "I'm not."

She smirked. "Good. Me, neither."

He kissed her again, a soft, lingering pulling of lips. "Thank you. The words aren't nearly enough, but I need you to know I appreciate everything you've done for me. And I wanted to say—"

Divine energy appeared nearby. A throat cleared.

Chrys growled. "Z, get the hell out of here."

Laney squeaked and sank lower in the water.

"I'm sorry, Chrys. For real. But we have to talk."

Seriously? Just when he'd resolved to tell her how he felt?

"It can wait."

"It can't."

"Z—"

"Chrys, it's Apheliotes. He's dead."

CHAPTER TWENTY-THREE

Rage a living monster coursing through his veins, Chrys guided Laney into Owen's living room. The pair of them were still dripping wet, having flown over after Chrys manifested them clothes. But none of that mattered. Aphel was dead. And Chrys had sent him right into the lion's den. Destruction and devastation. His fault. Again.

But not his alone.

No question that Chrys's existence had negatively impacted Eurus's when they were children. But enough was enough was e-fucking-nough. The child Chrys had been was not responsible—could never have been responsible—for the heinous evil that had become his brother's M.O. Once and for all, Eurus had to pay. Too many injustices had racked up. Thunder rumbled long and low overhead.

He surveyed the crowded room. His father, his brothers, most of the ordinal and inter-ordinal Anemoi. Owen had Megan and Teddy tucked under his arm. Boreas and Owen's neighbor, Tabitha, stood close together, whispering to each other. Without thinking about it, Chrys pulled Laney closer and wrapped his hand around hers.

Her touch felt natural, soothing, necessary. A small shining joy among the dark chaos.

Chrys turned to Zeph. "What the hell happened?"

"I don't know the specifics. We haven't found the body. I took Ella to stay with Mars until this passes. On the way back, the pall of divine death was suddenly palpable throughout the Realm of the Gods—the aching emptiness of it just made it feel like it was someone close, someone in the family. We were near Father's compound so we went to the Hall of the Winds. The light of the Southeast Wind was out."

Chrys pictured the enormous compass rose built into the floor of the ceremonial hall. Each of the sixteen points was tipped with a built-in lantern that contained the divine energy of the god who served as that wind's master. That any of the lights had been put out killed him. That it was one of his men, a god who'd served him true and faithfully for eons, was a blow to the heart. Chrys glanced at Laney. Was this the same light she saw surrounding the Anemoi? He shook his head and scanned his gaze over the group. "Hear me now. I will avenge Apheliotes." Whatever it took. However long it took.

Approving murmurs echoed around the room.

Aeolus stepped forward. "We are all expendable. It is not the god, but the wind he serves, that matters. So I ask each of you now. Are you prepared to stand and fight?"

The gods offered solemn agreement.

Aeolus moved to the center of the room. Anger and determination carved hard angles into his face. Thunder and lightning split the sky. "I say again. Are you prepared to stand and *fight?*"

A loud, fierce cheer of approval and commitment shook the room. Teddy fussed but didn't cry, as if even his divine energy understood the threat they faced.

"Make no mistake. We are at war. We will not all come out of it alive. Sacrifices will be made." He held up his maimed hand. "And you must understand the full extent of what you are up against. Eurus possesses the firestone ring. He has power over the winds, over each of you. This is my fault. I fully acknowledge it. And I stand ready to sacrifice myself to set this right." Murmurs sounded from around the room.

This...this was the resignation he'd seen on Aeolus's face. As many grievances as Chrys could voice against his father, he would fight to the last to prevent *any* of his family from dying. They'd lost enough. Had enough turmoil. For several lifetimes.

Aeolus continued. "Together, we are strong. He cannot take us all at once. We must fight. To avenge the death of one of our own who has fallen this night. To avenge wrongs against others of our numbers in recent days, weeks, and months. To preserve and protect the human realm, as is our duty and purpose."

Boreas pushed off the wall and stood tall. "In the name of the North Wind, I stand ready to fight."

Zeph nodded. "In the name of the West Wind, I, too, stand ready to fight."

"In the name of the South Wind, and in the name of vengeance for the Southeast Wind, I stand ready to kick some ass," Chrys said. "So what's our plan?"

Zeph's eyes flared deep blue light. "Take out Devlin."

Chrys held out his hands. "Wait. What? I thought—"

"He was standing on the cliffs," Boreas interrupted. "When we were attacked. It appears he led Eurus right to us."

Devlin was the cloaked figure he saw on Gibraltar? How the hell had he missed that newsflash? Chrys glared at Aeolus. "Sonofabitch. I *told* you."

"And I'll tell you what I told your brothers. There has to be another explanation. Devlin would not—"

"But he did," Zeph growled. "We all saw him there. Did he help Boreas? Did he intercede in the attack on our behalf?" He left the answers to the questions hanging there.

Boreas glanced at Megan and Teddy, then to Tabitha. He held her gaze for a long moment, then turned to face their father. "We can discuss Devlin further. A higher priority is getting out of the human realm before this fight breaks loose. We must take the war to the Realm of the Gods. If it happens here it will unleash unseen devastation."

Aeolus gave a tight nod. "Agreed." He looked from Chrys to Laney, then from Boreas to Owen's family. "We will go within the half hour."

Chrys heard his father's unspoken command: *say your good-byes.*

Aeolus began issuing orders to the lesser Anemoi, who resumed their sentinel duties in and around the house. Zeph and Boreas turned to Owen and Megan. Chrys couldn't hear what they were saying, but the looks on the couple's faces told him everything he needed to know.

Some of us aren't coming out of this alive. And everyone knew it.

Laney squeezed his hand. "Chrys?"

He turned to her and met her gaze. *I love you*, he thought. *You're the only woman I've* ever *loved.* Had it really only been a half hour ago that he'd nearly given voice to the words?

How could he possibly say them now?

How could he do anything to put Laney in any more danger? If he revealed his true feelings, she would throw herself more fiercely into protecting him and become an even bigger target.

The best thing he could do for her was stay away. Once and for all. The decision cut him deep, like a thousand icy shards filled his chest. He heaved a deep breath. "I regret it's not safe to take you home now."

"I'm not. I want to do something to help." She peered up at him, expectant.

Her willingness to help, to risk herself, was exactly the problem, wasn't it? It was why he admired her so completely and feared for her safety. He could never forgive himself if anything happened to her. Part of him would literally die.

He shook his head. "There's no place for you here." *It's too dangerous*. But he didn't voice those words, because he didn't want her to latch on to his concern as his reason for sending her away. He needed her to believe...*oh gods*... something it killed him for her to believe. That he didn't want her.

"But..." Hurt washed over her expression. Laney tried to mask it, she really did. "But I..." She shrugged. "My place is with you."

"No. Your place is your farm. Your human life, with the horses you love, and your friends. As soon as I can, I will take you back." The words were like crushed glass coming out of his throat. "I've enjoyed you, but I can't take care of you, Laney." He waved his hand at the room. "Not with all this going on, you know?"

Blue eyes flashed with anger. "I don't need you to take care of me. I love you."

The declaration pierced straight through him. He bit down onto his tongue until the taste of copper filled his mouth. "I told you I'm not the guy who sticks around. I'm sorry."

Laney's hands whipped to her throat. She tugged at the cord around her neck. "Here," she said, pulling it over her head.

He caught her hands. "I want you to have it."

A hard, fast shake of her head. "You said it has protective abilities. You should wear it. You're the one in danger." She pressed it into his palm. "Please, Chrys."

Even now, as he was breaking her heart, she thought of him first. The woman humbled him beyond all imagination.

Tears shimmered in her beautiful eyes. She pushed by, grabbed the molding to the kitchen doorway, and slowly walked into the next room. Away from him. His heart went with her, leaving a gaping, raw, empty place in his chest.

"Sure that's what you wanted to do, little brother?"

Chrys looked up into Zeph's concerned face. He stood where Laney had a moment before. Shaking his head, he said, "If you'd met Ella at this precise moment, would you have pursued her? Would you have drawn her further into this mess?"

Zeph's gaze bored into him.

"That's what I thought," Chrys said.

Over his brother's shoulder, Boreas caught Chrys's attention. Tabitha kissed his cheek, her worry and confusion apparent. The show of affection apparently caught him off guard, judging by the almost comical surprise the god wore on his face. But then Boreas cupped her cheek and kissed her softly on the lips.

Zeph's gaze followed Chrys's. "It's good to see, isn't it? It's like he's come back to life."

"Yes," Chrys said. And it was so true. Except for his white hair, which had spontaneously lost its brown color upon receiving the shocking news of Ori's death, Boreas was more his old self than Chrys had ever expected to see from him again.

Chrys couldn't have been happier to know that Boreas had found happiness again, that he might even be in the midst of finding love. Although why he'd open himself up to that now, of all times, he couldn't fathom. He looked away.

The hole where his own heart had been throbbed in empty agony.

But that was just his heart.

Nothing compared to what would happen if Laney died because of him. He'd lose his very soul.

ႸᎾᏟᎶ

Laney stood at the back door, staring at the great black nothingness, a combination of the dark and her night blindness. She couldn't be in the same room with Chrys. Not now. Not when she was so close to breaking down in tears, or begging him to love her back.

There's no place for you here. She hugged herself against the evening air.

The words echoed in her head until they ached a throbbing beat against her temples and behind her eyes.

In a short time, he'd take her back to Summerlyn and leave. And then, what? Was she supposed to pretend he wasn't out there somewhere? Was she supposed to forget that she knew *this* world—the one of gods and multiple planes of existence and divine wars—existed?

She'd feared that the brief return of her sight after they'd been in the elements would make it hard to go back to her blindness. But she already knew—it was going to be much, much harder to go back to her old life without Chrys than it would be if she could never see a single thing again.

Seth. What time was it? And where was he? Ever since the Anemoi had appeared out of thin air and she'd learned Chrys was hurt, the night had been a complete and total blur. In between realizing she was in love and getting dumped, she'd forgotten about the problem of explaining everything to her best friend. Now, there was nothing left to explain. Wasn't that convenient.

She retraced her steps into the kitchen and, after a few moments looking, found the handset to the cordless phone on the counter and dialed Seth's cell number.

"Hello," he barked.

"Where are you?"

"About two hours out. Trapped in stopped-dead traffic on 66. Accident. You okay?"

No. "Yeah. I was just getting worried about you."

"I figured with rush hour traffic, it would take me three or four hours to get to you, but this is ridiculous. This is the worst storm I've ever seen."

If only he knew. "Just take your time and be safe. I'll be here when you get here. You still have the address?"

"Yes." He blew out a long breath. "It's good to hear your voice."

"Yeah. Yours, too." She swallowed a knot that formed in

her throat. "See you soon."

They hung up and Laney sagged against the counter. She wanted nothing more than for Seth to get here. She didn't want to stay where she wasn't wanted, and Chrys had better things to be worrying about anyway.

The thought gutted her.

Shouts erupted from out back. A stream of gods ran through the kitchen, passing her in multicolored flashes of light.

Chrys paused in front of her just long enough to say, "Stay here." And then he was gone.

Heart in her throat, Laney crept into the mud room in the back of the house. Warm, humid air blew in through the screen door. Sticking to the shadows, she stepped as close to the screen as she dared. The yard beyond was now a riot of colorful auras, formed in a circle around a single god, judging by the dark, purple light. The newcomer's aura flashed and flared and rippled, sometimes appearing almost black, but occasionally a softer, calmer shade of purple pushed through the dark. Her heart tripped into a sprint. The flashes of black reminded her of the black light surrounding the god who had attacked her and Chrys.

"On your knees! On your knees!" someone shouted.

"I'm here to see Aeolus," a harsh voice said.

A number of angry responses rang out, and Laney couldn't hear who was saying what.

"What do you have to say for yourself, Devlin? What can you say to prove which side you're on?"

"There's no time for speeches. I have given you my word, Aeolus. Take it or don't. But you can all get off your high horses. Where have you ever been for me and my brothers while our father tortured us? Murdered one of us?"

"You work for your father. You do his noxious bidding," Chrysander said.

"And you make judgments without knowing all there is to know. Think what you will. I only came to warn Aeolus. Apheliotes is dead. Eurus tortured him. Knows he was on an errand for you." He paused. The purple light flared black. "He's coming. I'm sorry. I swear I didn't—"

The purple-black shot into the sky.

"After him!"

Other auras pursued. Shouting voices and frantic commotion made it impossible for Laney to follow what was going on. Where was Chrys? She couldn't perceive his gold light among all the others. And who was coming?

The lights of the Anemoi spread out, some on the ground, some in the sky.

An immense weight of anticipation hung in the air, which took on an almost electrical quality, like a storm approaching.

"Laney," a man's voice said. She turned, and the white aura revealed it was Owen. "Come away from the door."

"I can't see Chrys."

"He'll be okay. The safer you are, the more he'll be able to concentrate on keeping himself safe."

With one final look out over the dark yard, Laney moved toward Owen. He took her hand. She gasped and halted as an image sucked her in completely. Owen, standing in the middle of an overwhelmingly grand hall, silver fur robes hanging on his tall body. It disappeared as soon as it came, leaving a headache hammering against the backs of her eyes.

"Are you okay?" he asked.

"Yes." What was that? And why did it keep happening?

"Come on. Let's get you downstairs. Megan and Tabitha are already there."

"Is this necessary?" she asked as they descended the steps. Just how much danger was she in?

"Just a precaution."

Outside, thunder detonated. The house shook, and Laney hung on to the railing so hard her knuckles hurt. Somewhere, Teddy wailed.

"I'm going to pick you up." Owen scooped her off her feet and ran the rest of the way down. He made his way along a hall and into a room, where he placed her back on her feet. "Sorry."

She attempted a shaky smile. "I'll forgive you, this time." Truly, though, her knees were like jelly. Probably a good thing that Owen had carried her the rest of the way down. Seth would have a field day with an admission like that.

"What happened? Is she okay?" Megan asked over Teddy's breathless cries. "What's going on?"

"She's fine. I don't—"

Thunder exploded again. And again. Right overhead.

Laney shrank into herself and grabbed her head, like the sky might fall on it. Which didn't sound like an exaggeration.

"Come sit down," Tabitha said, taking her hand and leading her to a leather couch.

"Thank you," she said as she settled next to the other woman. Laney scanned her vision over the room, an office, it looked like, until she found Owen crouching on the floor in front of Megan.

"Is Eurus here?" Megan asked.

"Come here, big man." Owen took Teddy into his arms. The boy burrowed against his father's body, still crying, but less enthusiastically now. "I don't know if he's here. But I think he's coming. No matter what happens, I want you to stay here. All of you."

Eurus is coming? A shudder ripped through her.

An ominous rumbling sounded, as if from a distance. It got louder by the moment.

"What about you?" Megan asked. When he didn't answer, she said, "You're going to fight."

"I have to."

"Owen," she said, her voice tight with tears. "I can't lose you, too."

He pulled Megan's face in close to his, and whispered words Laney couldn't hear over the odd rumbling, then he spoke to Teddy in that same language Chrys sometimes used. "I love all of you," he said, passing the baby back to Megan.

He rose and left the room, pulling the door shut behind him.

Megan choked on a restrained cry. Laney eased down off the couch and made her way to Megan's side. Given how scared she was for Chrys, Laney could imagine some of what she must've been feeling. And, oh, God, what if Seth got here in the middle of this? She pushed the question away. She couldn't let herself go there, to a place where she might lose both Seth *and* Chrys.

"Owen loves you, Megan," she said. "He's not going to do anything stupid."

"I know," the other woman managed.

The rumble crescendoed to a roar and slammed into the side of the house. The whole building lurched. Upstairs, windows exploded. Laney screamed and flinched, her hands coming up to her ears. Crashes and thumps continued until she couldn't tell if she was shaking or if it was the house.

Tabitha joined them on the floor, forming a tight circle. "They're really gods?" she asked over the noise from above.

"Yes," Megan said. "I'm sorry about all this, Tabitha."

"Don't be. It's amazing, really. I'm just sorry—"

Thunder like an eruption shook the world. The lights went out.

Laney's cry was drowned out by Teddy's. God, she hated thunderstorms. *Hated* them. She gulped down a breath and forced herself to calm down. In the windowless room, it was pitch black—at least *that* she was more used to.

Megan groaned. "Oh, God, no."

"What is it?" Tabitha asked.

"Contraction," she gritted out.

"Give me Ted," Tabitha said. "I want you to breathe slow and deep. Have you had any false labor yet?"

"No," she said. "But that could be what this is, right?" The hope in her voice was plain.

"Yes, so just try to relax. Just breathe."

Laney found Megan's hand in the dark. She squeezed it through a series of percussive poundings. Thunder? Wind? Something else entirely? *Please don't let the baby come in the middle of whatever else is out there.* "I'm going to work on breathing with you so I don't hyperventilate." Megan gave a strained chuckle, and Laney talked to distract herself from the fear. Though she felt like she was shouting over the racket coming from all around the house. "When I was nineteen, I got turned around outside one night in a storm. I'd already lost my night vision and was completely blind in the dark. I couldn't find my way back to the house or the barn, or even find anything to try to take cover. I finally just sat down and waited it out. Felt like hours. I've been terrified of…storms ever…" She sniffed, once, twice. "Do you smell smoke?"

Neither did.

But with her diminished sight, Laney's other senses had strengthened. "I do. I swear I do."

"Hold Teddy. I'll go check it out."

"Be careful, Tabitha," Megan said.

Laney accepted the baby. He fussed and wiggled at the handoff. She could hear Tabitha's movements but not see. Even when the door opened, no light spilled in.

"She's right. It's stronger out here. Stay put for a minute."

Mere moments later, footsteps ran down the hall.

"Oh, my God. I'm so sorry, Megan. The house is on fire. It's coming down the steps. We have to get out of here."

CHAPTER TWENTY-FOUR

Chrys could hardly believe what he was seeing. Nor that Eurus was actually unleashing this horror upon the Earth.

The night sky was in chaos.

Bolts of multicolored lightning zinged through the air. Concussive blasts of thunder unleashed shock waves of turbulence that blew roaring winds this way and that. Rain slashed diagonally until it was almost impossible to see. Hail rained down in body-battering blasts. Trees had fallen—some brought down intentionally to close off the area. Homes had been damaged. Power lines were downed, wires twisting and sparking in the streets.

Aeolus wore the strain of attempting to rein in the elements in the tension on his face and in his muscles. Every time he was successful at drawing down the maelstrom of the storm, Eurus used the power of the ring to whip it up again.

Eurus had help in keeping Aeolus and the Anemoi distracted. A half-dozen Harpies swooped and screeched. And it appeared he'd lured a new ally into his malevolent cause—the Keres, female death daimons who lusted for the blood of dying and wounded men on the battlefield. The black-cloaked wraiths had gnashing teeth and vicious claws. Between the Harpies and the Keres, it was virtually impossible to get at Eurus.

Only Aeolus could get close. Father and son had engaged in nearly a half hour of grueling lightning-and-wind duels, neither making discernible headway.

Next to his father, Chrys was best equipped to take out the enemy. Between the season, the infernal dagger, and Laney's amulet, he was about as well protected as you could be. He pulled on his rage for Eurus and his grief for Apheliotes and threw himself into the confusion of the battle.

He flew up behind a wraith hard in pursuit of Livos. Fortunately, the Keres tended to prefer the easy pickings of those unable to fight back. Battle wasn't their specialty, and their situational awareness wasn't well developed. Chrys zoomed in close enough to slash the blade down the Keres's back, then veered hard left to avoid the imploding spray of blood into which it dissolved.

Chrys took out another and another, but there seemed an unending supply of the evil spirits.

Boreas and Zeph flew up. "We're going after Eurus. All of us. At once."

Chrys followed, determination flaring. They truly were strongest together. With the lesser Anemoi drawing away the Harpies and Keres, the three brothers launched themselves toward Eurus and all at once unleashed the combined power of their winds.

The blast knocked Eurus back, allowing Aeolus to get in an unblocked hit with a lash of lightning. Eurus screamed in thunderous rage, then unleashed a wild wall of wind that pounded into the Anemoi and scattered them uncontrollably.

Chrys slammed to the ground and rolled to the right just in time to avoid a swooping Harpy, talons out and ready to grab. Groaning from the impact, he saw the best news of the whole night. The flash of Eurus's lightning was dimmer, less frequent. *Almighty Zeus, please let that mean Father's strike hit something vital.*

"Chrys! Chrys!" Owen yelled from somewhere in the melee.

He shot to his feet and turned. "Holy fuck," he murmured. Owen's house was on fire. Every time rain smothered a section of flames, the winds breathed new life into it.

Laney. *Oh, gods, no.*

Owen raced up to him. "I can't get in. The fire's too hot. Megan, the baby—" He broke off, too choked up to continue.

He nodded. Chrys might not be powerful enough to defeat Eurus, as three solid months had more than proven, but he'd damn well use every bit of his power to save these humans, for whom he cared so deeply. "I've got it. Where are they?"

"Basement office. There's an exterior door around back."

Chrys whipped around to the rear of the house in an instant. He crashed through the door, sending glass and wood flying. "Laney? Megan?"

"We're here!"

Chrys rounded a corner and stopped. He could just make them out through the smoke, congregated outside of Owen's office door. Fire was roaring down the staircase along the wall that separated him from them. It had burned through the wall and ceiling above, which was sagging badly. The heat it gave off was enormous.

Come to Papa, he thought.

"I'm going to push back the fire and the heat," he shouted. "When I do, you run to the back door and stay there."

"Okay!"

Chrys shifted into his elemental form, moved to the center of the hall under the worst of the fire, called the heat into himself, and blew out the excess energy in a great gust that smothered the fire as long as he kept it going. *Run, run, run*, he thought. Because once he withdrew the current, the fire would come roaring back.

Relief flowed through him as the three women, Tabitha carrying Teddy, bolted beneath him and around the corner. Chrys retreated to the corner of the hall and watched as the fire tore back through the space. A section of ceiling collapsed, sending out a plume of heat and sparks. He stepped toward the conflagration and absorbed as much of the heat as he could. Deep satisfaction roared through him. As regretful as he was about the destruction of Owen's house, the fire's great heat replenished his energy and strengthened his body.

He materialized into corporeality as he rounded the corner, shaking with the force of the thrumming energy he now carried within. "Everyone okay?" he asked, looking to Laney. Thank the gods, she was unharmed. Rattled, but holding it together, and more beautiful than ever despite the smudge of soot on her brow.

"We're okay," Tabitha said. "But Megan's having contractions."

He nodded. "Okay if I take everyone to your house?"

"Of course."

"Everyone wrap an arm around one of mine. You have to be touching me, including Teddy."

Megan took his right. Tabitha took his left and wrapped the baby's arm around, too.

Laney came up behind him. "I'm sorry, but I have to do this." She pressed her front to his back and wrapped her arms around his stomach. She kissed his back, once, twice, and her love poured into him, warming and bolstering him, and making him realize he'd never given a second thought to the other women's touches. He pressed his hand over one of hers, and shifted them into the elements.

Chrys eased out the door and drifted to the corner of the house. Carrying this many beings into the elements drew on his reserves, but the fire had given him energy to spare. He moved slowly, carefully. The Harpies and the Keres could perceive divine energy, so being elemental didn't guarantee he wouldn't capture anything's notice. And if that happened with all these mortals, with Laney…

No. Focus, damnit.

He peered around the corner. Coast clear.

Pouring on the extra energy he'd imbibed from the fire, he shot across the long stretch of open space separating the houses. Half way across, a flash of light caught his attention.

Eurus had Owen pinned against the front of the house. With the fire at his back and Eurus and his lightning lance at his front, he was trapped. *Sonofabitch.* As a demigod, Owen had the least chance of any of them to weather an attack by Eurus.

Where the hell was Aeolus? Boreas? Zeph?

Chrys continued to the back corner of Tabitha's house and manifested. "Go inside," he said. He hated not seeing them in safely himself, but Eurus was raising the weapon for a death blow. Odd that Eurus was using his weaker hand to wield the lightning—Chrys didn't have time to think on it. He took off across the space, materialized the infernal dagger, and threw it with all his might.

A blast of divine energy blew in front of Owen, shielding him and throwing him off balance. He fell to the ground.

The lance of lightning struck right through the center of the energy signature, which flashed and flickered between its corporeal and elemental forms, just as the dagger stuck deep into Eurus's shoulder.

Two screams of agony rocked the nighttime world.

Eurus wrenched the dagger free and whipped it back toward Chrys who, with a massive guest of wind, blew it off course. Eurus staggered and weaved, and triumph roared through Chrys when he noted the gray mottled skin on the hand he'd slashed the previous day with the dagger. *Hell yes, it worked!* And now he'd struck him again.

Eurus shot off into the sky. The remaining Harpies and Keres retreated en masse.

Chrys reached the front corner of the house, and every bit of that triumph drained away. "No!" He skidded to his knees in the wet grass.

Boreas lay on his back in his human form, a great savage hole through his chest.

Owen crawled to him. "Gods, no. Boreas." Calling on his powers as a snow god, Owen cupped his hands over the gaping wound. White light slipped through the cracks of his fingers. His hands turned white and icy with frost, the cold energy a soothing balm for a god of the North.

"Keep going, Owen. I'll move us. We have to get him away from the heat of this fire."

Sweat streamed down Owen's face. He nodded.

Chrys grabbed Boreas's hand and reached for Owen's shoulder. He willed them into the elements and away a safe distance from the fire's heat. He manifested them in the soft, cool grass in front of Tabitha's house.

"B, you're going to be okay, man. Eurus is gone. It's over for tonight."

Zephyros and Aeolus burst into corporeality behind Chrys and knelt beside him. Footsteps squished in the wet grass and Megan, leaning on Tabitha and Laney, joined the circle of Boreas's family. She eased down next to Owen, tears streaking her face as she stroked her hand over Boreas's short hair.

"Oh, gods," Zeph said before he reined in his reaction. "We're here, Boreas. We'll fix this." He cupped his hands around Owen's. A golden, healing light spread over Boreas's chest. Of all of them, Zephyros's energy was the strongest and had the most powerful ability to heal.

Hope flared in Chrys's chest as the visible strain left Boreas's face. Chrys turned and sought out Livos, standing behind him on the street. He waved him over. Livos took a knee. "We need cover. All of you, draw in a fog. Thick as you can. And track down my dagger. We can't lose it." Livos nodded and left, and Chrys turned back to Boreas.

"We have to stop meeting this way," Zeph quipped.

"Yes." A great wracking cough seized Boreas. Blood spilled over his lips. "O-wen, son?" He scanned his gaze over the group, his normally silver eyes dulled to a flat gray.

"I'm here, Boreas. Right here," Owen grunted, his arms shaking as he poured the cold energy into his father.

Fog began to roll in around their position, dense and obscuring.

Boreas's head lolled toward Owen. "You...are great... father." He coughed again. More blood trickled from the side of his mouth. "I'm so...proud...you."

"Don't," Owen bit out. "Don't you even think of saying good-bye."

Boreas dragged his hand up, as if in slow motion, and placed it atop Owen's. "Have to. My...time's over," he slurred.

Megan pressed a kiss to Boreas's forehead. "Your time is just beginning. Do you hear? We love you," she said in a tear-strained voice.

Boreas managed a small smile. "You're best...thing ever... happened to him, Meg..."

Chrys saw what was happening. He'd seen the size of the hole, Boreas's blood loss, and now his struggle to speak and breathe. The cold energy Owen poured into him, the healing energy Zephyros spread over him—they were mere Band-Aids. Analytically, intellectually, he knew this. But his heart... his heart could not begin to accept the tragedy unfurling before him.

His beloved brother was dying.

Chrys whirled on Aeolus, kneeling at Boreas's feet, pale-faced and eyes filled with horror. "Do something!"

Aeolus dragged his gaze from Boreas and gave a nearly imperceptible shake of his head. He might as well have shouted, "There is nothing to be done." Their father turned back to Boreas and rested a hand on his shin. "I grant my permission, and my blessings, to transfer your godhood."

"Thank you," Boreas rasped. At the same time, Chrys, Zeph, Megan, Owen—all of them—issued a collective protest. Owen turned to look at Megan, regret and devastation on his face. Boreas's gasping coughs quieted the group. "Zeph, please keep your healing going long enough…"

To keep me alive, Chrys finished in his mind. And the words cut deep into his soul, unleashing a physical pain that raced through his veins until he could hardly stand it. "B, fight it."

But Boreas didn't respond, and Chrys didn't hold it against him, because it was an impossible request. Great waves of grief slamming his heart into his ribcage, Chrys found Laney's sad, horrified gaze across the small circle. He wanted to go to her, hold her, shield her from everything painful and unjust and tragic in the world. He wanted her heat and her compassion and her touch to bolster him when he felt he could stand no longer.

"Owen." Boreas patted his hands. "Release me."

"No."

"Owen."

"No, Boreas, no." Tears spilled from his mismatched eyes. "No."

With an unseen reserve of power, Boreas pushed Owen's hands away from the wound. "Closer," he said. "Lean…over."

Owen braced his arms on either side of Boreas's head and looked down onto his father's face. The younger god's back trembled with restrained grief.

Arms shaking, Boreas pressed one palm to Owen's heart, and one to his head. He spoke in low, rasping, stuttering words in the ancient language.

"*As m-master of the North…Wind, as guardian of Winter*"—he coughed for a long moment, more blood flowing forth—"*I command…the great, cl-cleansing winds of the…North t-to bow to the…n-new master now*"—he gasped, his breaths making a whistling sound—"*now before them.*

It is not the…vessel of the g-god, but…the wind that m-must be…honored and…protected." He sucked in a deep rasping breath. *"I command the North Wind, with…all of its powers, p-privileges, and…duties, into Owen, son of Boreas,…s-son of Aeolus, and c-commend him as…the next…Supreme God of the North Wind and Guardian of Winter. I have looked into his…heart…and his mind, and he is worthy."*

Owen's big shoulders shook. Megan's sobs rang though the pre-dawn gray, and Laney wrapped her arms around the other woman's shoulders.

The North Wind, called by the incantation, swirled in a light breeze, round and round. All about them, snow fell. The wind whipped it into a fragile cocoon around the whole mourning group. Inside, the breeze still circulated, as if waiting.

Chrys shivered mercilessly, more from the inconsolable grief overflowing his chest than the ravaging cold. It was nearly done.

"Repeat," Boreas gasped. He lifted his eyebrows in silent questioning. Owen nodded. Boreas haltingly stated three more lines.

Owen repeated them in the ancient language, his voice a raw scrape. *"I accept the power, the privileges, and the duties of the North Wind. I will be a fair and faithful master and a true and conscientious guardian. From this moment until I am no more."* A single sob escaped him. "I love you, Father."

Boreas had just enough time to offer a small, knowing smile. Silvery-white light lifted from Boreas's body, pushing Owen into an upright position on his knees. The light congregated in a blindingly beautiful orb and shot into Owen's chest. The North Wind inside the cocoon whipped into ever-tighter circles around the whole length of Owen's body. All at once, it seized him. Owen's body went rigid, and then seemed to absorb the swirling wind.

He collapsed to his side. Zeph just managed to catch him. The thin, snowy walls of the cocoon drifted to the ground.

"Owen!" Megan wailed, scrabbling around the group to him.

His eyelids eased open and he slowly pushed himself into a kneeling position. He grasped Boreas's still hand in his and tugged Megan in tight against his chest.

Boreas was gone.

Chrys's heart railed against the reality, his mind spun and scrambled for a different interpretation, for anything else in the world to be true.

Hot tears spilling down his cheeks, Chrys laid a hand on Owen's bent back. Zephyros's hand joined him, as did Aeolus.

Movement in his peripheral vision caught Chrys's attention. All the surviving lesser Anemoi surrounded them, kneeling, heads bowed.

Chrys dragged his focus back to the group, and his gaze found Laney's, her face a mask of grief. Hand over her mouth, tears streamed from puffy eyes. That she felt so deeply for his family made him love her even more. How that was possible, since he loved her beyond all reason already, he didn't know.

But that only added to the burden of his grief. Because Boreas's death reinforced every one of his misgivings where Laney was concerned. The danger of pulling a human into his life, his world was too great. The risks were too massive. And Chrys could make room for nothing more in his life right now than the vengeance he needed to exact.

He wasn't sure how long they stayed that way, encircled not as gods, but grieving together as a family.

Aeolus's head wrenched up. His gaze flashed to the side. Chrys tracked the movement and then heard what had captured his father's attention. A man's voice. Shouting. Calling. Calling Laney's name. The voice bounced off the thick fog, seemingly coming from multiple directions.

Chrys shoved to his feet. Aeolus followed.

Laney appeared next to him, her expression totally bewildered. "Seth," she rasped. "It's Seth."

"What?" Chrys bit out.

"Last night, with everything, I forgot to tell you," she whispered. "He threatened to call the police, so I told him…" She stepped forward, clearly searching for the other man in the fog.

His dark form suddenly appeared, maneuvering through the debris and devastation.

As he called her name again, Laney stepped further forward. It was clear the minute Seth saw her. He took off at a run toward her. Glaring at Chrys, he pulled her into his arms.

Laney gasped and stood rigid, as if caught off guard, but after a moment, she returned the embrace.

"Thank God. Are you okay?"

The hatred pouring off the human was nearly a physical thing, but Chrys was too numb with grief to feel it. And now, seeing the woman he loved in another man's arms—it was nearly more than Chrys could take.

"Jesus, it's like a war zone. There was this whirling cloud and lightning like I've never seen. The police have everything cordoned off for blocks and blocks. But I found a way in. I thought—" Seth shook his head. "What the hell is going on?"

Right there. Right there was a man who would take care of Laney Summerlyn. If Chrys walked like he should—like he'd said he would—Laney wouldn't be without someone. Cold desolation filling him up until he could hardly breathe, Chrys turned away.

Dawn approached. Light enough existed to show the devastation of the neighborhood. Damaged houses, including the still-smoldering ruins of Owen's, downed trees, smashed cars, the corpses of otherworldly creatures, including some of the inter-ordinal Anemoi, who would turn to dust when sunlight laid upon them.

"We must go," Aeolus said in a low voice, as if he didn't want to disturb the solemnity that still hung over Boreas's body.

Slowly, the others all rose. Owen lifted Boreas's body into his arms. Zeph stepped forward to support Megan, weak with exhaustion and grief.

Chrys let his gaze drift back to Laney, now standing beside Seth. The man's expression was part lethal, part bewildered. "Father, the humans must seek shelter with us until we can figure this out," Chrys said. They had to get their dead back to the Hall of the Winds before sunrise, but no way he was leaving Laney here unprotected. Not with Eurus and Devlin still out there.

Owen's gaze cut to Aeolus. His eyes. Still brown and blue, but now the light that flared from them was brighter, lighter, infused with flecks of silver.

Aeolus looked from Megan to Laney and Seth to Tabitha. "So be it." He turned to the lesser Anemoi. "Gather the dead. Leave no one behind."

"We're not going anywhere," Seth said. "I'm taking Laney

home."

Chrys refused to meet Laney's eyes. He couldn't bear to see whether she *wanted* to go. "Not up for discussion."

Seth got right up in his face. "I agree completely. We're *leaving*."

The man's eyes. They possessed an odd reflective quality Chrys hadn't noticed before. Rage washed off Seth and, with it, the same hint of supernatural energy he'd felt before.

Aeolus shoved the two of them apart and glared down at Seth. He jerked his hand away from the human and stared a long moment. "What are you?"

Seth frowned, but Lacey stepped between him and the god. "He's my friend."

Aeolus gave the man another long, assessing look, then nodded. "Bring them," he said to Chrys, then turned away. "Time is short."

Laney wrapped her arms tight around herself. For a moment, she looked so lost and alone that Chrys had to go to her, hold her, touch her. He pulled her into his arms. Her fingers fisted into his shirt, as if holding on for dear life.

He held her for a long minute, and then he tipped her chin up with his fingers. "I am sorry beyond measure that I pulled you into the middle of this."

She glanced away, toward Seth, then opened her mouth as if to speak.

"Please, let me finish," he said. "We have to get Boreas back to the Realm of the Gods before the sun rises, and I can't leave you here. Not now."

Her eyes went wide. "I can go to the Realm of the Gods?"

"Normally, it is forbidden. But Father can invite you into his home if he so chooses." When the Olympians found out humans had been there, there would likely be hell to pay, but really, so much shit was waiting to hit the fan that one more thing wouldn't make much of a difference. "However, I must make you sleep for this trip." Human consciousness couldn't well tolerate the transition between the human and divine dimensions.

"I trust you, Chrys. Whatever you need, I'll do."

Were his heart not already buried under so much grief, the words would've pierced him.

One hand around her back, he pressed his other to her forehead. A warm, soothing wind poured over her and dragged her under. She went limp, and he caught and lifted her into his arms.

Seth lunged, but Aeolus blocked his path and forced him into unconsciousness. He hefted the man over his shoulder. "There's something about this one," he said.

Chrys nodded, but now wasn't the time to figure it out.

Zeph and Livos repeated the process with Megan and Tabitha.

In the east, the first slivers of dawn threatened.

One by one, they shifted into their elemental forms and shot skyward toward a future that no longer made any sense.

CHAPTER TWENTY-FIVE

Dressed in long ceremonial robes, Chrysander stood at the South point on the giant compass rose inlaid into the floor of Aeolus's Hall of the Winds. The ceremonial hall was huge and round, with a domed ceiling that gave it the soaring feeling of a temple. Murals telling the stories of the exploits and service of the Anemoi decorated the walls in muted hues.

At the start of the private installation ceremony, five of the sixteen spots stood open, the corresponding lanterns dark. A sixth spot stood open while the light still burned — Eurus's cardinal spot in the East. In addition to Boreas and Apheliotes, the gods of the North Wind and Southeast Wind, the compass rose stood empty on its East-Northeast, West-Southwest, and South-Southeast positions.

They'd lost five good, nay, *great* men last night. His heart hurt so badly, Chrys still found it nearly impossible to draw in a full breath.

Aeolus made his way around the circle, first installing three new inter-ordinal Anemoi, all the eldest sons of their deceased fathers. He promoted Phoenicias from god of the East-Southeast Wind to become Apheliotes's successor in the Southeast, and Phoenicias's son succeeded his father. One by one, the new gods filled in and fortified their circle. New lights shone in each of their lanterns.

The ceremony was needed and it would strengthen them, but it also emphasized that nothing would ever be the same.

And then Aeolus stepped to the top of the circle, where a large ornate 'N' was tiled into the floor. Owen stood back from the circle, outside of it, in long fur robes reminiscent of the kind Boreas used to wear.

"Owen, chosen son of Boreas, son of Aeolus, step forward to claim your godhood and your rightful place as Supreme God of the North Wind and Guardian of Winter."

For a long moment, Owen stared at the dark blue 'N.' Chrys could only imagine the grief weighing down on Owen now. In one fell swoop, he'd lost his father and the quiet life he'd chosen and built with Megan, Teddy, and the baby on the way. As a full god, his life was no longer wholly his own, and he came to power in the midst of war, when nothing was certain and no one was safe.

Owen stepped into place as the master of the North Wind. He repeated the words he'd said for Boreas during the night: "I accept the power, the privileges, and the duties of the North Wind. I will be a fair and faithful master and a true and conscientious guardian. From this moment until I am no more." His voice was heavy with sadness.

Aeolus lifted the circular glass lantern out of the floor and opened a door on the side. Since Boreas had already bestowed his northern energy, the interior was empty. Except... Aeolus reached in and removed something. "Open your hand," he said quietly. "The day you married Megan, Boreas arranged for these to be placed here. They each now contain remnants of his divine energy."

Owen extended his hand and received the gift. For a long moment, he struggled to rein in his grief. His brow furrowed, his eyes squeezed closed, his lips pressed tight together. And then he nodded and opened his eyes. "Thank you," he rasped. Just like Boreas to do something so unexpectedly thoughtful, whatever it was.

"Your light will guide and lead the North Wind. Place it within so all will know you as its master."

Owen raised his other hand and turned it palm up. He looked at it, concentration plain on his face, and a small orb of bright white light lifted from his skin, hovered. He placed it within the lantern.

Aeolus secured the door with a skeleton key and lifted the lantern high. "Long live the North Wind."

"Long live the North Wind," everyone answered, the joined voices echoing against the cavernous ceiling.

Aeolus gave the key to Owen to safeguard, for the only one who should ever have access to that divine energy was the god himself, then he settled the lantern into its space on the floor, completing the circle. Once again, sixteen lights shined, although one threw a pall over each of the other fifteen.

But Chrys had seen proof in Eurus's desiccated hand that the infernal dagger was effective against him. And that gave him hope.

As the group began to break up, Owen stood looking a little lost. Zeph must've seen it, too, because they both crossed the compass rose to him at the same time.

Owen glanced up, pain shining out of his strange eyes. He

opened his palm. Three faceted crystal snowflakes glimmered in the low light. "He always gives us snowflakes." He cleared his throat. "Gave."

"You brought him back to life, Owen. These past few years were the happiest he'd had in a very long time."

Chrys nodded. "That kind of happiness means everything, and the three of you gave it to him." He felt Zeph's gaze on him. "What?"

His brother arched a brow. "If happiness means so much, why are you throwing yours away?"

Owen crossed his arms and tilted his head, as if waiting to hear the answer, too.

"I don't know what you're—"

"Don't," Owen said, his eyes flaring with that new silver light. "Don't pretend you don't know what he's talking about. Not on the day we lay my father to rest. Honor Boreas's death by living your life."

Chrys planted his hands on his hips, pressure filling his chest. Didn't they know how badly he wished he could just have what he wanted, consequences be damned? "It is *her* life I am trying to protect."

"We are in the shit right now, Chrys. There's no doubt about it," Zeph said. "But this war will end. She's here. She's seen the worst. Maybe you should give her a say in it." He gripped Chrys's shoulder. "Just be sure before you throw away forever. It doesn't come along very often."

"That's for damn sure," Owen said. "Speaking of forever, I'm going to go find Megan. Thank the gods, her labor pains stopped, but I think she's in shock." He tugged his hand through his black hair. "We have a lot to figure out."

"And you will," Zeph said. "Go. She must be eager to see

you." The new god of the North Wind stepped away. "Oh, and Owen?"

He turned, the fur robes swirling around him.

"You are our brother as surely as Boreas was. Don't hesitate to ask for anything."

Chrys nodded. "That's the damn truth."

"Thank you…brothers."

As he watched Owen stride toward the ornate doors, Chrys didn't envy the challenges the new god of the North Wind and Megan now faced. At least Ella was a goddess, and she and Zeph could live together in the Realm of the Gods. While Boreas had found a way to extend the span of Megan's life, she was still a mortal, still human, and as such could not live in this realm. Zeus strictly forbade it.

Now that he thought of it, their situation offered yet another reason why Laney was better off without him. How many sacrifices did he expect her to make for him? Not that he'd ever voice such a thing. Owen had enough to deal with right now, and Zeph often regretted that Ella never had the chance to choose her goddesshood for herself. He'd made that decision for her, though there wasn't a chance in hell she would've chosen any differently.

What would Laney choose? The thought slid insidiously through his brain.

He knew the answer. He could still hear her voice declaring her place to be with him. No matter how much he yearned to make that come true, he wasn't worth that kind of sacrifice, and Chrys would never ask her to make it.

৪৩৫৪৪

Laney woke up with a start and sat bolt upright. For a moment, she had no idea where she was. The bedding below her fingers was silky soft. Ahead of her, the wall seemed to be made of light. She scanned her vision over the space, attempting to assemble the puzzle. The details she gathered told her it was a bedroom…

Memories returned to her in a rush. The fire, the battle, Boreas's death. Her throat went tight as she recalled the devastation in everyone's voices as they'd said their good-byes. The love they'd all shared was one of the most beautiful things she'd ever witnessed, and their loss of it, one of the most tragic.

"I don't want to lose you, Chrys," she whispered into the silence. But she already had, hadn't she? Her heart of hearts demanded that he loved her, too, that he'd showed it time and again even if he'd never said the words. Wishful thinking, no doubt.

Now, it was just a matter of time before he returned her to Summerlyn.

Nearly overwhelmed just about every way you cut it, Laney took a moment to scan her gaze over the floor. It appeared clear of obstacles. She got up and crossed the room. Was this truly the Realm of the Gods? How long had she slept? Where was Chrys? And what had happened to Seth?

Seth. Laney sucked in a breath and spun her feet to the floor, a strange memory flooding back to her. When Seth had hugged her upon their reunion, Laney had gotten the oddest image in her mind. It was Seth, but not as a man. As a lion. Sorta. He'd had wings, too, and a great bird's head.

Voices sounded outside in the hall.

Debating for a moment, she slowly crossed the room

toward the muffled conversation and dragged her hand along the far wall. Her fingers found a handle and she cracked open the door.

Owen's bright white aura was the first thing she noticed— brighter than it had ever been before. Megan walked beside him.

"Dada, Dada," Teddy's voice called out.

After everything they'd been through, she didn't want to intrude, but they spotted her before she could retreat.

"Are you okay, Laney?" Megan asked.

"Oh, yes. I just woke up and I…" She shrugged.

"Things just broke up," Owen said. "I'm sure Chrys'll come find you in a few. Aeolus has had a feast prepared."

"We're going to get Tabitha," Megan said. "We'll see you there."

Laney's stomach flip-flopped. A divine feast in the Realm of the Gods. How much more magical and fantastical could her day get? That strange lion-bird image shot into her mind and she didn't let herself answer that. "All right. Thanks."

Owen lifted Teddy into his arms and turned. A flapping of heavy fabric sounded out.

She scanned her gaze over the retreating family. It was very possible her sight was failing her, but she would've sworn that Owen was wearing long, silvery robes. Just like the ones she'd seen in her mind's eye when he had taken her hand to lead her to safety.

"That's not possible," she said to herself.

"Oh, but it is," a voice said from behind her.

Laney whirled, her heart in her throat. Judging by the grey, metallic aura, another god stood before her. "Who are you?"

He hobbled closer. "You don't remember?"

"Should I?" Now that she thought about it, there was something familiar about his short height and gruff voice… The old man from her dream. She gasped. "But it was just a dream," she murmured.

"Incorrect. It was a visitation. And I bestowed upon you a gift."

"Gift?" She focused on the god and struggled to bring his details into focus. Unkempt brown hair. Hunched back. Gnarled hands. It *was* the man from the dream she'd had the day Chrys posed as a contractor.

"The gift of prophecy. Life is about balance. You lost one sight. I gave you another."

Another? Dizziness threatened. "I don't understand. You mean…the things I've seen were visions? Like, the future?"

"Yes. Your ability will get stronger with time."

"Seth," she whispered, her mind reeling. How could what she'd seen be his future?

"Is safe. And he is also a griffin. Or, at least, he could be. The blood runs through him, if distantly."

"A…griffin? What is that?" she asked, not sure she really wanted to know.

"King of the beasts. Guardian of priceless treasure. Part lion, part eagle. Very strong. Very courageous. Paired with your line long, long ago. For protection, of course."

"My line?" she asked, mind absolutely swirling with all this information.

"Distant descendant of Auxesia, one of the three Horae— the one who watches over nature's growth in summer."

Laney shook her head, absolutely speechless. Both their names actually *meant* something? Actually connected them, even if only in a small way, to this magical world? Her heart drummed a fast beat against her chest. She pressed her palm there to keep it from flying away. This was all so crazy. Starting with the idea that she would be able to see the future. What could she do with an ability like that? How could she help people with it? The possibilities were overwhelming. "Your gift…it's truly amazing," she finally said. "Thank you. "

He gave a small bow. "I am Hephaestus. I have been keeping an eye on you."

His words should've brought fear, but for some reason they didn't. "Why have you watched me?"

"Because I am always curious how things work and what makes people tick. And because we are alike."

A nervous laugh spilled from her. "How so?"

"Both of us have bodies that could hold us back, but we haven't let them now, have we?"

She thought of the hunched over way he walked, recalled an image from her dream of gnarled feet and hands. This god felt some affinity with her because of her blindness? As if he hadn't already honored her enough with his gift. She grappled with how to respond. "We all have our challenges," she finally said.

"Indeed. And there's that genuine, selfless character again, rare and unusual qualities in my experience. "

She struggled to keep up with the unusual god's pronouncements. "I don't…really know what to say to that. Thank you," she rushed to add. "But…I'm just like anyone."

"Ach. You are not. Three times you have risked your life for another."

"Chrys? It's what anyone would do for someone they—" Heat spread across her face. She hugged herself.

"Ah, yes. So you *do* love him?" He stepped closer, and

Laney realized she was taller than him because of the way his back and shoulders had curled.

What did it hurt to answer? If he'd truly watched her, he already knew. "Yes."

"Then I have a question for you."

The hair raised on her arms and the blood raced in her veins. Laney's stomach tingled, like she was balanced on the edge of a vast cliff. "Dare to know," she whispered to herself. She met the god's expectant gaze. "Okay. What is it?"

"If you had the choice between the return of your visual sight or remaining blind and gaining long life, which would you choose?"

A shiver passed through Laney's chest and over every inch of her skin. Such a thing was possible? And this god had the power to offer it? Laney's whole life narrowed to this one moment. "What do you mean by long life?" she asked, nearly breathless.

"The ability to stay with immortal Chrysander for as long as you wish, but mostly blind, as you are now."

The walls of the room swam and buckled. Laney swayed.

Hephaestus's rough, calloused fingers gently caught her arms. "Steady, lass."

"I wouldn't grow old or die?" She shook her head. "I don't even know that he wants me."

"And what if he did?"

Her heart thundered, sending blood roaring through her ears. If there was even a chance, Hephaestus was offering them a way to be together forever. "The choice would be easy. I would choose love, so I would have to choose long life and blindness."

"Would you like to make this choice?"

"Laney," a voice behind her rasped. She turned. Chrys stood in the doorway. How long had he been there? She dragged her gaze up his big body to his face. He was shaking his head. "Don't do this. I'm not worth it. You could see again."

Hope and fear filled her chest in equal proportions. "I don't want my sight. I want you."

"Hephaestus, please," he said.

"The choice is hers, Chrysander Notos. She has earned it."

"Remember your joy when we flew in the elements," Chrys said, his voice desperate. "Remember your wonder at getting to see again. The sun, Laney. Sappho, your farm, your books…a million things. You could have all of it again."

She shouldered back the side of her psyche that latched on to his rejection, and listened to what he wasn't saying. It *wasn't* that he didn't love her. It *wasn't* that he didn't want her. It was that he didn't think he was worthy of her sacrifice of these things.

Her heart ached for him. "You *are* worthy, Chrys." Her choice would prove it to him. As soon as the words left her mouth, certainty flooded over her in a warm rush. She turned back to Hephaestus. "I would like to make the choice. Long life and blindness."

"So be it." Hephaestus pressed one gnarled finger to her forehead and another to her heart. Electric tingles ran through her, and a white haze descended over her mind. Chrys's voice sounded out, but Laney couldn't decipher the words. She seemed to float outside herself for a long moment. Then, in a rush, she slammed back in. Her knees buckled, and she fell.

Warm arms caught her, cradled her against an even warmer chest. The rightness of the feeling flowed through her. The hazed lifted. Was it done? Was it really true?

Hephaestus leaned over her. "Indeed it is."

"I said that out loud?" The old god grinned and nodded. She grasped his hand and kissed a gnarled knuckle. "Thank you."

"You have chosen powerfully, Laney Summerlyn. You shall keep your prophetic sight." He straightened, at least as much as he could. "This is for you, Chrysander. Do not open it until you've made *your* choice." He hobbled two steps backward and lurched to a stop. "Oh, and we finished your barn roof. No thanks to you, Notos."

Then he disappeared.

⊱⊰

Chrys looked from the now empty floor in front of him, still echoing with the series of wild pronouncements, to the incredible woman lying in his arms. Overwhelmed by the sheer magnitude of her sacrifice, he sank the rest of the way to his knees.

Every reason he'd used to convince himself they couldn't be together fell away, and, in a great rush of faith, Chrysander surrendered. To need, to want, to love.

She had given up something for which she had long yearned for the mere *possibility* of a love, and a life, with him. With *him*.

Yet, she had no idea how he felt about her. How powerfully love and admiration and pure, simple *awe* flowed through him for her. All she knew were the lies he'd told— that he didn't want her, that his life had no room for her. The lies were a shameful disgrace in the face of the enormous gift she'd bestowed on him. A disgrace he needed to correct right now.

"Chrys—"

"I love you," he rasped, his throat so tight the words were barely audible. He swallowed, hard, and crushed her to him. "I love you," he said louder. "I want you. And I'm so sorry—"

"You love me?" Joy scattered every doubt from her beautiful eyes. A smile brightened her whole face, even as her eyes glassed over. "I love you, too. Nothing means more to me than you."

Chrys cradled her face and kissed her for all he was worth. Every longing, every yearning, every hope he'd ever had for and about her, he poured into the kiss. Her love and acceptance were like a balm to his soul, warming those places that had been left cold and unattended his whole, long existence. Breathing hard, he pulled away. "I want to make love to you."

Cheeks flush, lips swollen, she nodded. He saw his desire mirrored back to him on her lovely face. "I'm yours. Always."

He rose in one movement and crossed to the big bed, sending a rush of the South Wind behind him to secure the door. Willing their clothes away, he sprawled her on the center of the bed and climbed between her spread thighs. His cock twitched and throbbed, already aching for their joining. He dragged his fingers from her throat to the soft curls between her legs. He rubbed his thumb over the hard nub of her clit. She was already wet and wanting with desire. For him.

"Jesus, you are gorgeous and so damn sexy. I want to spend the rest of my life exploring you, bringing every one of your fantasies to life. But right now, I have to get in you."

She grasped his cock and guided him to her opening. "I need you."

He thrust forward and filled her in one slick penetration. An ecstatic groan tore out of him. Nothing had ever felt more right, like he was exactly where he was supposed to be. Like he was home.

Laney threw her hands above her head and arched beneath him. "You feel so good, Chrys."

Bracing his fists on either side of her stomach, his body took over, moving in deep, fast strokes through her tight heat. The iron amulet knocked against his chest in time with the grinding rhythm. He dragged his gaze down her body, alive and writhing with arousal. Her hips rocked, her breasts shook, her teeth scraped at her bottom lip, her hands fisted and grasped at the covers above her.

Seeing a lover this way wasn't something he was used to. And Laney…she was absolutely breathtaking to behold. And he wanted to feel her, feel *this*, every bit of it.

"Laney," he rasped, the foreign desire to *touch* resurrecting a hint of his ancient anxiety.

"I love you," she panted.

The declaration, so freely given, so deeply felt, blanketed the apprehension just enough that he thought he could take the chance… "Touch me." His heart tripped into a sprint. "Oh, gods, touch me."

Eyes wide, she reached up and grasped his face in gentle hands. "Shh, it's okay." Her fingers stroked his cheeks. "You can trust me. I'll never hurt you. I'll never do anything you don't want."

He swallowed, hard, his breath rushing from his chest. "More."

She lifted her legs and wrapped her calves around him, rubbing and stroking his ass as he thrust.

The sensation was electric. Warmth and pleasure overloaded his skin and crawled down his spine, gathering in his balls. "Aw, gods, I want—" He lowered his body fully onto hers, his hands fisting in her hair, his hips thrusting wildly. Everywhere they touched, her heat seared and soothed him until his head was spinning with the incredible, foreign sensation. She smelled so good, warm and feminine and sweet. He breathed her down deep, but couldn't get enough. Would never be able to get enough. "Hold me," he gasped against her lips.

Her arms came around his back in a tight, warm embrace.

He groaned and claimed her in a fierce kiss. Their tongues swirled and licked, their lips and teeth nipped and pulled. Their breathing was rough and panting. Chrys dropped kisses everywhere he could reach without giving up one iota of her touch.

His hands were filled with black silk. His torso pressed against the firm mounds of her breasts. Their stomach muscles, damp with sweat, rubbed and slid. Her thighs squeezed his pistoning hips and her heels spurred into his ass, completing the mind-blowing full-body experience. He'd never felt anything like it before. "You're the only one," he said, emotion raw in his voice.

A high-pitched whimper tore out of her. He captured the sound with his mouth and worked his hips against her clit. His cock stroked hard and deep, and he angled his thrusts until she was mewling and whimpering into his mouth.

"Gods, Laney, give it to me. Give every bit of it to me."

For a long moment, she held her breath and her whole body went tight. Her orgasm tore through her—her slick sex milking the part of him deep within her, her body thrashed and bucked under him in great waves, and her nails dug into his back. Gods, he hoped she marked him.

As her orgasm went on and on, Chrys got lost in her clenching heat. His grinding rhythm grew jerky, a glorious pressure filling his balls. He went light-headed at the overwhelming sensation, and then his orgasm slammed into him, shooting up his spine and down his legs. His release erupted into her, filling her up and spilling over them both.

When his body finally calmed, he lifted his head. Laney smiled up at him, her eyes full of love, her expression totally blissed out. Her hands dragged lightly up his back and found his hair. She combed her fingers through it, her nails soothingly scratching his scalp. He could've purred.

She'd touched him. Every part of him. Until he couldn't feel where he stopped and she began. And he'd felt...good, right...alive.

Awed, he shifted his hands to stroke the damp hair off her face.

She stretched beneath him, a long, luxurious movement. Grimacing, she reached beneath her hip. "What's this?" The little leather bag Hephaestus had given him.

"I don't know." *Do not open it until you've made your choice*, that's what Hephaestus had said. And Chrys had made his choice—he'd chosen Laney. They worked together to release the thin string holding the top of the satchel closed tight.

"How much of my conversation with Hephaestus did you hear?"

"Most of it. Enough to know you and Seth have ancient divine connections, and that you did the most amazing thing anyone has ever done for me."

"I did it for me, too."

He kissed her, just a light, worshipful brushing of lips. They finally got the strings untied. "Hold out your hand." Chrys dumped the contents into her palm.

Two rings, both made of brushed infernal iron, one band thicker, the other thin.

Certainty and gratitude roared through him.

Laney brought her other hand to explore the objects. She gasped. "Are these—"

"Yes." He picked up the smaller ring. "When the chaos is behind us, we will do this right. But until then, Laney Summerlyn, I promise to love and cherish and honor you, forever. Will you be mine?"

Her breath caught and her eyes went glassy. "Yes."

Chrys slid the ring, a perfect fit, on her finger. *Thank you, Hephaestus.*

She grasped the remaining piece. "Chrysander Notos, I promise to love you and take care of you and be there for you in every way you need me, for the rest of my long life. Please be mine."

"Always," he rasped as the cool iron settled on his finger. His cock hardened at the sight, slow but sure. "I want you again," he said, slowly moving his hips.

She nodded. "Anything you want. Everything you want. I love you."

"As I love you, Laney, and I always will."

Dark days lie ahead—only ten sunrises separated them from the fall equinox and Eurus's ascension. He and Laney would face every challenge, together. Everything else was uncertain, but not this. Never this.

ACKNOWLEDGMENTS

From his very first breath, Chrysander Notos had his own way of doing things, never easy, never straightforward, never boring or dull. And that made bringing him to life one of the most challenging and fulfilling writing experiences I've ever had. I know so many of you have waited to spend more time with the golden boy of the Anemoi, and I hope you love him as much as I do.

I have to offer thanks first and foremost to Christi Barth, who read the entire manuscript and pushed me again and again to go deeper. To have such an incredible critique partner and wonderful friend in the same person is a true privilege. I must also thank my best friend Lea Nolan, who brainstormed with me, cheered me on, shared Panera cookies, and held my hand more times than I can recount. Stephanie Dray, Joya Fields, Marta Bliese, and Laura Thompson (my horse expert!) provided encouragement, moral support, and tough love that kept me going when life went off the rails. Again. And again.

Thanks, always, to Heather Howland, for loving the

Anemoi as much as I do, for making me shine, and for never letting me get away with a thing! She's the kind of editor authors dream of working with. A special word of thanks to Kari Olson of A Good Addiction blog, who won an Entangled Publishing contest and got to name Boreas's love interest, Tabitha. You did great! Thanks to Jenn Schober for always being there with an encouraging word!

I also need to offer thanks to someone who doesn't know she inspired me. My former graduate student, Dana S., was diagnosed with retinitis pigmentosa and faced the news with such courage and determination. Dana, I hope I've done RP justice here. To learn more about RP or donate toward finding a cure, visit the Foundation Fighting Blindness at www.blindness.org.

Huge love always goes out to Laura's Heroes, the best street team an author ever had. To Brian and my girls, thank you for supporting me so completely. I love you. And, as always, I have complete love for the readers, who welcome characters into their hearts and minds and let them tell their stories over and over again. ~ LK

See where it all began with Owen and Megan in

NORTH OF NEED

book one in the Hearts of the Anemoi series
by Laura Kaye

Her tears called a powerful snow god to life, but only her
love can grant the humanity he craves…

Desperate to escape agonizing memories of Christmas past, twenty-nine-year-old widow Megan Snow builds a snow family outside the mountain cabin she once shared with her husband, realizing too late that she's recreated the very thing she'll never have.

Called to life by Megan's tears, snow god Owen Winters appears unconscious on her doorstep in the midst of a raging blizzard. As she nurses him to health, Owen finds unexpected solace in her company and unimagined pleasure in the warmth of her body, and vows to win her heart for a chance at humanity.

Megan is drawn to Owen's mismatched eyes, otherworldly masculinity, and enthusiasm for the littlest things. But this Christmas miracle comes with an expiration—before the snow melts and the temperature rises, Megan must let go of her widow's grief and learn to trust love again, or she'll lose Owen forever.

The series continues with Zeph and Ella in
WEST OF WANT
book two in the Hearts of the Anemoi series
by Laura Kaye

Betrayal is all he's ever known, but in her, he'll find a love
strong enough to be trusted...

When Marcella Raines' twin brother dies, she honors his
request to be buried at sea, never expecting the violent storm
that swamps her boat. Though she's gravely injured—and still
emotionally damaged from her recent divorce—Ella fights to
survive.

Zephyros Martius is the Supreme God of the West Wind
and Spring, but being the strongest Anemoi hasn't protected
him from betrayal and loss. Worse, he's sure his brother Eurus
is behind it. When Zeph's heartbreak whips up a storm that
shipwrecks a human, his guilt forces him to save her.

Ella is drawn to the vulnerability Zeph hides beneath
his otherworldly masculinity and ancient blue eyes. And her
honesty, empathy, and unique, calming influence leave Zeph
wanting...everything. When Eurus threatens Ella, she and
Zeph struggle to let go of the past, defend their future, and
embrace what they most want—a love that can be trusted.